HIGH PRAISE FOR
SHERIDON SMYTHE!

THOSE BABY BLUES
"A compelling, sexy romp that leaves you smiling!"
—Christine Feehan, *New York Times* bestselling author

"The interaction between the characters is first rate and highly entertaining . . . a fast, fun and tender story sure to touch the reader's heart."
—*Romance Reviews Today*

"Sheridon Smythe has created a warm and touching tale of love that just keeps expanding."
—*Romantic Times*

A PERFECT FIT
"Lots of good chuckles and a modern relationship that goes from zero to racing speed in seconds flat."
—*Romantic Times*

"Brooke and Alex's sexy interactions will keep you reading."
—*All About Romance*

MR. HYDE'S ASSETS
"A warmhearted and charming tale of secrets, lies and true love."
—*Romantic Times*

A REVEALING ENCOUNTER

"Now *that's* a sight for sore eyes," a familiar voice drawled from behind her.

Ashley froze, painfully aware that not only was her behind exposed as she bent over the suitcase, but she was also topless.

Michael . . .

She grabbed the first thing her fingers could snag—a slinky red and black nightie—and clutched it to her bare chest. Slowly, she turned, wanting to confirm the impossible. Michael. Her ex-husband. Here. In her cabin on board a cruise ship heading for the Caribbean.

"You look great, baby."

The low, masculine whistle that followed Michael's observation scalded her from head to toe. She swallowed dryly, her voice nothing short of a croak. It's the way she felt—as if she would croak any moment. "What—what the hell are *you* doing here?"

Other *Love Spell* books by Sheridon Smythe:

HEAT WAVE (anthology)
THOSE BABY BLUES
A PERFECT FIT
MR. HYDE'S ASSETS

Hot Number

SHERIDON SMYTHE

LOVE SPELL NEW YORK CITY

LOVE SPELL®

December 2003

Published by

Dorchester Publishing Co., Inc.
200 Madison Avenue
New York, NY 10016

If you purchased this book without a cover you should be aware that this book is stolen property. It was reported as "unsold and destroyed" to the publisher and neither the author nor the publisher has received any payment for this "stripped book."

Copyright © 2003 by Sherrie Eddington

All rights reserved. No part of this book may be reproduced or transmitted in any form or by any electronic or mechanical means, including photocopying, recording or by any information storage and retrieval system, without the written permission of the publisher, except where permitted by law.

ISBN 0-505-52523-2

The name "Love Spell" and its logo are trademarks of Dorchester Publishing Co., Inc.

Printed in the United States of America.

Visit us on the web at www.dorchesterpub.com.

Hot Number

Chapter One

"As you can see for yourself, the house is just the right size for a small family."

Ashley Kavanagh moved slowly from room to room as she spoke. From the corner of her eye, she could see that her prospective buyers—a young doctor and his very pregnant wife—looked suitably impressed. Good. Ashley had shown the house a dozen times this month; maybe this time would be the last. With her furnace on the blink, she could use the income. "Upstairs we have four bedrooms and two full baths, with a large linen closet in the hall. One of the bedrooms could easily be converted into an office."

"Hmm. You'd like that, wouldn't you, hon?" The blonde linked her arm with her husband's and flashed him a teasing, totally devoted grin.

Ashley cleared her throat to get their attention, casting a quick glance at the big window fronting the street. Driven by a wild north wind, sleet and snow pinged against the glass in ever-increasing fury.

The storm reminded her of her marriage to Michael—something she definitely did *not* want to think about.

It had just begun to storm when the couple arrived, but from the look of things it was going to be every bit as bad as the Weather Channel had predicted. Great, Ashley thought, gnawing the lipstick from her bottom lip. The snowstorm would go really well with her frigid house if the serviceman failed to fix her cranky old furnace today.

At least the man they'd sent from the garage had managed to get her car started this morning. First her furnace, then her car. Could the day get any worse?

"Is this a working fireplace?" the young doctor asked, snagging Ashley's attention.

"Yes. The previous owners—" Ashley paused a beat as her cell phone gave a muffled peal from the depths of her coat pocket. She studiously ignored it, making a mental note to remind her new assistant that she didn't like to be interrupted during a showing. "—put a lot of work into the house, and it shows, don't you agree?"

The cell phone stopped abruptly. A few seconds later her beeper—located in her other coat pocket—began to emit an urgent sound.

The doctor chuckled at her exasperated frown. "Go ahead, take care of business. I'm surprised *my* beeper hasn't gone off."

"Not as surprised as *I* am," his wife quipped.

Even as Ashley extracted her compact phone from her pocket, she explained, "I'm sorry. I'm breaking in a new assistant. I guess she forgot I was showing the house."

"Take your time. Lori and I will take a look around upstairs."

When they disappeared from sight, Ashley quickly rang her office. Traci answered on the first ring. She sounded agitated and breathless. A shiver of premonition danced along Ashley's spine. What else could go wrong today? she wondered, instinctively sensing another disaster.

"Miss Kavanagh! I'm so glad you called—"

"This had better be an emergency," Ashley broke in.

"It is, I think. I mean, I guess it *could* be a prank call, but this lady sounded ancient. I just couldn't picture her as the prank caller type, you know?"

"Get to the point." *She would have to say something about that irritating, popping gum.*

"Do you know a Mrs. Abernathy?"

Ashley frowned impatiently. "She's my neighbor. Why?"

"Because she called and said that your house was on fire."

"Excuse me?"

"Your house . . . Mrs. Abernathy said she called the fire department when she saw smoke rolling from the basement window."

Frozen to the spot, Ashley slowly snapped the phone together, cutting Traci off in midsentence. Okay, so she was wrong; the day *could* get worse.

"But I thought you guys replaced that old furnace when you bought the house."

Ashley scraped the bottom of the ice cream carton and shoved a spoonful of Rocky Road into her mouth as she considered Kim Wallace's words. She stared at the muted television with an intensity that made her eyes water, determined to speak without bitterness.

It wasn't easy. Any time she thought of her ex-husband, Michael, she got this harsh, metallic taste in her mouth, not to mention a queasy feeling in the pit of her stomach. Or maybe it was an entire half gallon of Rocky Road that was making her queasy.

"I was all for replacing it, but . . . *Michael* was adamant that it had a few good years left," Ashley told Kim, placing the blame squarely where it belonged. From the moment the fire chief explained that the old furnace had caused the fire,

Ashley decided it was Michael's fault. If he had listened to her, she wouldn't be sitting on someone else's couch eating someone else's ice cream and watching someone else's television.

Not that Kim was bad company. She and Kim had been friends throughout high school and beyond. Unfortunately, Kim was Michael's half sister, which had made their friendship a bit awkward since the divorce.

When they were together, the subject of Michael always managed to pop up, despite Ashley's blatant hints that she preferred to forget her two-timing, faithless ex. But Kim, it seemed, was a hopeless romantic and just couldn't accept the fact that Ashley and Michael were finished.

Kim suddenly blocked her view of the television. Bracing her hands on her hips, she faced Ashley. "If you think it's Michael's fault, maybe you should call him and suggest that he help pay for the damages."

The idea was ludicrous—and obvious. Ashley sighed and set the empty ice cream carton on the coffee table. Gently, she said, "Kim, Michael and I have been divorced for two years. I bought him out, so that makes the house my responsibility—not his."

"But—"

"No buts. Just period. End of subject." She added a warning glare but wasn't surprised when

Kim ignored it. Kim and Michael had disturbing similarities.

"Michael's changed, you know."

"Good for him." Ashley stubbornly ignored the sharp pain that squeezed her heart.

"I mean, he's changed a *lot,*" Kim added, her eyes narrowing slyly. "He's thinking about getting married again."

Ashley managed a delighted smile, crushing Kim's hope that the news would arouse jealousy. "Great! Maybe we can have a double wedding, because Tom and I are thinking about setting a date as well." She was kidding about the double wedding, but she wasn't kidding about the rest. She and Tom *had* talked about setting a date.

Kim's face crumpled. "You can't marry Tom!" she cried.

"Oh, yes I can, and I'm going to. Tom is definitely Mr. Right." Ashley's grin became genuine at Kim's disgruntled expression. She waved her hand. "Now, will you please move? They're about to announce the winning lottery numbers."

Her friend obliged and moved aside, her voice taunting, relentless. "If you're truly over Michael, why do you still use those sentimental numbers for the lottery?" When Ashley remained stubbornly silent, Kim continued. "What were they? Let me see . . . I believe it was the anniversary of your first date with Michael, and your wedding date."

"What makes you think I haven't changed them?" Ashley demanded flippantly, then spoiled it by flushing. She never could lie to Kim, dammit! "Tom and I intend to pick out new numbers. We've just been . . . busy." Even to her own ears, her explanation sounded a little lame. The truth was, she'd never told Tom the significance of the numbers. To discuss it would be to remember how Michael teased her about her silly belief that she'd win one day.

Bittersweet memories she'd much rather keep buried, thank you very much!

"Hey, aren't those the numbers . . ." Kim's voice trailed away as she stared, openmouthed, at the numbers scrolling across the television screen.

Ashley laughed outright. "After the rotten day I've had, it's hardly likely that . . . I . . . would . . ." Her scornful glance landed on the flashing numbers.

Familiar numbers. Numbers she knew by heart. Numbers she had played faithfully for three years.

The blood drained from her face. Her heart stopped for a scary moment, then lurched against her rib cage. Very slowly, as if she feared the numbers would disappear, she leaned forward.

And gulped loudly.

She'd won the lottery!

* * *

Normally if the phone rang while Michael Kavanagh was in the shower, he'd let the answering machine do its job.

Not tonight. Tonight was the night he was going to pop the question to Candy, and if that was her calling with some excuse not to see him tonight, he wanted the opportunity to change her mind—before he changed *his*.

Thus his mad dash out of the shower, clutching a damp towel to his still-dripping body.

He snatched the phone from the hook on the third ring. "Hello?"

"Michael, you'll never believe what's happened!"

Not Candy but his little sister, Kim. "Kim. What's up?"

"Ashley's car wouldn't start this morning."

At the mention of his ex, Michael frowned. "So?"

"Then her furnace stopped working."

He winced, remembering their heated argument about getting a new one. Still . . . he didn't see what any of it had to do with him now. Someday—please God—Kim would accept their divorce. "I'm sorry to hear that. Listen, Kim, I'm dripping all over the—"

"Michael, her house caught on fire."

Now *that* was cause for pause, Michael thought, a thrill of fear streaking through him,

8

mocking his outward nonchalance. "Is she all right?" he demanded roughly.

"Yes, she's fine. She wasn't there." Kim sucked in another deep breath. "Michael, I'm calling to tell you that Ashley *won the lottery!*"

Michael held the phone away from his ear as Kim followed her garbled announcement with an excited squeal. "She what?" he asked, certain he'd heard her wrong. He was surprised he could hear *anything* after that ear-splitting scream.

"She won the lottery!!! She wouldn't call and tell you herself, stubborn wench, so I had to. She never changed the numbers, you know. Of course, she has to share it with someone—some other lucky stiff who picked the same numbers. Still," Kim prattled on, "five hundred thousand dollars is a big pile of dough."

But Michael was no longer listening; he'd just remembered something. Something momentous. Something wonderful.

Something shocking.

Gently laying the phone on a pillow, Michael grabbed his jeans from the floor where he'd dropped them and stuck his hand in the right pocket. He withdrew a crumpled lottery ticket and carefully smoothed it out on the bed. The one and only lottery ticket he'd ever bought, purchased that morning at a convenience store on a silly, nostalgic whim as he thought about his relationship with Candy, and his past with Ashley.

He could still hear Kim talking as he stared at the familiar numbers on the crumpled paper. Numbers he'd teased Ashley about. Numbers that brought back bittersweet memories of the happiest times of his life. Numbers that reminded him of what he'd lost—what her mistrust had cost them.

Wouldn't Kim be surprised to know that *he* was the other lucky stiff?

Chapter Two

"If you need anything, Mrs. Kavanagh, just let me know. The ship's casino is open from noon till midnight—unless we're in port—and dinner is at seven."

Ashley hid a cynical smile at the young steward's rehearsed speech and handed him a five-dollar bill. She didn't bother correcting her marital status.

He flashed her a toothy grin, set her suitcases on the floor, and left, closing the cabin door with a soft click.

She turned in a slow circle, her gaze moving around the luxury cabin on board the cruise ship *Funstar*. There was a king-size bed, a mini-bar, a built-in refrigerator, and plenty of closet space. Carved-wood accenting lent the room a rich, personal feel, and there was a small table and two chairs positioned in front of the port-hole.

It was bigger than she expected, more luxuri-ous than she could have dreamed, and for the next seven days, it was all hers, compliments of her hometown travel agency. In return she agreed to pose for a publicity picture that would grace their new brochure advertising *Funstar* cruises.

Winning the lottery certainly had its perks, Ashley mused, testing the king-size bed. And the unexpected cruise couldn't have come at a more convenient time. She literally needed a place to stay while workers cleared the basement, re-paired the damage, and installed her new fur-nace.

Being temporarily homeless was one of the reasons she'd agreed to board the ship without Tom. Ashley let out a rueful chuckle as she thought of all the sexy lingerie she'd bought with Tom in mind, not to mention a daring, slinky black cocktail dress she intended to wear to the farewell party that was rumored to be the high-light of the cruise.

She had decided it was time to take her rela-tionship—so far platonic—one step further. She'd even gotten a prescription for birth con-trol. After all, this was the new millennium; time to leave behind her old-fashioned idea of waiting for marriage.

Imagine how disappointed she was to learn from a red-faced Tom that he suffered seasickness so violent that just looking at water made him ill.

"Well, my luck had to run out eventually," Ashley mumbled to herself. Shaking her head, she pitched a suitcase on the bed and began to search for her new bathing suit. She'd flown to Ft. Lauderdale from Kansas City that morning to catch the *Funstar*, and she couldn't wait another minute to bake the chill from her bones. After that she planned to enjoy a leisurely dinner, drink a little wine, and maybe visit the casino.

She found the bottom of her bikini bathing suit beneath a stack of underwear—the skimpy, silky, slinky thong kind that she normally avoided. Shucking her jeans and panties, she slid into the blushingly skimpy bottoms, then stared down in dismay. She didn't remember the suit being *that* skimpy! Her eyes narrowed as she remembered that Kim had been with her when she bought it. She wouldn't put it past her devil of a friend to exchange the suit for a smaller size when her back was turned.

With a sigh, Ashley removed her top and bra, then dived back into the suitcase for the bathing suit top, reminding herself that it was unlikely she would run into anyone she knew aboard a cruise ship. Besides, she went to the club twice a week—not one of Michael's clubs, of course—

and had acquired an artificial tan to start her trip. The five pounds she'd shed in the two weeks anticipating the cruise hadn't hurt, either. Too bad Tom wasn't here to—

"Now *that's* a sight for sore eyes," a familiar voice drawled from behind her.

Ashley froze, painfully aware that not only was her behind exposed as she bent over the suitcase, but she was also topless.

Michael . . .

She grabbed the first thing her fingers could snag—a slinky red and black nightie—and clutched it to her bare chest. Slowly, she turned, wanting to confirm the impossible. Michael. Here. In her cabin on board a cruise ship heading for the Caribbean.

"You look great, baby."

The low, masculine whistle that followed Michael's observation scalded her from head to toe. She swallowed dry, her voice nothing short of a croak. It was the way she felt—as if she would croak any moment. "What—what the hell are *you* doing here?"

Michael. Definitely here, and dressed in nothing more than a damp towel tucked casually—and all too carelessly for Ashley's peace of mind—at his waist. Her burning gaze dipped to the bulge beneath the towel, then jerked back to his handsome face.

Apparently he'd been in the bathroom while

14

she thought herself alone. She had mistakenly assumed the shower sounds she'd heard were coming from the cabin next to her own.

"I should ask you the same thing," Michael said, leaning against the door and crossing his arms. "I gather Kim didn't mention to you that I would be on this cruise?"

Ashley shivered as his dark eyes slid over her again, slowly, thoroughly. Her knees went weak, but she resisted the urge to brace herself against the bed. So, Michael could still make her weak-kneed. All the more reason to avoid him.

"Get the hell out of my cabin before I call security."

Michael's dark brows shot upward at her threat. His handsome lips curled into a mocking grin that made her mouth go dry and her mind go numb from a flood of bittersweet memories. Just seeing him again—something she'd managed to avoid for long stretches—reminded her of just how dangerous he was to her.

Dammit.

"It's not like I haven't seen you naked before, Ash," Michael said, his voice dipping low. "Besides, this is my—"

"Get out!" Ashley was shaking now as she tried to cover herself with the sheer material of the negligee. Being in the same room with a half-naked Michael was paramount to being caged with a randy lion—an irresistible, silver-tongued lion. Unfortunately, she knew the dangers all too well. . . .

"I can't get out."

To her discomfort, he strode past her to the closet on the opposite side of the room. The towel—she noticed but wished she hadn't—slipped dangerously, revealing the smooth, tanned skin of his buttocks. Apparently she wasn't the only one who had prepared for the trip. Gulping, she watched him as he opened the closet doors and pulled a shirt from a hanger.

Ashley looked past him and gasped. There were men's clothes hanging in the closet. Lots of them. "You—you—" She stopped, swallowed hard, and began again. "What are your clothes doing in my closet?" This was a nightmare, one she'd had many times—that of being close to Michael and unable to control her libido.

"I tried to tell you," Michael said mildly, slipping the shirt over his broad chest. "This isn't *your* cabin—it's mine. There must have been a mix-up." He waved a hand to indicate the clothes. "As you can see, I was already in residence when *you* came barging in."

" 'Barging in'?" Ashley sputtered, taking the opportunity to slip the negligee over her head while he buttoned his shirt. The suitcases containing her day clothes were still sitting by the door, and she wasn't about to take her eyes from the enemy long enough to look for the shirt

16

she'd been wearing. "For your information, Michael, I didn't *barge* in! A steward brought me here—obviously by mistake."

Carelessly, he dropped the towel as he reached for a pair of pants.

Ashley slammed her eyes shut, but the image left behind was enough to send shock waves throughout her body. Her knees buckled. She sat abruptly on the bed, trying to picture anything—*anything*—but the sight of Michael's glorious semi-arousal. Her voice was horribly faint and husky as she repeated, "There's obviously been a mistake."

She jumped a foot in the air and shrieked as strong, familiar hands landed on her upper arms. Out of self-preservation, she kept her eyes shut. Had he put the pants on? Or was he . . . still naked? She didn't want to know. No, of course not. Not at all.

"Ash . . . are you okay? You look like you're going to faint."

Concern. Warmth. And something else she couldn't and didn't dare define in his voice. Little by little, she opened her eyes. She let out a relieved sigh to find him dressed. "I'm okay, just a little shaken." The confession was out before she could snatch it back. To her surprise, he nodded.

"I know what you mean." The sound of his rueful chuckle slid over her like hot suntan oil.

"When I opened the bathroom door and recognized your . . . bottom, I was a little shook up myself. It's been a while, hasn't it?"

Ashley licked her lips, trying not to stare at the oh-so-handsome line of his mouth. Forcing herself instead to recall in vivid detail the night she'd made a surprise visit to his hotel room. It was the night her heart had shattered into a million pieces.

Evoking the bitter memory worked all too well.

"Not long enough," she said coldly, shaking his hands loose. "Now, unlike you, I have a little modesty, and I'd appreciate it if you'd step outside the cabin while I get dressed."

"The bitch is back."

"She never left." Ashley pointed at the door. "I need five minutes. Is that too much to ask?"

"Not at all." Michael had lost his smile. His eyes had grown dark with grim anger. "Just remember, I was here first."

"Whatever."

Outside the cabin door, Michael unclenched his teeth and his fists and forced air deeply into his lungs. He turned and braced his hands against the door, giving in to the temptation of imagining Ashley lifting that sexy nightie over her head and baring her breasts. From what he'd seen, she was golden all over, so that meant her nipples would be duskier than he remembered. . . .

He stifled a groan and shoved himself away.

After two years and countless self-lectures, he'd laid himself wide open within ten minutes in her company. Why? Why did he let her hurt him again? The woman was poison! Because of her mistrust, she'd nearly destroyed him.

Yet here he was, lusting after her on the other side of a closed door.

Michael paced a rectangle in the hall, concentrating instead on how the mix-up with the cabin could have happened. When he'd gotten the free package from the travel agency, he hadn't meant to take the offer. Then he'd thought about Candy, and the fact that he still hadn't proposed. So he'd said yes, allowing Kim to make the arrangements.

Mistake number one.

Then, when he'd discovered that Candy had no intention of going with him anywhere, ever, he'd let Kim talk him into going alone.

Mistake number two.

He pivoted, frowned, and paced again. Kim must have known that Ashley would be on this ship—apparently without Tom.

The opportunity to throw them together had been too much for his meddling little sister to resist. She had never accepted the fact that his marriage to Ashley was over.

Michael ground to a halt. Elated to have solved the puzzle and eager to share it with Ashley, Michael opened the door to the cabin and rushed in.

Ashley stood by the bed, her breasts jiggling as she struggled with the nightie that covered her head. Her hips, encased in the skimpy bikini bottom, swiveled to and fro. Frozen at the delicious sight, Michael shamelessly watched.

Slowly, her struggles ceased. He could hear her breathing hard through the satin material, see the enticing movement of her breasts with every breath she took.

Golden-tipped. Luscious. Firm. Familiar.

"Michael?" she panted.

Michael cleared his throat, glad she couldn't see the color that rushed into his face. "Need some help?"

"Oh, God!" She sounded adorably frustrated and embarrassed. "I—the damned hook on this thing is caught in my hair."

He began to walk toward her, his gaze hot and burning on her squirming body. Need slammed into his groin, bringing him to a painful arousal within seconds. Yearning filled his heart, pushing aside iron-clad barriers.

"Um, Michael?"

He paused, wondering if she could hear him breathing hard as well. "Yes?"

"Will you please close your eyes? I—I can feel you watching me."

I'm not surprised. After a quick swallow, he said, "Sure." It was a bold lie, perhaps one of the boldest he'd ever told her. Reaching out, he gently found the hook and released her hair, then helped her pull the nightie clear.

Her nipples grazed his chest, knocking another inch into his arousal. Her hands fell to his shoulders as she staggered.

Nose to nose, their harsh breaths mingled. He saw the fear in her eyes as he inched his mouth toward hers, and wondered if she could read the same in his.

"Michael?" she whispered.

"Ashley?" He sounded just as bewildered.

"I love Tom," she stated weakly.

Her stinging declaration wrenched the lie from his lips. "And I love Candy." He grabbed her bottom and hoisted her up. She wrapped her legs tightly around his waist.

His arousal pushed against the flimsy material of her bathing suit. Michael reached down and pushed it aside, plunging into her in one swift, soul-shattering stroke.

He was home.

Chapter Three

Ashley didn't smoke, and she drank only occa-
sionally. In fact, she had no hard vices that she
was aware of, but the moment Michael shoved
the damp crotch of her bathing suit aside and
thrust his hard length into her, she would have
eagerly traded places with the worst crack addict.

In Ashley's mind, being addicted to Michael
was far, far worse than any drug. Like a drug, he
brought humiliation and shame. Like a drug, he
was intoxicating, even while she cursed his existence. Like a drug, she was not only helpless to
resist him, she was helpless against the rush of
euphoria that turned her blood into liquid silver.

She was addicted to Michael, and she knew it.
Just as a smoker might avoid a crowd of smokers,
or a junkie might avoid an alley full of other
junkies, she had avoided Michael since their divorce.

And *this* was why.

"Oh, God, Ash," Michael moaned against her mouth as he withdrew, then plunged into her again. He did that little swiveling thing with his hips that made her insides go into wild spasms. "You are so *tight!* I'd forgotten how tight you are, baby. So tight and hot and delicious."

And that was another thing, Ashley thought, biting her bottom lip hard as with the third stroke, Michael pushed her closer to the edge of the abyss. The way he talked when they were making love. It might have distracted other women, but no, not her. Not the way Michael talked. Not the things he said. Coupled with the way he moved, it intensified their lovemaking to a volcanic degree.

"You make me so hard, baby," he whispered, then covered her mouth in a deep kiss that sucked the air right out of her lungs.

Kissing Michael was another addiction entirely. When she kissed Tom, her feet remained firmly planted on the ground. The experience was mildly pleasant, yet safely forgettable.

When kissing Michael, she was jerked up and shot into the sky like a rocket heading for space. The heat of his mouth . . . the erotic way he sucked her tongue . . . the pleasurable ripples that made their way along her spine.

"Michael." Without conscious thought, she moaned his name. Ashley held on to his rock-hard forearms, wishing he would slow down, knowing she would scream her protest if he did. She was a second away from exploding, could feel deep inside her the contractions beginning, the ones that signaled her impending release.

"Are you close, baby?" he whispered roughly, echoing her thoughts as his fingers tightened on her hips and his thrusts became deeper and faster. "I hope you are, because it's been so long I can't help myself . . . Ashley?"

She recognized the significance in the rise of his voice. Recognized and responded as she always had to Michael: mindlessly. She tightened her arms around his neck and held on, wildly anticipating one mother of an orgasm—

"Oh, dear. Oh, dear. The door was cracked, so I thought—oh my, dear!"

And if one strange voice wasn't enough of a shock during this most intimate moment, Ashley heard another.

"Newlyweds, darling. Wouldn't you say?"

It was immediately obvious to Ashley that Michael hadn't heard the intruders. His grip had tightened on her hips to a painful degree and he was drawing back for what she suspected was a final thrust. If she remembered correctly, that thrust would be followed by Michael's shouting her name to the heavens.

"Michael," she whispered urgently into his ear, trying to ignore the deep, warning spasms inside her own body that begged her to keep quiet just a moment longer. "Oh, God, Michael! Stop! We've got company!"

"Huh?"

Another time and place Ashley might have laughed at the absolute shock on Michael's face as her words sank in. Slack-jawed with disbelief, he turned to stare at the outrageously beaming elderly couple in the doorway.

Deep inside her, she could feel him pulsing, hovering on the brink of an orgasm.

The elderly woman smothered a giggle with her hand and continued to stare. Her husband, Ashley assumed, shook his head, his smile widening. He looked as if he'd just caught a couple of teenagers necking in the porch swing, instead of locked together in the most intimate of embraces.

Neither looked the slightest bit embarrassed.

Ashley felt a full-body blush race across her exposed skin like a wildfire out of control. She buried her face in Michael's shoulder, totally mortified. "Put me down, Michael. *Please!*"

He did, slowly and reluctantly, giving her legs time to adjust before he let go of her hips.

She lifted her head and peered around his shoulder, allowing him to shield the rest of her body. She slumped in relief. "They're gone. Oh, God!"

Michael whirled around and stomped to the

door, slamming it shut and belatedly twisting the lock. He leaned against the door with his forehead to the varnished wood, breathing hard. "Unbelievable."

Was he talking about the outrageous couple, or the way things had gotten out of control? Shaken, Ashley sank onto the edge of the bed and buried her burning face in her hands. Her body tingled and ached, but her mind had already begun to grasp the reality of what had happened.

What had she done? The fact that they had been thwarted seconds before the grand finale did not ease or excuse her guilt. Not one tiny bit. Not even a hair.

She had been unfaithful to Tom, her fiancé.

With Michael. Her ex. Her rotten, faithless ex-husband. The man who had shattered her heart into a million pieces. The very man she had vowed to avoid for the rest of her life.

Not only had she been unfaithful, but unfaithful in front of strangers, as if that made it ten times worse.

And for some perverse reason she couldn't explain, it did.

"I—I had a weak moment. It can never happen again,"

At her whispered words, Michael slowly closed his eyes. He had his back to her, and he was glad.

Without turning around, he shoved his painful erection into his jeans and managed to zip them.

What the hell *had gotten into him?* The woman was poison. He *knew* that, yet . . . yet he'd reacted like a randy convict just out of prison. As if she were the only woman in the world. As if there weren't hundreds of women he could have. Hell, he encountered a dozen invitations every day at one of his health clubs. From women ten times prettier. Ten times firmer. Ten times less lethal.

His throat worked until he found his voice. He could do nothing about the hoarseness and he knew it. She would know. Hell, she *already* knew, unless she was deaf, dumb, and paralyzed.

And she would gloat.

He couldn't allow it. Had to make some excuse. Had to convince her that it was a brain funk or something. And he couldn't let her know about Candy. He could only pray that Kim had taken his advice about keeping his private life private.

Michael turned abruptly, his gaze locking with hers. She looked shocked as hell. And her cheeks were flushed with excitement in a way he remembered. Good. She hadn't been faking her arousal just to get him to the brink of exploding.

Small comfort, but comfort nonetheless.

"You're damned right it can't happen again." He clenched his jaw, then let go. "It wouldn't have happened at all if you hadn't been flashing me." Her eyes widened to an incredible degree, but before she could respond, Michael plowed recklessly onward. He had to convince her that what had happened between them had meant *nothing*. "But you're not completely to blame. Candy's a bit old-fashioned, so it's been a while for me. I'm sure you understand."

To his relief, there was nothing in her expression to hint that she knew the truth about Candy.

"I understand perfectly, Michael." Her voice was winter cold and filled with uncharacteristic sarcasm. "But you'd better get a handle on your starving libido, because I don't think the other women on this ship will be wearing much more than I was wearing when I tackled you and forced you to have sex." Her chin went up a notch, and her glittering gaze raked him with unmistakable scorn. "I'm going to have to search for my clothes, and I can't do that while you're in here. Would you please leave?"

"It will be my pleasure," he drawled, stalking to the closet to retrieve his sneakers. He slipped them on and left them untied, then retrieved a lightweight jacket that he folded over his arm and held in front of him to hide the telltale bulge in his pants.

He didn't think it would be disappearing anytime soon.

"I'll go find you another cabin while you get

dressed." He had his hand on the door when he added, "I guess you've figured out by now that Kim is probably behind this not-so-innocent little mix-up."

There was a tiny, stunned silence.

So she *hadn't* figured it out, Michael thought, feeling a thrust of unwelcome pleasure at the idea that she might have been too distracted.

"Kim might have been behind *your* reason for being here, but the travel agency offered me a free cruise in exchange for a publicity shoot for their brochure. Your sister had nothing to do with it."

"Kim has friends everywhere."

"I won the lottery, Michael."

"I know." She hadn't said *we*, Michael realized with knee-weakening relief. Was it possible that for once in her life Kim had respected his wishes? That Kim *hadn't* told Ashley about Candy—or about his shameful secret? The last thing he wanted was for Ashley to find out he'd bought a lottery ticket using her own sentimental numbers. The thought of giving her that kind of power over him made his gut churn.

He'd rather jump overboard into shark-infested waters. And if he had to do that, he was taking little sister with him.

"What's *your* excuse for being here?" she prompted.

The suspicion in her voice almost made him

laugh. "Don't think for a moment that it was because *you* were going to be on this ship. I didn't know, and if I *had* known, I wouldn't be here." Every word he spoke was the solid truth.

"Me neither."

"Good. Then we both agree to stay out of each other's way?"

"Sounds fine to me."

"I'll be back as soon as I can clear up this mistake."

"Thanks for the warning."

Despite his inner turmoil, Michael found himself biting back a smile at her heartfelt comment as he let himself out and closed the door behind him. Ashley had once, laughingly, called their intense sexual attraction a perfect example of "spontaneous combustion."

Michael was not amused to realize that nothing had changed.

"I am *so* over him," Ashley said loudly and sternly once Michael was out of sight—and out of mind. Just because she was obviously still attracted to him sexually did *not* mean she loved him.

She was attracted to Michael because he was a fine specimen. He owned and operated two health clubs, for heaven's sake. He ate all the right foods and worked out every day, and it showed in his well-toned, muscled body. He also had a handsome face to go with that eye-catching physique.

And, as she well knew, she was not the only one who found Michael attractive. He could get just about any woman he wanted—and had before their marriage, if the rumors were true—so there was no reason he had to take his desperation out on her.

Unless, of course, he had an ulterior motive.

Ashley frowned at this new, alarming possibility. What if Michael had lied about Kim being involved? What if Michael had decided following her aboard a cruise ship would present an excellent opportunity to sabotage her happiness with Tom?

The blood drained from her face as she realized Michael already had enough evidence, if this was what he planned, plus two witnesses. And poor Kim! In her desperate attempt to throw them together, she would never suspect her brother of devious intentions.

As the possibility continued to alarm her, Ashley leaped to her feet and began searching every inch of the room for a hidden videocamera. Yes, she told herself when her resolve wavered and she found herself feeling ridiculous, Michael *was* capable of filming them having sex. She couldn't forget how bitter and furious he had been when she served him with the divorce papers.

In return, she had been dumbfounded that he

had had the nerve to be mad when *she* was the wronged party!

No, Ashley thought as she stood on the bed so she could reach the smoke alarm attached to the ceiling next to the vent shaft, Michael hadn't changed, as Kim had claimed, but he might have gotten better at hiding his deceitful, conniving ways from his little sister.

She yanked on the outside case of the smoke alarm until it came off in her hand, then peered inside for a hidden camera. Nothing there but a nine-volt battery. After she replaced the cover, she propped her hands on her hips and gave the room one last careful survey before giving up.

So maybe he hadn't set up a camera. Maybe she was being ridiculously paranoid. Of course she was. Michael had a knack for bringing out the worst in her.

Ashley let out a frustrated sigh. She'd been looking forward to a relaxing cruise, and she knew she would never relax as long as Michael was on the ship.

Which brought her back to the same question: *Why* was he on the ship? Was it innocent, as he claimed?

Her mind ran in circles as she found her clothes and quickly dressed. Later, when she was in her own cabin and able to think calmly, she would figure out what to do about Michael.

Snapping her suitcase closed, she sat on the bed and waited for Michael to return.

"Is this your credit card number?"

Michael glanced at the number. The cruise was free, but he'd had to give his credit card number as a show of faith. "Yes."

The woman in the purser's office shoved the clipboard closer to Michael's face, her smile one of benign patience. "And is this your signature?"

"Yes." Michael silently ground his teeth. "But there's been a mistake."

"I don't understand. It says here that you clearly reserved a luxury cabin for Mr. and Mrs. Michael Kavanagh."

"I know, but—" Michael felt himself flush. Dammit! Out of respect for Candy, he'd signed her on as his wife. Now his little deception was backfiring, because it was obvious that Kim hadn't made the changes he'd requested when Candy backed out of going. "Look, can you just get Mrs. Kavanagh another cabin? We can't share one."

Miss Beech was shaking her head before Michael could finish. "This is peak season for us, Mr. Kavanagh. I'm afraid there are no cabins left." Her voice lowered to a confidential whisper. "Give it a little time. Maybe you two will kiss and make up."

Michael couldn't deny that they might kiss,

but he knew for certain they wouldn't make up.
"Thanks, anyway," he muttered ungraciously before heading to the door. He wasn't looking forward to giving Ashley the bad news.

"Sorry I couldn't help, Mr. Kavanagh. Oh, by
the way, you might not have noticed, but it's at
least eighty degrees." Her gaze dipped suspiciously to the folded jacket shielding his stubborn erection. "We wouldn't want any of our
passengers suffering heat stroke, you know."

He might suffer heat stroke before the trip was
over, Michael thought darkly, but it wouldn't
have anything to do with *that* kind of heat. He
slammed the door with unnecessary force and
tried to imagine taking a cold shower.

It didn't work. He could still feel her around
him, against him, torturing him, bringing him to
the brink of the sort of wild orgasm only Ashley
seemed capable of giving him.

Her scent was firmly planted in his nostrils.
Her taste clung to his tongue. Her image took
over his mind, an erotic image of Ashley's
flushed face and passion-glazed eyes.

Damn her.

With a muffled curse, Michael went in search
of the ship's bar. He needed a drink before he
faced Ashley again, something to dull his senses.
What was it about her? Why didn't other women
affect him this way? He'd had no trouble at all
keeping his hands to himself around Candy, who

was twice the knockout. She oozed sex appeal and drove men to a frenzy. Her double D bustline alone made men drool.

The fact that he *had* kept his hands to himself was probably the very reason Candy had suggested they take a breather.

A *permanent* one.

He found the bar and ordered a straight whiskey. He preferred beer but knew that whiskey was quicker. The bartender lifted a questioning brow at his gruff tone.

"Two hours out to sea and already you've got problems?" The bartender let out a low whistle of disbelief. "That ain't good, my friend. Not good at all. The *Funstar* has a reputation for making people happy."

Michael's lips twisted in a rueful smile. "Don't worry, it isn't the ship's fault." He draped the jacket over his lap, wondering if Ashley had planted a curse on him. What if he stayed this way the entire seven days? He'd have to wear baggy pants, carry his jacket in front of him, and lurk in the shadows.

The thought prompted a groan.

"That bad, huh? The name's Rick."

Since the bartender, a young man with bleached hair and friendly blue eyes, seemed determined to play the proverbial confidant, Michael found himself sharing information he wouldn't normally share.

"Michael. Yeah, it's that bad. There was a mix-up, and it looks like my ex-wife and I will be sharing a cabin for the next seven days."

Seven days. To Michael, that seemed like a life-time—and a lot of cold showers.

"Can I get a strawberry Margarita?"

Michael glanced at the woman who had taken the stool beside his own. She wore a skimpy, off-the-shoulder white dress that complemented her deep tan and petite, shapely figure. Her arms, he noted, were firm and slightly muscled. Her honey-blond hair looked natural.

With a guilty start, he realized that she'd caught him looking. She smiled, revealing dazzling white teeth.

"Hi. I'm Tanya." She held out a slim hand.

To Michael's mystification—and exasperation—the moment he touched her hand his stubborn erection took a nosedive. "The name's Michael."

Her smile wavered, then disappeared. She gazed at him with obvious disappointment. "You're married."

Had he given her a false signal? Frowning, Michael wasted no time correcting her. "No, I'm not. Divorced two years, actually."

"Sure." Tanya didn't sound as if she believed him. She paid for her drink and left, leaving Michael wondering what the hell he'd done wrong.

"What did I say?" he asked Rick, who was

watching Tanya's departure with a wistful expression.

Rick blinked, then looked at Michael. "You've got it written all over your face, my friend."

"What?"

"That you're unavailable," Rick explained with a matter-of-fact shrug. "Chicks are sensitive to stuff like that."

"But, I'm not—" Michael clamped his lips shut. If he wanted Ashley to think he and Candy were still a couple, then he couldn't go blabbing the truth to bartenders or anyone else on the ship. "She's right. I've got a girlfriend. She had an emergency at the last moment, so she had to back out of the cruise. Give me another shot, will you?"

Rick happily complied. "So, how long have you and your ex-wife been divorced?"

Michael tipped the glass and swallowed its entire contents. It burned a satisfying path along his throat and made his eyes water. How many more would it take? Two? Three? "Two years," he said, shoving the glass in Rick's direction again.

"And how long have you been with your current girlfriend?"

He had to think hard. "Um, six or seven months." It could have been four. Or twelve. Another reason Candy had jumped ship.

Rick poured the whiskey. "What color are her eyes?"

Without thinking, Michael said, "Blue. Sometimes violet. When she gets mad, sometimes they turn a deep gray."

He was staring into his whiskey when Rick asked somberly, "And what color are your ex's eyes?"

"I just told you—" Michael looked up at the bartender. Shock hummed along his nerve endings. At that moment, he wanted to plant his fist right in the center of the smug bartender's kisser. Instead, he growled, "What the hell are you? My conscience?"

Rick held up his hands in surrender. "Hey, take it easy! It's pretty obvious you've still got your ex-wife under your skin." He shrugged and began wiping the gleaming counter. "Maybe you should take this opportunity to purge yourself."

"Purge myself?"

"Yeah. You know." Rick winked suggestively. "Get her out of your system."

Chapter Four

Ashley nearly jumped out of her skin when the cabin door crashed open. "Michael!"

"In the flesh," he drawled, shutting the door. His eyes held a glittery quality she couldn't define. "Looks like you and I are stuck with each other, babe."

"Don't call me babe, and what do you mean? Stuck with each other? No way!" The idea didn't just fill her with dismay, it terrified her.

But she wasn't about to let Michael know that. Oh, how he would gloat if he knew how afraid she was of him. Not afraid of him physically— never that—but afraid of him emotionally. Sexually. Big time.

Michael leaned his back against the door, his hands behind him. He studied her long enough to make her nipples pucker in reaction. Ashley quickly crossed her arms over her breasts, cursing her body's betrayal.

"They don't have another cabin, sweetheart."

"I'm not your—" Ashley closed her eyes and mentally counted to ten. Finally, when she could trust herself to speak, she said, "Michael, there is no way in hell that I'm staying in this cabin with you for six nights and seven days."

Softly, Michael taunted, "What's the matter, you chicken? Can't trust yourself around me? Afraid you might *enjoy* my company?" He pushed away from the door and started walking toward her, his eyes dark with intent.

Ashley hastily vacated the bed and moved around him to the door. He turned, a mocking smile on his handsome face. She glared at him. "There has to be another cabin. Maybe you didn't stress the importance—"

"Oh, I stressed it, all right. Stressed it loud and clear, but it didn't do any good. There is no cabin available, so you're stuck with me."

She couldn't be stuck with Michael. The idea was not only out of the question but totally impossible. She scrambled for the doorknob, found it, and yanked the door open. "I'll talk to the person in charge myself."

"That would be Miss Beech in the purser's office, up on Deck Two. Knock yourself out. In the meantime, I'll just wait right here . . . in *my* cabin." He turned to the bed, then swung back around. "By the way, do you still sleep on the right side of the bed?"

Ashley couldn't get the door shut behind her fast enough, and nearly clipped her heels trying. Then and only then did she let out a shaky breath.

Michael was insane if he thought she was going to share a cabin with him. This Miss Beech person would just have to come up with another cabin. If Ashley had to bribe her, she would. She had the money and she was just desperate enough to use it for her own gain.

After asking a steward for directions, Ashley quickly made her way to the upper deck. She found Miss Beech in her tiny office and came right to the point.

"There's been a mix-up, I'm afraid. I'm supposed to have a cabin to myself, but you've got me paired with Mr. Kavanagh."

Miss Beech blinked at her, then calmly removed her glasses and massaged the bridge of her nose. Finally, she looked at Ashley with studied patience. "It's like I told Mr. Kavanagh, I can't just give you a cabin because you've had a fight—"

"Miss Beech, Michael and I have been divorced for two years—"

"I'm sorry to hear that but glad that you're making an effort to patch things up—"

"We are *not* making an effort to patch things

up!" Ashley realized her voice had risen and quickly lowered her tone. "Look, you've got to give me another cabin. I can't stay with him." Ashley no longer cared how desperate she sounded. "He's—he's—my fiancé wouldn't understand the situation." Which, Ashley suspected, was what Michael hoped.

"I'm sorry. There's nothing I can do."

The woman sounded final, but Ashley was too desperate to give up. "I want to speak to the captain."

To her chagrin, Miss Beech laughed.

"Oh, you can't. Even if you could, he would know nothing about cabin arrangements. That's *my* job."

There was nothing left to do but offer a bribe. Feeling like a criminal, Ashley dug into her jeans pocket and pulled out her emergency cash. She knew it was somewhere in the two-hundred-dollar range. She slapped it down on the desk. "Is that enough? If it isn't, I have more in my cabin."

Miss Beech didn't even glance at the money. "Even if I could come up with an empty cabin—which I can't—I wouldn't take your bribe. I'm sorry."

Ashley hated to admit defeat, she really did. But this appeared to be one of those times when she had no choice in the matter. Mumbling an ungracious thank you, she gathered her money and left the impossible woman's office. She didn't want to return to the cabin and Michael, not while their recent encounter, as she preferred to call it, was still so fresh in her mind.

Not to mention her body, which tightened each and every time she thought about Michael inside of her.

Desperate to take her mind off her illicit thoughts, Ashley followed the corridor signs directing her to the Coconut Lounge. She wasn't much of a drinker, but right now she was determined to do whatever it took—as long as it dulled her electrified senses. What was it about Michael, anyway? Tom never made her feel this . . . *agitated.*

Which was exactly why she loved him. With Tom, she didn't have to worry about heartaches and unsatisfied throbbing in unmentionable places, which led to sleepless nights and tear-soaked pillows.

No, she would never go there again. It was total insanity.

"Can I get you something?"

Ashley gave a start at the bartender's question. She smiled and shook her head. "Sorry, I was daydreaming. I'll have something strong. Surprise me."

"Okay, you asked for it."

The bartender, whose short, cropped hair had obviously been bleached platinum and whose flirty blue eyes betrayed his youth, made a flourish out of mixing her drink. His hands moved so fast on the various bottles that Ashley's head was already spinning by the time he handed her the pink concoction.

She flashed him a rueful grin. "Dare I ask?"

The bartender shrugged, grinning back. "It's my own speciality. It's called Rick's Remedy."

"I take it you're Rick?"

"In the flesh."

She gave a start at the familiar words. Why did everything remind her of the one person she was trying to forget? With a sigh, she asked, "And the remedy is for . . . ?"

"Your gloomy face."

"Oh." Ashley swallowed a laugh. "I'm Ashley Kavanagh. You can charge the drink to my cabin."

"Nice to meet you, Ashley. Want to tell me about the long face?"

Ashley grimaced and took a cautious sip of her drink. It was strong and sweet, but just flavorful enough to tolerate. "I wouldn't want to bore you."

Rick glanced around, then leaned close to whisper dramatically, "Don't look now, but we're being watched. You see, it's my job to make people smile. You leave here without smiling and I could lose my job."

Rick sounded so sincere that Ashley had to

laugh. She didn't believe him for a second, but she liked him. "Well, you probably won't think it's a big deal, but there was a mix-up with the cabin arrangements, and I'm having to share with my ex-husband."

"Hmm. Same last names, I take it?"

"Yes."

"I can see how that could happen."

Reluctantly, Ashley agreed. "I suppose it would be an easy mistake to make." She took a deep breath. "The thing is, I just can't stay in that cabin with him."

"So the old flame still burns, eh?"

Surprised by his shrewd observation, Ashley glanced sharply at him. He stared back at her without blinking. She frowned. "I wish I could say it didn't, but I'd be lying. It's—it's just a physical thing."

"How long were you married?"

"A year. We've been divorced for two years, and I'm engaged to be married to someone else. So is he."

"Ahh." Rick nodded, as if he understood completely. "Want another one of those?"

Ashley stared at her empty glass in surprise. "Yeah, sure. Why not?" She *did* feel more relaxed, she thought, wondering how many more it would take before her thighs stopped quivering and her breasts stopped aching. A quick glance down revealed that her nipples were still standing at attention as well.

Michael had that effect on her. It seemed that nothing had changed in that department.

"I guess it's just plain, old-fashioned body chemistry," she said, sipping her drink.

"So you're engaged."

"Yeah. To Tom."

"What's he like?"

"Hmm. He's taller than me by about three inches, and very solid. Broad shoulders, broad chest, narrow waist and narrow hips. He's got dark brown hair that gets these golden streaks in the summer, and his eyes are brown, but not just an ordinary brown." Absently, she turned the empty glass in her hands. "They're more like a rich dark chocolate, and sometimes they turn as black as midnight."

"And your ex-husband? What's *he* like?"

With a start of pure shock, Ashley jerked her gaze to the bartender's. "I—that's who I was describing." When Rick's eyebrows rose, she flushed. "You tricked me."

"I didn't," he denied, replacing her drink with a fresh one. He wiped the counter in front of her until it gleamed beneath the overhead lights. "But if you ask me, I think you've still got issues with your ex-husband. Maybe this mix-up was fate, something you needed."

Ashley's mouth went bone dry. She knew, but

she had to ask anyway. "What do you mean?"

Rick shrugged. "Maybe you need to purge yourself. Get him out of your system. Bring some closure to the relationship."

"Closure." Although his suggestion alarmed her, she liked the sound of that one word. Closure. Perhaps she *did* need closure with Michael. It was something to think about.

The speaker overhead crackled as a cool, feminine voice announced that an informal dinner would be served in the ship's dining room in thirty minutes.

"You won't want to miss it," Rick said. "They're serving petite lobster tails and coconut shrimp."

"Yes, well . . ." Ashley slipped from the stool and had to steady herself against the bar. "How many of those drinks did I have?"

"Three." Rick grinned. "Harmless . . . unless you haven't eaten today."

"Oh." *Now* he told her! "Well, thanks for the advice, and the drinks."

"My pleasure. Come back and see me anytime, Ashley. Michael's a lucky guy."

Ashley stumbled and grabbed the back of a chair. "Don't you mean Tom?"

"Yeah, Tom."

Funny, she thought, as she made her careful way back to the fated cabin. She couldn't remember telling Rick her ex-husband's name. But she must have. Otherwise, how would he have known?

She found the cabin door locked. Ashley used her key and let herself in, muttering a prayer beneath her breath that Michael would be gone.

The cabin appeared to be empty.

She heaved a grateful sigh and quickly locked the door, although she knew that it would be useless if Michael decided to return. She changed into a sleeveless blue summer dress, slipped into a new pair of matching sandals that had cost her more than what she would normally spend on a month's worth of groceries, and spent the remaining fifteen minutes hanging the rest of her new clothes in the beautiful armoire adjacent to Michael's.

She tried not to think about the coming night and sharing the cabin with Michael, but it was impossible not to. Should she take Rick's advice and get Michael out of her system? And what if the plan backfired? What if she fell in love with Michael again?

Oh, no, there was no chance of that happening. She would never put herself through that again. Never allow it to happen. In the last two years, she had come a long way from that silly, lovesick, naive girl Michael had swept off her feet.

She was a knowledgeable woman now, and the

blinders were off. Men like Michael couldn't remain faithful to any one woman.

Which was why she had picked safe, sedate, gentle Tom. She knew she could trust Tom. In fact, it had been Tom's idea that they wait to consummate their relationship. He'd wanted everything to be just right, and she had agreed.

Ashley's rueful chuckle startled her. After her crazy reaction to Michael, she wasn't certain Tom's decision to wait had been the right one. Apparently, she'd been steadily building up sexual steam.

And Michael had touched off her release valve.

But now she was prepared, and he wouldn't surprise her again. If something happened between them in the next seven days, it would happen because she *allowed* it to happen. Because she *wanted* it to happen.

And if she wanted it to happen, it would be to purge herself of Michael once and for all so that she could have a happy life with Tom.

Ashley locked the cabin door behind her and followed the flow of people to the enormous dining room. A hostess consulted her dinner card and led the way to the table assigned to her during the cruise.

"Everyone, this is Ashley Kavanagh," the hostess said, clapping her hands to gain their attention.

The three men sitting at the table immediately rose, including Michael. Ashley sucked in a sharp breath at how handsome he looked in dark green khakis and a pullover polo shirt in the exact same shade.

"Mrs. Kavanagh will be your dinner companion for the duration of the cruise." The hostess indicated that Ashley be seated. "Please introduce yourselves," she added before disappearing into the crowd.

Ashley avoided Michael's heated gaze, concentrating on her companions. She froze as she recognized the elderly couple beaming at her. Heat rushed over her in a fiery burst.

It was the same shameless couple who had interrupted their furious coupling. Ashley didn't know whether she should thank them or curse them.

The elderly woman was the first to speak. "Oh, we've met, haven't we, Mrs. Kavanagh? And your husband, Michael. I'm Birdie Scott, and this is Bart, my husband. This is our fourth cruise."

"Our sixth, sweetheart," Bart corrected gently, giving her hand an affectionate pat.

"Nice to meet you," Ashley mumbled. She knew her face was flaming, and she knew Michael was amused by it. So she ignored him.

The next introduction came from a gorgeous honey blonde with full, red lips and a skimpy dress made of a daring, sheer material that revealed more than it covered. Ashley fancied she could actually see the dark shadow of the woman's nipples through the dress. She appeared to be in her late twenties.

"Hello. I'm Tanya Reeves. I'm recently divorced from a doctor who was obviously already married to his work, and this is my first cruise."

Her soft, husky voice scraped over Ashley's nerves like nails on chalk. She glanced at Michael to catch his reaction, and found him watching Tanya with a bemused expression on his face, as if he didn't know quite what to make of her. The sharp pang she felt was *not* jealousy, Ashley told herself.

"And last but not least, I'm Deckland Jennings. I'm a psychologist-slash-writer, currently on hiatus while I finish my book."

Deckland was a tall, big-boned man somewhere in his early to mid-forties with an easy smile and intelligent blue eyes. Ashley liked him instantly. "What is your book about?" she asked politely. Taking her cue from the others, she began eating the salad the waiter had placed before her. After three of Rick's remedies, she figured it would be in her best interest to get some food in her stomach.

"I'm writing about body chemistry."

Ashley choked on her salad. Beside her, she heard Michael inhale sharply. Then he was pounding her back so hard he brought tears to her eyes.

When the dust settled, Deckland joked, "Was it something I said?"

"If anyone would know about body chemistry," Birdie said outrageously, "it would be those two." She nodded at Ashley and Michael. "Maybe they can help you with your research."

Ashley wanted to melt into a puddle and slip beneath the table. She knew that her face must be beet red.

"They're on their second honeymoon," Bart informed everyone. "Michael and I had a nice chat before everyone else arrived, didn't we, Michael?"

"Indeed we did, Bart."

She heard the laughter in his voice but couldn't believe it. Wasn't he embarrassed? Was it so very different for men?

"I remember the good old days when I could make love standing up, don't you, Birdie?"

"Yes, I do, Bart," said Birdie, without a trace of embarrassment. "But when your knee gave out and I hit my hip against the kitchen table, we decided it was time to use the bed."

Bart leaned in to kiss her wrinkled cheek. "Ah, you remembered."

Was this couple for real? Ashley wondered, speechless with shock. She had always thought the older generation more reserved, even prudish.

Obviously, Bart and Birdie came from a different planet!

"Don't be shy, Mrs. Kavanagh," Birdie teased. "It's our duty to make certain Mr. Jennings gets his facts straight. Right, Bart?"

"Right, Birdie. We haven't forgotten that fellow who wrote the article about our nudist colony." Bart waved his fork at his audience. "Mangled the facts badly. Talked about orgies and voodoo rituals! It was nonsense."

"*All* nonsense," Birdie echoed, sounding offended. "Except for that time Merle and Jake—"

"You mean Dan and Charlotte—"

"Ah, here's our main course," Deckland exclaimed, smoothly ending what Ashley was certain would have been another embarrassing revelation.

She had never been so humiliated in her life! It wasn't enough that the senior couple had witnessed their wild sex—they had told everyone at the table about it. And what had gotten into Michael? He'd obviously led Bart to believe they were on their second honeymoon.

Why would he tell such an outright lie?

Chapter Five

Moonlight dancing across the ocean set a romantic scene that Ashley knew she'd never forget. Overhead, the stars were visible, lighting up the sky like a scattering of diamonds against a black velvet blanket. They looked so close she felt she could reach up and scoop them into her hand.

The air was warm and wet and tasted of salt. Waves lapped against the sides of the ship, lulling Ashley into a false sense of serenity as she stood by the railing on the upper deck.

How could she feel serene when she was about to put her heart in jeopardy? Did she truly think that she could spend time with Michael without throwing her heart into the ring? He was a ruthless womanizer, something she mustn't forget, not for an instant.

She had foolishly forgotten . . . once upon a time.

"It's beautiful, isn't it?"

Ashley stiffened but didn't turn around. Looking at Michael beneath a full moon would be courting a madness she wasn't prepared to handle. Heck, she couldn't look at him in the daylight without her knees buckling. "Yes." Then, very deliberately, she added, "I wish Tom was here."

"And why isn't he?"

"He gets seasick." She wished she didn't sound so defensive; another trick of Michael's. "How about Candy? Why didn't she join you?" She felt the warmth of his breath an instant before his arm brushed against her hip as he moved to stand beside her at the railing.

Her nipples sprang erect as if he'd touched them instead of her hip.

"An important job came up."

A snort escaped her before she could stop it. "She's a stripper, Michael. What kind of job could she have that was more important than joining you on a cruise?"

"She's an exotic dancer, not a stripper."

"An exotic dancer who does lap dances?" For the life of her, Ashley couldn't keep the sarcasm from her voice.

"Kim should get her facts straight," Michael

said. "Candy doesn't do lap dances . . . unless she and I are alone."

And just like that, he thrust the arrow deep.

The pain petrified Ashley. After two years of self-therapy, she should feel nothing, nothing at all! Determined that he would never know the extent of her wound, Ashley rallied. "Earlier you said Candy was old-fashioned," she pointed out. "Now you're implying that she performs private lap dances for you. So which one is it?"

"There are ways to make love without sexual intercourse, Ash. You know that."

Graphic, painful images immediately swamped her mind. Ashley gave herself a mental shake as she lied, "I know exactly what you mean. Tom and I tried to wait, but we just couldn't."

Beside her, she felt him jerk. Intense satisfaction flooded her. Touché, she thought.

"You never did have much control, did you?"

Well, she supposed she deserved that one. "And you did?" she challenged, moving slightly away from him. She didn't want him touching her; it muddled her train of thought.

"We were hot for each other. That hasn't changed."

"Maybe for you it hasn't," Ashley lied baldly. "But for me it has. I told you, I had a weak moment."

In a flash, Michael was behind her, pressing against her buttocks and thighs in a flagrantly sexual way that bordered on primal. She could feel the entire length of him nestled between her cheeks.

He was hard, hot, and throbbing.

His breath washed over her bare neck, then his hot mouth scalded her skin as he kissed her shoulder, her neck, and her ear. She shivered violently and tried to move away, instantly aroused.

He caught her around the waist and hauled her back against him until there was no doubt that he was ready to take her then and there.

"There's no one else up here," he whispered hoarsely. "I could bend you over and take you right here." He moved his hand between her legs, finding her moist and ready. His other hand moved up to cover her breast, his fingers finding and kneading her hard nipple until she moaned.

"Just say the word," he coaxed, breathing hard. He took her hand and thrust it between them, urging her to feel his rock-hard erection. "And I'll make you scream."

For one insane, mind-melting instant, Ashley closed her fingers over him. She felt him throb and swell. And the heat . . . the heat he radiated was incredible.

"No!" She wrenched the word from her constricted throat, then followed it through by wrenching herself free of him. She stood there on the deck, the wind blowing her hair in her eyes and her breath coming in painful bursts. "No, Michael! This isn't going to happen. It's—it's just lust, and we're strong enough to resist. We *have* to resist!"

"Why?" he demanded, his eyes black and glittering. He took two steps in her direction and she scrambled back, holding her hands up to ward him off.

"Because of Tom, and Candy," Ashley cried desperately. "It would be wrong."

"They wouldn't have to know."

Michael knew the moment the words were out that he'd said the wrong thing. He watched as her eyes flared wide, then narrowed. He saw the way her mouth trembled, then firmed into a straight, unyielding line.

Then her shoulders went back, her chin came up, and her voice turned to frost.

"Is that what you told the women you lured into bed while you were married to me?" Her voice dropped another ten degrees. "That she doesn't have to know?"

Michael knew from past experience there would be no reasoning with her now. He knew, yet he still muttered the same old denial. "There weren't any women, Ash. Just the one, and we weren't—"

"Don't. Just stop right there. We're divorced

now, Michael. You don't have to explain, and I certainly don't want to hear your explanations. I've heard them all, remember?" She swept her hair from her face with a furious hand. "I don't intend to spend the remainder of this cruise beating a dead horse with you, so let's just drop it, okay?"

Finally, the anger Michael had been hoping for. He welcomed it with open arms. "I can drop it . . . if *you* can drop it, Ashley. I don't think I was imagining that you want to make love every bit as much—"

"Make *love?*" she asked incredulously. "At least call it by its real name, Michael. It's sex with you. Pure animalistic *sex*. Nothing less, nothing more."

"I don't remember you complaining."

"You bastard."

"Bitch."

"I'm out of here. When you come to bed, don't even *think* about touching me."

"Don't worry!" Michael shouted after her retreating form. "I've lost my appetite!" Which was a damned lie, and all she'd have to do was look at the bulge in his pants to know it.

But Ashley wasn't looking back. She was forging ahead, determined to run from this crazy attraction between them.

Well, she could run, but she couldn't hide, Michael thought, rubbing the back of his neck. Finally, his anger melted away and he found himself chuckling ruefully. He'd forgotten how alive he felt around Ashley. She excited him in more ways than one.

He turned to the railing and gripped it, staring out across the moonlit sea. By the time he returned to the cabin, he suspected he'd find her wearing enough clothes to smother an elephant. She'd probably pretend to be asleep, hugging the edge of the king-size bed.

He never had and never would force himself on her, and Ashley knew it, which told him that she didn't trust herself any more than she trusted him.

After another half hour of stargazing, Michael made his way to their cabin. He let himself in as quietly as he could, then locked the door. She'd left the bathroom light on and the door ajar for him, he noted, his gaze moving to the bed.

There was a dark mound in the middle of the mattress. A very large, unidentifiable mound.

Frowning, Michael walked closer.

Pillows. She had stacked half a dozen pillows in the middle of the bed to form a barrier between them.

He shook his head, smiling as he got undressed.

Completely.

* * *

Ashley felt something heavy pressing against her chest. She came awake with a startled scream locked in her throat, thrusting at the weight on top of her.

It was the pillows, she realized finally. The barrier she'd made had toppled onto her. In her panic, she had pushed most of them to the floor.

Slowly, she sat up. The bathroom door was cracked and the light still on; it cast a thin sliver of light onto the bed. She peered over the remaining layer of pillows.

Her heart slammed against her chest at the sight of a naked Michael stretched out on the bed. He had one arm flung over his head onto the pillow and the other stretched along his side. His hand cradled his semihard erection.

It was the way he'd always slept, she recalled. She'd teased him unmercifully about guarding the family jewels.

Sternly, she dragged her gaze away from the unsettling sight and onto his sleeping face. Her breath caught. He was so beautiful, she thought, her throat aching. She could watch him for hours.

Had watched him for hours.

Now they were divorced. Strangers to each other. Committed to other people. Yet here they slept, together in the same bed, an ocean away from the people they claimed to love.

No, that wasn't right. She *did* love Tom. Yes,

she was attracted to Michael. Desired him sexually. But that didn't mean she loved Michael. It could never mean that. The sex had always been incredible. Dynamite.

And was it any wonder she was obsessed with it now? She and Tom didn't sleep together. Never had. In fact, Michael was her first and her only. She could honestly—although painfully—accept that she missed it.

She would die before she would admit any of those facts to Michael. Oh, he would love to have that kind of power over her! She still couldn't figure out what he was doing on this cruise. It could have been a coincidence, but Ashley highly doubted it. The odds of Michael deciding to take the same cruise at the same time as she were about as fantastic as the odds of her winning the lottery.

But she *had* won the lottery.

"Take a picture," Michael whispered in a sleep-roughened voice, making her jump. "It'll last longer."

To cover her embarrassment over getting caught ogling him, she said, "I haven't heard that old saying since grade school."

He smiled. "Me neither." He shifted suddenly, thrusting a pillow behind his back and sitting up in the bed.

From the corner of her eye, she could see his erection growing. She steadfastly kept her gaze on his face. The light wasn't great, but there was enough to show her that Michael was now good and awake.

And she had destroyed the makeshift barrier between them.

His gaze roamed over her, reminding Ashley that she wore a next-to-nothing nightie. She hadn't packed anything comfortable or concealing, since she'd had seduction on her mind.

Only the seduction had involved Tom, not Michael.

"I was convinced you'd be wearing flannels," he said, making no attempt to cover himself.

He was shameless, Ashley thought with an inward groan. And so was she. Her nipples were poking holes through the sheer gauze of her nightie, and the crotchless, matching panties did nothing to absorb the sudden moisture that gathered between her legs.

"Earlier . . . when I was inside you, I nearly lost my mind."

Ashley swallowed hard. She found it suddenly impossible to draw a deep breath. And impossible to move.

"Afterward, I couldn't stop thinking about it."

His voice was deep and sexy, husky with desire. It turned the moisture between her legs into a drench. Ashley bit her lip and shifted, squeezing her legs together.

"Just shut up, Michael. Please." Oh, what a pitiful, weak request! She turned her face into the pillow, aching all over. Aching for Michael. Only Michael.

Michael, of course, ignored her plea. He continued to topple her puny defenses with whispered, sexy words of love play.

"All day long, I thought of how tight you felt. How hot you were. How wonderful it was to be inside you again." His sigh sounded more like a groan. "I can tell you've been lying in the tanning bed. Your nipples are darker than I remember. Unbelievably sexy."

"Stop."

"And your mouth. God, your mouth! It's made for kissing and nibbling and sucking—"

"Michael. Don't."

"Don't stop? I don't intend to. You've known all day this was going to happen. We've both known it. There's no reason to torture ourselves any longer. I want to be inside you . . . and you want me to be inside you. We are hot together . . . dynamite, Ash. We don't just come, we *explode*. Tell me it isn't so."

She tried. She couldn't.

"Give me your hand."

She squeezed her eyes shut and shook her head. She gave him her hand.

He guided it to his erection, curled her fingers around it and began to rub her palm against his silky skin. The heat burned into her, spreading its delicious warmth along her arm and into the rest of her body.

She reached out and grabbed a pillow, throwing it to the floor. She grabbed another, and another, until there was nothing between them.

He pulled her against him, suddenly urgent as he found her mouth and kissed her until she was mindless. Within seconds they were frantic to get closer, touch each other, feel each other, taste each other.

She took him in her mouth and he growled once, twice, before pulling her roughly away. Then he retaliated by lifting her high onto his shoulders and planting his hot mouth right against her throbbing core.

She had less control, convulsing around him within seconds. The orgasm went on and on, and just when she thought she would die, Michael settled her onto his erection and thrust her downward, impaling her to the hilt.

"*This* is heaven," he panted.

Ashley watched him as he threw back his head and clenched his jaw, fighting his release. She knew he wouldn't allow himself the luxury of letting go yet. Not until she was exhausted and begging him to stop. Still watching him, she flattened her hands against his granite-hard chest, then curled her fingers.

He moaned but didn't move.

She leaned forward and scraped her teeth

across his nipples, first one, then the other.

He moaned again, and squeezed her hips.

She clenched her inner muscles around him, then slowly rose, smiling when he opened his eyes to glare at her. He went after her, thrusting hard and deep, bringing her back to him.

"You're killing me," he growled, suckling her breasts until she whimpered.

With a move that stole her breath, he flipped her onto her back and came down on her, still inside her.

Now he had full control, and it was Ashley's turn to plead as he began a torturous rhythm that had her squirming and begging him to go deeper, faster.

And then he did that swiveling move with his hips and Ashley was spinning out of control as another orgasm snagged her and shot her into space.

Michael muffled her scream with his mouth, and she felt him began to shudder. He pulled away and threw back his head.

"Ahhh . . . Ashley!"

She watched him, and her heart seemed to stop at the sheer beauty of his release.

Michael was right; they didn't just come together, they exploded.

Chapter Six

The sound of voices outside the cabin door startled Ashley awake. She sat up, staring at the chaos around her in complete confusion. It looked as if she'd had an overnight party with her girlfriends, and a pillow fight had been the main attraction.

Heat rushed into her face as she recalled what had really happened last night.

With Michael.

Oh, Lord. Definitely with Michael. *Deliciously* with Michael.

She should regret it, but she didn't.

But it wasn't going to happen again. She'd gotten him out of her system, all right, just as the bartender had suggested. Now she could go about the business of enjoying her cruise. And after the cruise she would marry Tom and Michael would marry Candy and everything would be fine.

They were, after all, incompatible in almost every way. Okay, okay, so they were dynamite together in bed. Michael was her first and only. How did she know it wouldn't be the same with Tom?

Ashley groaned and shook her head as she got out of bed and kicked her way to the shower. She knew because when Tom kissed her, she didn't melt. So what? Who said a girl had to see Fourth of July fireworks every time she kissed? Such a thing could quickly become exhausting.

She turned on the shower and removed the shreds of her nightie, unable to stop the smile that came and went at the memory of Michael literally stripping her naked. He'd gotten his toe caught in the hem of the nightie, and that was that.

Nobody messed with Michael's big toe. He'd broken that same toe three times. If you wanted to see a grown man cry, then step on Michael's toe.

It wasn't until Ashley finished her shower and was searching through her wardrobe that she saw the note on the nightstand. It was propped against one of the sandals she'd worn the day before.

Stomach quivering, she picked it up and tore open the envelope, compliments of *Funstar* cruises. It was Michael's surprisingly neat handwriting, all right. The message was brief and crystal clear: *Ashley—I know you're probably thinking the same thing, so I'll say it first. Last night was dynamite, and I can't bring myself to regret it, but you were right. It's wrong. You're engaged to Tom and I'm involved with Candy. So let's chalk it up to a rogue itch and try to remain on good terms the remainder of the trip, okay?*

It was signed, *Yours truly, Michael.*

Rogue itch? That was a first for Ashley, but it fit them to a *T.* They weren't compatible; hardly liked each other, if the truth be told. So what else could it be but a *rogue itch?* And last night they had scratched that itch. End of story.

"I'm *so* over you," Ashley muttered, crumpling the note and pitching it in the direction of the trash can. She missed, of course, but what did it matter, considering the mess the room was in? If the maid possessed an ounce of Cajun blood, she'd probably put a curse on them.

Maybe she'd be willing to teach Ashley a little voodoo.

By the time Ashley was dressed and ready to go to breakfast, her resolve was ironclad. If Michael had hoped to hurt her with that little note, then he would be disappointed. She *had* been thinking the same thing. So what if he'd beaten her to the punch?

To strengthen her resolve even further, she

would call Tom right after breakfast. Yes, hearing Tom's voice was just the medicine she needed.

When Ashley opened the cabin door, she found the hallway crowded with stewards and official-looking men in white uniforms. In the middle of the crowd was Birdie, looking agitated and near tears. Bart stood beside her, his arm firmly around her shoulders.

Alarmed, Ashley pushed her way to Birdie's side. The couple was eccentric, but they seemed harmless enough, and they were not only her neighbors but her dinner companions. "What's going on, Birdie?"

Birdie sniffed. "Someone broke into our cabin and stole my grandmother's brooch, that's what's going on! It was a priceless heirloom."

One of the stewards patted Birdie on the shoulder, his voice sympathetic. "I'm sorry, ma'am. We've got your description of the brooch, and we'll be changing the lock on your door immediately. Maybe whoever took it will have a change of heart and return it."

"Let's go to breakfast, darling," Bart said, gently leading her through the crowd. Catching his meaningful glance, Ashley flanked Birdie's left side and took her arm.

"I'll walk with you, if you don't mind," Ashley said, concerned over the woman's pallor. She looked as if she'd seen a ghost. And who could blame her? Birdie was seventy if she was a day, and she'd said the brooch belonged to her grandmother.

Which meant the piece of jewelry was definitely an antique. And then there were her feelings of violation, knowing that someone had been rifling through her things.

Ashley shuddered. She'd never been robbed, but she could imagine how Birdie felt.

As they approached the dining room, Ashley braced herself. If by chance Michael thought she'd be crushed by his note, then he was in for a surprise.

"Are you enjoying your cruise, Michael?" Tanya asked him the moment he settled into his appointed seat at the table.

He accepted the coffee a passing waiter offered before he replied. "What's not to enjoy? The weather's great, the food is superb, and the women are gorgeous." She blushed and he smiled, but behind his smile he was grimacing.

On the second day of the cruise, Tanya had opted for short shorts and a crocheted halter top that revealed more of her breasts than it covered. She'd piled her honey-blond hair onto her head in a loose, careless knot that made her look young, fresh, and sexy.

A casual glance around proved Michael's theory that there wasn't a man in the dining room who wasn't fantasizing about Tanya.

With one exception.

He wasn't fantasizing about Tanya. In fact, he wasn't the slightest bit attracted to the blond bombshell.

And then he caught sight of Ashley entering the dining area with Birdie and Bart.

Raw desire shot into his groin, igniting a fire that had apparently been slumbering. With a muffled oath, Michael grabbed his napkin and dropped it into his lap to cover his reaction.

Ashley wore a sunny yellow summer dress with a plunging neckline and a belted waist. Her tanned legs were bare, right down to her matching sandals and painted toes. She wore her rich brown hair loose around her shoulders and a shade of lipstick that made her lips look ripe and full.

Just hours ago, he'd sucked on her little painted toes and nibbled on those luscious lips. In fact, he couldn't remember a part of her body that he hadn't nibbled, tasted, or licked. How many love bites had he left in his wake? A dozen? Two dozen? In the bright light of day, he wanted to take off her dress and examine every inch of her body—

Michael groaned again and dragged his gaze away. He found Tanya watching him with raised eyebrows and a wistful little smile on her pouty mouth.

"Damn," she said, then sighed. "I want a man

who looks at me like that when we go on our second honeymoon." She laughed and shook her head. "In fact, I don't think I've *ever* had a man look at me the way you look at your wife."

He had to swallow a denial, reminding himself that it was his fault. After Bart and Birdie had caught them in the act, he had instinctively sought to protect Ashley by letting the older couple believe they were married.

"Good morning, everyone," Bart said as he reached the table. With infinite tenderness, he led a pale-faced Birdie to her chair. Ashley took her seat next to Michael's, accidentally bumping his thigh with her own.

Michael let out a soft hiss, and his erection grew beneath his napkin. He knew he wouldn't be one of the first to leave the table when breakfast was over. Get her out of his system? Ha! He felt the same this morning as he had before their wild night.

"Birdie, is something wrong?" Tanya asked, passing Bart the cream. "You look pale."

Bart poured cream into his wife's coffee, then his own. "We've been robbed, I'm afraid. Someone took Birdie's grandmother's brooch."

Birdie's eyes filled with tears. She grabbed her napkin and touched it to the corners of her eyes. "It must have happened while Bart and I were out taking our morning stroll around the ship."

"What did I miss?" Deckland inquired as he took his seat.

Bart began to fill him in, and Michael took the opportunity to look his fill at Ashley. She leaned forward to reach the tiny pitcher of cream, causing her daring dress to gap.

Michael saw a trail of love bites along the inner side of her left breast.

He tried to muffle the groan that rose in his throat, but he wasn't in time.

The sound startled Ashley. She jerked around, knocking her napkin to the floor between them.

With a deep sense of foreboding, Michael watched her bend over to retrieve the napkin. She paused on the way up, her gaze fixed on his lap.

She lifted her eyes to his pained expression, her brow creasing in concern. "What's wrong, darling? Is that rogue itch bothering you again?"

"Tom?"

"Um, no. Just a moment."

Ashley frowned, trying to put a face to the groggy male voice that had answered Tom's phone. He didn't have a roommate, and the voice wasn't familiar.

She plugged her free ear with her finger, straining to hear over the casino noises behind her. There was a slight rustling sound on the other end, and then Tom came on the line.

He sounded just as groggy. "Hello?"

"Tom? Did I wake you?" *And who's there with you?* It wasn't a woman, so why was she concerned? But she knew why. Tom lived in a one-bedroom apartment, with the bed in a loft above the living room, and if the guy who had answered the phone had been sleeping on the sofa downstairs, he wouldn't have had time to get the phone to Tom that quickly.

So what was she thinking?

"Ashley? Is that you? You sound a million miles away!"

"Close." Ashley bit her lip. "They told me I might have trouble hearing you, or vice versa. Who answered the phone?"

"Oh. That was Lindsey. He had a little too much to drink last night, so he crashed here. I was just bringing him my hangover remedy when you called."

Relief washed over her. She felt silly for her suspicious thoughts. Tom wasn't gay. Of course he wasn't gay. She managed a laugh. "Poor Lindsey." Whoever Lindsey was. "He won't know what hit him until it's too late."

Unlike Rick's sweet concoction, Tom's "remedy" was three-fourths vodka and one-fourth tomato juice.

"Well, I'm glad to hear you're not pining away for me," she said, only half-joking.

"Oh, but I am, Ash. I miss you like hell. I can't wait until you get back."

Ashley couldn't speak for a moment. She was imagining Michael saying those exact same words, and how much more sincere they would sound coming from him.

When Tom said them, they were devoid of passion. He could have been talking to any number of his friends.

Stop it! Ashley pinched the bridge of her nose until tears sprang to her eyes. Damn Michael! And damn Kim, too, if she was behind this, as Michael suspected.

"So, have you met the other lottery winner?" Tom asked, snagging her attention and reminding her of something she had totally forgotten.

"Um, no. Not yet." The only information she had about the other winner was that he or she was from her home state. They weren't allowed to give her any further information, so she was on her own. She would have to play sleuth, and had actually been looking forward to it.

Until Michael. Once Michael entered the picture, she'd forgotten a lot of important things.

Like fiancés and lottery winners and self-respect and shame.

Why are you here, Michael? Just to torment me?

She and Tom said their good-byes, and Ashley hung up the phone with a deep sense of impending doom. She had hoped the call to Tom

76

would make her feel guilty, but it hadn't.

Before she could change her mind, she quickly dialed Kim's number. If Kim truly was behind Michael's presence on the ship, she would confirm it.

"Hello?"

"Kim?"

"Ashley? Oh, my God, Ash! How's the cruise? Is it fabulous? Have you spent all your money? Did you buy something for me?"

Ashley didn't feel like exchanging idle chit-chat. She had a situation on her hands. "What's Michael doing on this ship?"

"Who?"

"Michael. Your brother. My ex-husband. The man I do my best to avoid." The man who had rocked her world last night.

"Oh. Him. What was the question?"

"For heaven's sake—what is he doing on this cruise?"

Kim was silent far too long for Ashley's peace of mind. What was she doing? Preparing her lie? Stalling?

"Well, he, uh . . . the truth is, he made me swear not to tell anyone."

"Tell anyone what?" Ashley demanded.

"I just told you, Ash, I can't tell you!" Kim sounded agitated. "I know we're best friends and all, but this time Michael made me swear on Mom's grave."

"You have to tell me."

"I can't."

"Yes, you can. And you will." If Ashley had to call her back a dozen times, she would find out the truth.

"I can give you a tiny hint, but you have to *swear* not to tell him, or let on that you know."

A sharp thrill raced along Ashley's spine. Kim had never before sounded so cloak and dagger-ish. "Okay, I swear."

"On your mother's grave?"

"Kim, my mother's still alive."

"Oh. That's right." Kim sighed. "He's going to kill me for this. . . ."

"He won't ever find out," Ashley promised.

"Just a hint. That's all I can give."

"Can you give it to me *today?*" Ashley asked, exasperated. "As in right now?"

"It's about money, and that's all I can say."

"Money?" Ashley was dumbfounded. "*Money* is the reason he's on this cruise? Come on, Kim! You can do better than that."

"No, I can't. I've told you more than I should have already." Kim's voice dropped low as she pleaded, "Please don't make me break a promise to my brother, Ash."

Ashley wasn't convinced, and wasn't fooled by Kim's pleading tone. "You're lying. You threw us together on purpose, and now you're trying to distract me—"

"I *did* throw you two together," Kim confessed hurriedly, but without apology. "I admit that. When I found out Tom wasn't going with you, the opportunity was too sweet to resist. But I'm not lying about the money."

For the next several moments, Ashley pleaded, threatened, and cajoled, but to no avail. Kim had buttoned her lip. Finally, Ashley gave up. "Okay, but after this cruise you and I are going to settle this Michael thing once and for all. Michael and I are divorced. I'm going to marry Tom. Your brother's going to marry Candy." The name almost got stuck in her throat. Ashley swallowed gamely, trying not to imagine Candy performing a back bend on Michael's lap. "So get over it, Kim."

"Yeah, sure."

"Kim . . ."

"Gotta go, Ash. Give Michael a kiss for me, would you?" With that cheeky remark, Kim hung up the phone.

"She's impossible!" Ashley muttered, slamming down the receiver. Just like her brother! Impossible and contrary and devious.

Ashley spent the next two hours in the casino, recklessly feeding the slot machines . . . determined that she would find *something* to take her mind off Michael and the stark image of the tent pole in his shorts.

And the look of pure lust in his eyes when he realized she'd noticed.

How could he be so quick to arouse after the night they'd spent? How could she be so quick to react to his arousal? How could either one of them have the energy left to think about it?

And what the heck had Kim meant about Michael and money? Was he broke? It didn't make sense. Broke people didn't go on expensive cruises. They stayed home and counted their pennies and tried to figure out ways to get out from behind.

She was still playing the slots when she happened to glance up and catch sight of Michael across the room. He was seated at a blackjack table, and he'd already drawn a crowd around him.

Like a magnet to steel, Ashley crossed the room and merged into the expectant crowd to watch Michael.

"Hit me."

"Are you sure you want to bet the entire two thousand, sir?"

"I don't need a nursemaid, I need a card," Michael growled. "Now hit me."

Ashley held her breath as the dealer turned up a seven of diamonds to Michael's queen. As one, the crowd leaned forward.

Hot Number

The dealer turned up his own card, a ten of spades to go with his king.

Michael had just lost two thousand dollars on one hand of blackjack.

Chapter Seven

Michael walked to the far end of the upper deck, where he could have a little privacy. He flipped open his cell phone and dialed Kim's number, turning to face the warm salty breeze.

To his left, he saw a school of dolphins leaping in the air as they raced to keep up with the ship.

The phone rang twice before Kim picked up. Before he could announce himself, she said, "If you're calling to badger me into telling, you're wasting your time."

"Kim?" Michael frowned. There was a small, awkward silence on the other end of the line. "Are you there? It's Michael."

"I realize that now," Kim said, sounding suspiciously guilty. "I forgot your phone has a certain ring on my end so that I know you're calling."

"So I gathered," Michael said grimly. "I've got bad news."

"Do I need to sit down?"

"Probably." He gave her enough time to do just that before he said, "I lost the entire two thousand."

"Oh, that!"

She was laughing in relief. Michael held out the phone and tapped it a few times. Maybe they had a bad connection. Just in case, he said, "Kim, I lost your money. I told you I was lousy at gambling."

Kim remained oddly cheerful. "Did you play blackjack, like I asked you to?"

"Yes."

"And did you play the entire two thousand on one hand, like I asked you to?"

"Yes."

"And did you enjoy it?"

"No." Michael ran an exasperated hand through his salt-damp hair. "I'm going to win your money back for you, and then I'm finished with gambling."

"You would think," Kim drawled, heavy on the sarcasm, "that after winning the lottery you might be willing to take a risk now and then."

"You could have used that money to expand your catering business," Michael pointed out.

"Which is why I'm going to win it back. *I* can afford to lose it. *You* can't."

"Instead of using your money to win mine back, why don't you buy Ashley something nice when the ship docks in St. Thomas or Barbados?"

"You cheeky little brat." Michael was amazed at her gall. "You're not even going to *pretend* you didn't know she would be on this cruise."

Kim snorted. "Give me a little credit for giving *you* a little credit for having some brains, bro. You would never have believed me."

"You're right, I wouldn't." Michael shook his head, knowing he should be furious. He'd always had trouble staying mad at Kim. "But you'd better hope she doesn't figure out that I came to be on this cruise for the very same reason *she's* here."

"She won't. Think about it, Michael. Ashley knows you. She knows how you are about gambling. She would never in a million years consider that you won the lottery."

Michael chuckled, knowing Kim was right. It would be the last thing Ashley would dream of.

"I mean, the absolute *irony* of you buying a lottery ticket using the same sentimental numbers—"

"I told you, I was mocking her. I never thought for a moment that she'd win—that *I* would win." At least he was telling the truth about not believing either of them would win. The rest he would take to his grave.

"Right. So how's the fire?"

"The fire?" Michael was lost. "I don't get you."

"The fire. The big blaze. The inferno you two create when you're within a few feet of—"

Without hesitation, Michael slapped his phone together, disconnecting her. He held out his arms and squeezed his fingers together, imagining Kim's neck.

From the corner of his eye, he caught sight of a boy, about six or seven, watching him with wide, frightened eyes.

With a sheepish smile, Michael dropped his arms and stuck his hands in his pockets, whistling nonchalantly as he walked away.

Michael didn't show for lunch.

It took every ounce of willpower Ashley possessed to remain at the table throughout the meal, listening to Birdie's constant chatter and trying to pretend that nothing was wrong.

When everything was wrong.

She'd left the casino in a state of horrified shock. Watching Michael carelessly throw two thousand dollars away on a card hand, swift on the heels of her murky conversation with Kim about money and Michael, had left her shaken and imagining the worst.

Michael never gambled. Just the shock of seeing him *in* a casino should have triggered an alarm, but she'd been so busy trying not to think naughty thoughts about him that she hadn't been thinking straight at all.

Michael made fun of people who gambled. Not because he was trying to be righteous—that would be a laugh, because Michael had always been a risk-taker—but because he considered the odds laughable.

Once he'd snatched her lottery ticket from her hand and pointed to the list of rules typed on the back in red ink. "See the odds, Ash? One in *two million* chances that you'll get these numbers. You're wasting your money, and the state of Missouri is getting rich."

To her knowledge, he'd never bought a lottery ticket, and she doubted he ever would, not even after she'd managed to beat the odds herself. She could hear him now: "It was a fluke. It will never happen again to anyone we know."

Yes, that sounded like something Michael would say all right. And after saying it, nothing would persuade him to participate in the lottery . . . or any other type of gambling.

So what happened? And *when* did it happen, and why hadn't Kim mentioned it to her? She was, after all, his ex-wife. She still cared about him—oh, not *that* way anymore, of course—but as one human being to another.

How could Kim keep it from her? How dare

she, when she took every opportunity to throw them together?

"Penny for your thoughts? Or is it a dollar these days?"

Ashley gave a start and looked up to find Deckland watching her with a concerned smile. She forced herself to smile back. "I'm sorry. Did I miss something?"

"We were all wondering where Michael was," he said.

Tanya caught the sleeve of a passing waiter pushing a dessert tray and snatched a couple of decadent-looking chocolate mousse dishes from the assortment. She set one in front of Ashley. "Yes, tell us where Michael is. He may be totally devoted to you, but he has a way of making *all* women feel pretty, and I could use a lift right about now. The most interesting guy I've met so far is Bart."

"Thank you, my dear," Bart said, sounding pleased.

The chocolate mousse looked loaded with calories. Ashley gave a brief thought to the five pounds she'd lost before she dug in. It was delicious, and just what she needed. She swallowed her second bite before she said, "Truthfully, I don't know where he is at the moment." She had her suspicions, but nothing she wanted to share with her lunch companions.

"And you're not worried?" Tanya pointed her

fork at Ashley. "Honey, if I had a man like Michael, I would never let him out of my sight. The women are drooling all over him. Haven't you noticed?"

Suddenly, the chocolate tasted bitter. Ashley shoved her uneaten dessert aside and reached for her water. She hadn't noticed, because she'd been too busy drooling over him herself.

Deckland saved her from having to answer the unanswerable. "Does she look worried? I don't think she does. Anyone with a scrap of intuition can plainly see that Ashley and Michael are soul mates."

Tanya turned her wide-eyed gaze to Deckland. "You believe in soul mates, Dr. Jennings?"

"Call me Deckland, please. I'm officially off duty." He shot Ashley an odd, knowing look that froze her on the spot. "Unless I'm needed, of course. And yes, Tanya, I do believe in soul mates. Michael and Ashley are perfect examples."

"Bart and I are perfect examples too," Birdie inserted. "And though we no longer get it on the way Ashley and Michael do, we had our day." She exchanged a heated look with Bart before locking in on Ashley's mousse. "If you're not going to finish that luscious-looking dessert, may I?"

Absently, Ashley handed her unfinished dessert to Birdie, no longer shocked by anything the elderly couple did or said. She was still thinking about what Deckland had said, and the funny look he'd given her. Almost as if he knew she and Michael were not the happily married couple everyone thought them to be.

Could the man be that astute? She supposed he could be. He was, after all, a psychologist. A certain amount of perception was probably a necessary attribute in his profession.

Maybe she could talk to him about Michael and his gambling problem, see what he suggested she do. And maybe while she was at it, she could find out what Deckland knew about the mystery of body chemistry, since he was writing a book about it. What Ashley wanted to know was how two people who were so obviously wrong for each other could be so insanely attracted to one another.

And whether there was a cure for that attraction.

Suddenly, the air was shattered by the sound of a loud foghorn. Birdie let out an excited cry and leaped to her feet, knocking the empty dessert dish from the table. Bart caught her wayward chair before it hit the floor, casting the others a sheepish smile.

"Come! Come!" Birdie shouted, waving her arms. "They've spotted whales! Let's go see the whales!"

Tanya immediately rose to follow the charge of people heading for the lookout deck. Ashley rose too, but Deckland stopped her with a hand to her wrist before she could take a step away from the table.

Surprised, she turned to look at him.

"Won't you stay and talk? We'll have another chance to see the whales. I promise." When she hesitated, he tugged on her wrist. "I know that you've got something on your mind."

"Is it that obvious?" she asked with a rueful twist of her lips. He nodded, then patted the chair Tanya had vacated. The dining room was deserted.

More than a little embarrassed, Ashley allowed him to pull her down. "You're on vacation. I'm sure the last thing you want to do is deal with someone else's problems."

Deckland smiled. "Believe it or not, I didn't enter into this profession for the money. I did it because I care about people, and I want to help them."

"How did you know that I—that I—"

"Had something on your mind?" he finished. "Let me see. You might have tipped me off when you glanced at Michael's empty chair for the hundredth time. Or it might have been that frown between your brows. Then there was the fact that you ate your garnish, which happened to be made of wax."

Ashley dropped her face into her hands. "Tell

me you're joking," she mumbled between her fingers. Her face was on fire.

"Sorry. You really did eat your garnish, and it really was made of wax. But don't worry, it won't hurt you. I asked one of the waiters."

She lifted her head to peek at him. "Did anyone—"

"No. Nobody else saw you eat the wax seashell. In fact, if it will make you feel better, Birdie ate hers, too." Ashley couldn't resist a smile. "That's better. Now, would you like to talk here, or would you rather go somewhere more private?"

Ashley didn't hesitate. She didn't want to take a chance that someone else might hear what she had to say. "Let's go to your cabin."

Michael emerged from their cabin just in time to catch the flash of Ashley's yellow dress disappearing into Deckland's cabin down the hall.

His jaw dropped and a wave of jealousy swept over him, causing him to stagger back into the cabin and shut the door. What the hell was Ashley doing in Deckland's cabin? While he'd been attempting to drown his relentless erection in cold water, she, apparently, had had no trouble at all putting him from her mind—*replacing* him.

She's none of your business, Michael. She is history. Old history.

Oh, the sweet voice of reason. Michael hated it, but he knew that it spoke the truth. It would be wise of him to listen, too, and if he couldn't bring himself to listen to reason, he had only to recall the dark days, weeks, and months following Ashley's unjust desertion. Her complete lack of faith in him—*them*—had nearly ruined his life.

She was poison. Pure poison.

He knew better. Which was why he'd written that note, before she'd had the chance to hurt him again. He couldn't stop his body from igniting when he was around her, but he could damn well keep his mind and his heart out of it.

Let her have her little fling with the shrink if that was what she intended. Perhaps having a fling before settling down with Tom was what she'd had in mind when she accepted the free cruise and left her fiancé behind.

Michael's college buddies had encouraged him to do the same thing when he and Ashley had become engaged, unable or unwilling to believe that Michael was capable of settling down with one woman for the rest of his life. Michael, the playboy, who had often dated several women at the same time, settling down? Impossible. Highly unlikely.

But he'd fooled them all by proving to be a loving and devoted husband, and they had retaliated by planting a woman in his hotel bed when he was too drunk to realize he was alive.

It should have ended the same way it had

begun—as a harmless prank played by well-intentioned friends.

Instead, the strange woman had gotten curious about the same time Ashley, who was supposed to be in Kansas City, not Aspen, decided to surprise him.

Michael had awakened with the devil's own hangover to find a strange woman in his bed, examining his manhood at close range. He hadn't seen Ashley, but he'd heard her gasp just seconds before the door slammed shut again. At the time, he'd thought it was the maid.

Later, when he'd come home to find Ashley gone and a cryptic note informing him of their impending divorce, he realized that it hadn't been the maid after all.

In the blink of an eye his wonderful marriage had crumbled.

Chapter Eight

"Wow. You have a great cabin," Ashley said, nervous now that she was alone with Deckland. What was she doing? If Michael had gambling problems—and the cards were pointing in that direction—then it was certainly none of her business.

He wouldn't appreciate her butting in, and he definitely wouldn't appreciate her sharing the information with a total stranger.

Not a stranger, she reminded herself, but a professional.

Deckland slid a glass door aside and gestured to a small table and two chairs out on the balcony. "I've got friends in high places," he explained with a lopsided grin that made him look years younger. When she followed him and sat down, he took the chair opposite her. "So, tell me. What's going on with you and Michael? I know it's just our second day, but I already feel as if I know everyone at our table."

Ashley hesitated, thinking again that Michael wouldn't appreciate her talking about his private life with a stranger. She took a deep breath. "Well, I have this friend—"

"No, you don't." At her dumbfounded expression, Deckland laughed. "Sorry. I've always wanted to say that, and I just couldn't help myself."

"Oh." Ashley tried to look offended, failed, and ended up laughing with him. "Are you always this informal with your patients?"

"I try to be. I find that it helps for them to know right off the bat that I'm human, too."

"With a sense of humor," she added.

He shrugged, still smiling. "In my line of work, it pays to have a sense of humor. If it helps, think of me as a friend, not a doctor. I *am* officially off duty."

When he fell silent again, Ashley knew it was time to talk. Seriously. About Michael. "I think Michael has a gambling problem. I want to know how I can help."

"What makes you think he has a gambling problem?"

"Right before lunch I saw him lose two thousand dollars on a single hand of blackjack."

Deckland whistled. "That's a pretty good sign. How long has he been gambling like this?"

Ashley glanced out at the sea, so beautiful and vast. If it hadn't been for the spectacular view and the smell of salt spray, she would find it hard to believe they were on a ship. In fact, it was hard to believe a lot of things that had happened to her lately, beginning with winning the lottery. "I honestly don't know."

"Hmm." Deckland drummed his fingers on the tabletop, his expression thoughtful. "I find myself wondering why you agreed to go on this cruise if you were aware of his problem. Most ships have casinos."

"I didn't—" Ashley bit her lip. Did she really want to go into a long explanation about her relationship—or lack thereof—with Michael? No, she decided, she didn't. She'd rather use the time to figure out how to help Michael. It was the least she could do for him, considering they had once been married *and* he was her best friend's brother. "It was either come with him or let him go alone. I decided to come with him, hoping I could keep him distracted enough so that he wouldn't have the opportunity to gamble." She was amazed at how easily she told the lie. Only it wasn't all a lie. She really did want to distract him, now that she knew.

Deckland's brow rose. "From what Birdie and Bart told me, you started off on the right foot."

Despite the heat that rushed to her face, Ashley said, "Obviously I haven't distracted him enough."

"Well, there you have it. Try harder. Don't let him out of your sight. Keep him busy, in whatever way you can. I can tell by the way Michael looks at you that you could have him wrapped around your little finger in no time."

Ashley had to swallow a disbelieving laugh at Deckland's sadly mistaken observation. The doctor had no idea how very wrong he was, and she didn't have the heart to tell him. "You've been very helpful. Can I pay you? I have plenty of money—"

"Yes, I heard that you'd won the lottery," Deckland surprised her by saying. "That must have been exciting."

"You did?"

"When Michael told us you two were on your second honeymoon, he said you'd been given the cruise by your hometown travel agency after winning the lottery. Something about posing for a brochure."

Michael, it seemed, had been doing a little sharing of his own, Ashley mused. It went a long way toward easing her guilt over talking to Deckland. Besides, talking to Deckland about Michael wasn't like talking to Tanya, or the Scotts. Deckland was a professional. Anything she told him would be kept confidential.

But just in case . . . "You won't tell him that we talked, will you?"

"Okay. *Now* you can think of me as a psychologist," Deckland said with a rueful shake of his head. Then, more seriously, he added, "Michael's a lucky man to have you."

Ashley suffered a pang of guilt over lying to Deckland. She wasn't entirely certain why she hadn't told him the truth, that meeting Michael and sharing a cabin aboard ship was either a wild coincidence or, if Michael could be believed, a devious, stubborn plot hatched and carried out by her best friend.

Possibly *ex*–best friend, by the time the cruise ended. Instead of a nice, relaxing vacation, she had not only slept with her ex-husband, she was now thinking about sticking to him like glue for the remainder of the trip to keep him away from the casino.

Why? Why was she so concerned about a man who had trampled her heart in the dust and now threatened her well-ordered, hard-won stress-free life?

It was a question, a very reasonable question, that she couldn't answer.

"Ashley?"

Ashley gave a start, realizing she'd been so deep in her thoughts that she hadn't heard Deckland's question. "I'm sorry. Could you repeat that?"

"I asked if you would mind helping me with my book. Maybe answer a few simple questions? I won't use your name, of course."

With a straight face, Ashley asked, "Could I get that in writing?" Now it was her turn to laugh at Deckland's dumbfounded expression. "Gotcha."

His smile was rueful and boyish. "I guess I had that coming."

"Yes, you did. And yes, I'll answer your questions to the best of my ability."

"They're personal," he warned.

"I've already discovered that nothing is personal or sacred when you share a cruise with Birdie and Bart."

"They *are* a pair, aren't they?" He chuckled and shook his head. "You definitely have a point."

"So shoot. I'm anxious to go find Michael before he loses his shirt." She wasn't joking, and Deckland didn't laugh.

"This body chemistry between you two . . . is it *only* with Michael?"

Ashley's first instinct was to lie. But she couldn't. Deckland had helped her, or tried to help her. She at least owed him honesty, no matter how reluctant she was to admit the truth even to herself. With a sigh, she said, "Yes. It's only with Michael."

"Since . . . ?"

"College. No, even before that. I developed a

99

crush on Michael when I was in high school, and he was a freshman in college. We started going steady when he was a senior, and I was a sophomore at the same college." Just talking about those days brought a nostalgic lump to her throat. She and Michael had been so in love. The perfect couple. She swallowed hard, and reminded herself that those days were long gone. "His sister and I are best friends."

"Kim approved of the relationship?"

"Oh, yes." Ashley laughed at the memory. "She's a matchmaker, and good at it, too. In fact, she's still—" She bit her lip before she gave herself away. "Kim is a very determined person."

"Sounds like someone I would like to meet," Deckland said.

"You'd love her." In fact, Ashley thought, Kim and Deckland *would* get along well together. It would serve Kim right if she turned the matchmaking tables on her for a change. Warming to the idea, Ashley tried to sound casual as she said, "So, Deckland, where are you from?"

"Missouri."

Ashley felt a jolt of shock, followed by a surge of excitement. "So am I. You wouldn't happen to know another person on board from our home state who won the lottery, would you?" To her disappointment, he shook his head.

"Sorry, no. I wasn't aware that you had until

Michael mentioned it. Would you mind if I asked you one more question?"

With a shrug, Ashley said, "Go ahead."

"Is Michael the only lover you've had?" She must have flushed, for he added quickly, "It's personal, I know. But vital to my research for the book. You don't have to answer if you don't want to."

Very reluctantly, Ashley answered. "Yes, he is." But not for long, she added silently. The moment she got home, she and Tom were going to get down and dirty if it killed her. She *would* get Michael out of her mind and out of her system if it was the last thing she did.

Right after the cruise. Six more days. With Michael. Sharing a cabin. And a bed. And sticking to him like glue for the next . . . six . . . days.

And nights.

Oh, Lord. What was she thinking? What if he got the wrong idea? What if he started thinking that she was gullible enough to fall for him again?

Then she remembered his note. How could she have forgotten it? He'd wanted to forget about last night and just have a jolly old time for the rest of the cruise.

But he'd said nothing about not being friends. Close friends. The kind of friends who did everything together. She could be his friend. Once upon a brief time, they had been friends as well as lovers and husband and wife.

She had to give it her best shot. For Kim. Yes, for Kim. Kim was her best friend now, and she must be worried sick about Michael and his problem. He'd worked very hard to get where he was today, as owner and operator of two successful health clubs. How could he risk everything this way?

But then, she had to remind herself that gambling was an addiction like any other.

Sort of like her addiction to Michael. She had a handle on *her* addiction, so maybe she could help him get a handle on *his*.

Later, back in her cabin, she was dressing for dinner and thinking about her interesting conversation with Deckland when she realized something peculiar.

She hadn't mentioned Kim's name to Deckland, yet Deckland had known about her. With a shrug, Ashley slipped into her high-heeled sandals, deciding that Michael must have mentioned his sister's name to Deckland earlier.

What other explanation could there be?

The first time, he'd done it Kim's way.

This time he would do it *his* way. Slowly. Cautiously.

"Hit me." Grim-faced, Michael watched the dealer flip the card next to his king. Another king. He grunted with satisfaction. Unless the dealer had an ace to go with his queen, Michael would be up another ten dollars.

So far, he'd won back fifty dollars of Kim's money. If it took the rest of the cruise, he would get that two thousand dollars back. He shouldn't have let Kim badger him into betting a chunk of her savings in the first place, all on one hand of blackjack, but she'd kept on and on until he'd had to agree or go stark, raving mad.

Kim was like that: deadly persistent, and totally unwilling to accept defeat. She could also be eccentric, something he believed she had inherited from their grandfather, who had over 200 birdbaths in his front yard to attest to that fact.

How much time, energy, and money had gone into Kim's most recent plot? Michael wondered as he counted out ten more dollars to bet on the next hand. She'd obviously gotten to someone at the travel agency, for starters. He suspected the cruise package hadn't been entirely free at all, now that he knew Kim was involved.

And he hadn't been exaggerating when he'd reminded Ashley that Kim had friends everywhere. She was like the mafia; they all owed her favors, and she called them in when she needed them.

"Sorry, sir. Dealer takes all."

Michael swallowed a growl and kept his peace as the dealer took his chips. He really did hate to gamble. It was all luck, pure luck, and he didn't like those odds. He preferred to play games that required skill and brains to win.

Like chess. Now there was a game a man could sink his teeth—

"Hey, gorgeous. I'm looking for a date. You interested?"

"Sorry, I'm not—" Michael froze as the familiar, husky voice registered. And not just the voice, but the endearment. And the perfume.

He slowly turned around, his eyes nearly popping out of his head. It was Ashley, wearing a skimpy, strapless, backless, *short* short red dress. She wore her hair swept to one side and fastened with a silver comb, leaving the rest hanging over her bare shoulder in a dreamy, sexy flow of soft curls and golden highlights.

His gaze moved slowly down. He swallowed hard. Red sandals. Three-inch heels. Red-painted toes. She'd never been what anyone might call a conservative dresser, but she'd never dressed like a high-class, expensive hooker, either.

Tonight she was. Definitely.

It was like a fantasy come true.

Only he couldn't. After his jealous reaction when he saw her enter Deckland's cabin, he'd come to terms with the scary fact that maybe, just maybe, he still had some feelings for Ashley.

Which gave her power.

She'd nearly destroyed him once; he couldn't go there again. He might not survive the second time around.

So there couldn't be a second time.

She leaned forward abruptly, giving him a close-up view of her succulent cleavage, reminding him of something else he could sink his teeth into.

"Hey, I'm just asking for an escort to the show," she whispered, her voice slightly amused. "I'm not asking you to strip and dance on the table."

When she moved back to look at him, Michael saw that her eyes had darkened to violet, which he knew from experience happened when she was scared, pissed, or aroused.

He didn't think she was scared or pissed, although the latter was a possibility after the note he'd left her. He hoped Ashley would never know that fear and ego had prompted that note.

He'd wanted to say it first, before she had the opportunity, as she had the first time when the Scotts had interrupted them. He hadn't thought at the time that he'd regret it.

But he was regretting it now as he imagined cradling her luscious breasts in his hands and kissing her full, painted lips.

Without taking his eyes from hers, Michael reached behind him and pulled his jacket free of the chair where he'd draped it. Very casually, he folded it over his arm and held it in front of himself as he rose.

He was becoming very talented at hiding his instant reactions to Ashley, he realized, taking her arm with his free hand and leading her away from the blackjack table.

"It's warm tonight. Would you like to drop your jacket off at the cabin?" Ashley asked.

Michael shot her a sharp look, but she merely smiled back at him innocently, her provocative perfume teasing his nostrils. "Um, no. I think I'll keep it handy. It might get chilly later."

What a laugh. If anything, he would need a cold shower.

Chapter Nine

The comedian was a hoot.

At least, Michael assumed he was a hoot, since the audience was laughing at his jokes.

But Michael wasn't listening.

He was thinking about Ashley, who was sitting beside him at a small table near the back of the room. Sitting with her long, gorgeous legs crossed so that her short red dress rode high on her thighs.

Why was she being so friendly? Was she *that* relieved over his note? He'd thought—no, that wasn't right—he'd been *hoping* she would be furious.

He could handle Ashley mad, or sad, or cold.

He couldn't handle Ashley sexy, flirty, and friendly.

Because it made him want to do something

very naughty with her. Like strip her naked and pull her onto his lap.

Everyone was watching the comedian. Maybe no one would notice.

Michael downed half his cold beer and cut her another secret glance. She was watching the comedian, laughing with the others. Apparently having a high old time. Oblivious to the fact that he was painfully aroused.

Why was she dressed to kill? And why had she picked him as her date tonight? It wasn't a secret that she despised him, and had ever since their divorce. They lived in the same town, yet she avoided him like the plague.

So what was up? If he didn't know better—and he definitely knew better—he'd think she was out to seduce him.

Ha! As if she had to try. As if he wasn't very ready and extremely willing to race back to their cabin and begin a repeat performance of the night before. And maybe this time he'd let her scream, instead of smothering her ecstasy with his mouth. Let their fellow passengers know that he could make Ashley scream.

Let Deckland Jennings know that he wasn't the only bag of wild oats in the barn.

From the corner of his eye, he saw Ashley shiver, as if she was cold. He pretended not to notice.

She couldn't have his jacket.

She could *not* have his jacket.

He needed it to cover the bulge in his pants.

Several feet separated them, yet Ashley could feel Michael's tension. He seemed distracted and irritated.

As if he regretted his decision to join her, and wished he'd never left the casino.

Not for the first time, Ashley questioned her decision to try to help Michael. After what he'd done to her—to their marriage—why would she put her heart and her ego in jeopardy? She owed Michael nothing.

Absolutely nothing.

Well, then, she wasn't doing it for Michael, she decided; she was doing it for Kim.

The sudden applause startled Ashley. She hastily joined in. The comedy show was over. What now? It was only nine o'clock by her watch.

The casino didn't close until midnight.

Before she could change her mind, she rose and held out her hand. Michael stared at it, unmoving. Ashley swallowed hard and said, "They've got a live band in the Coconut Lounge. Would you like to go have a drink, maybe dance a little?"

Michael's gaze moved from her hand to her arm. Then farther up, slowly, until it reached her smiling face. Ashley gamely held on to her smile as his dark eyes studied her. Inside, she was shaking. Just being with Michael set her teeth on edge and made mush of her insides.

"Why not?" he drawled, taking her hand.

His skin felt hot. So hot it made her strangle a gasp. A jolt shot along her arm, reminding her that touching Michael was dangerous.

Insanity.

Her nipples sprang erect, tingling with anticipation, with the memory of his mouth, hot and sometimes rough, sometimes tender.

She closed her eyes and bit her bottom lip until she felt the pain.

"Are you okay?" Michael asked, his voice low and raspy in her ear.

Ashley managed to nod. She opened her eyes and began to walk to the door, hoping to tug free of his hand, praying he didn't know what was *really* wrong.

He wouldn't let go. Instead, he pulled her back to him. Passengers milled around them, a few grumbling.

Beneath his penetrating, heated gaze, Ashley tried to keep from shivering. "I told you, I'm fine."

"No, you're not."

She shook her head. "I don't know what you—"

"Yes, you do. You know *exactly* what I mean." Michael tugged her closer, until her aching breasts touched his chest. His voice turned gravelly, almost angry, but with an underlying sexual tension Ashley couldn't miss. "What are you doing, Ash?"

Ashley tried not to pant. Why did the man have to be so sexy? She licked her lips. "Trying to be friends. Is that so unbelievable? We're on the same ship. We're sharing the same cabin. We used to be married. It would be childish to try to avoid each other."

"It would be wise, is what it would be," Michael muttered, his gaze lingering on her mouth. "After last night—"

"I agree that we should forget last night," Ashley said hastily. "Let's just be friends and try to enjoy the cruise." They had only been married a year, she thought with genuine despair. So why did it seem as if she'd known him all her life?

Michael laid a burning hand on her hip, then slowly ran it along her thigh until he reached the top of her short dress. He grasped the hem with his fingers, rubbing her skin with his knuckles until it tingled and burned. "A dress like this makes it very hard to forget," he whispered.

Ashley's knees went weak at his words. She had to do something, and she had to do it fast. People were beginning to stare. "I'll go back to the cabin and change. I—I didn't realize it would have this effect on you."

A tiny smile danced at the corners of his mouth, mesmerizing Ashley. "You didn't?"

"No, I didn't. I bought these clothes with Tom in mind." The moment the words were out, she knew she'd said the wrong thing. Or was it the right thing? Yes, yes, it was the *right* thing to say. Of course it was.

Last night had been a mistake, a weakness on both sides. One of them needed to say something to remind them they each had someone waiting back home.

She had Tom.

He had Candy.

The air between them instantly chilled. Ashley told herself that she was glad, glad, glad. Helping Michael was one thing; sleeping with him again was something else entirely.

Sleeping. Ha! To call what happened between them *sleeping* was ridiculous.

"Tom. Right." Michael's smile didn't quite reach his eyes, Ashley noted. "Let's go get that drink. We can celebrate our engagements."

"Yes, we should." But why didn't she feel like celebrating? With a frustrated sigh, Ashley allowed Michael to lead her through the door and in the direction of the bar.

She wanted Michael, but she didn't *want* to want Michael. Was Michael feeling the same perverse tug-of-war?

"Yoo-hoo! Ashley! Michael!"

They both turned in the direction of that singsong voice, spotting Birdie and Bart, along with

Deckland and Tanya, at a table by the bar.

Birdie was waving madly.

"I guess we should join them," Ashley said reluctantly, glancing at the bar to see if Rick was working.

He was nowhere in sight.

"Yeah, I guess we should."

Michael slipped his arm around her waist, and together they weaved their way to the table.

"Don't you two look *marvelous!*" Birdie exclaimed, her eyes literally gleaming as she looked them up and down. "Isn't she a knockout?" she demanded of Michael.

"Yes, she is."

He sounded so sincere, Ashley couldn't help blushing. Her gaze met Deckland's. He winked and she smiled, trying to silently let him know, so far so good.

"Oh, great!" Tanya said, looking young and sassy in a slinky black skirt. "Someone new to dance with. No offense, Deckland, but you're a bit too tall for me. I'm getting a crick in my neck looking up at you."

Michael took the seat next to Tanya, leaving Ashley to sit next to Birdie. Ashley told herself that she didn't care if he sat on Tanya's *lap*.

And when he immediately led Tanya onto the dance floor, she assured herself that she wasn't a bit jealous.

Birdie, apparently, didn't believe her. She patted Ashley on the shoulder, her tone matter-of-fact. "Don't worry, dear. He's just using Tanya for cooling-off purposes."

Ashley turned to her, completely confused. "Excuse me?"

"I said, he's using Tanya to cool off." Birdie pointed to the jacket Michael had left behind as she added outrageously, "He's always aroused when he's around you. That's why he keeps the jacket held in front of him. He's not attracted to Tanya, so when he talks to her, or dances with her, it takes his mind off *you.*"

Ashley burst out laughing. She'd never heard of anything so wild and preposterous in her life! But considering the source, she supposed she shouldn't be surprised.

"She's right, Ashley," Bart put in. "The boy can't keep it down around you. And he's having trouble hiding it, too."

Convinced she'd been thrown into an old episode of "The Twilight Zone," Ashley tried again to laugh it off. This odd couple was not only embarrassing but persistent.

"If you don't believe us," Birdie said, "watch him when he comes back to the table. The moment his eyes land on you, he'll throw his jacket over his lap."

Pressing her hand to her hot face, Ashley tried to change the subject. "Have you heard anything about your stolen brooch, Birdie?"

"No, but the captain assured us personally that he would do everything in his power to find the thief." Birdie nudged her in the ribs, proving that Ashley hadn't succeeded in distracting her. "Here comes your man, dear. Just watch."

Tanya was laughing as she took her seat, her face flushed and her eyes sparkling. Michael had a way with women, Ashley thought, ignoring another stab of jealousy. How could Michael *not* be interested in Tanya? She was gorgeous. And single.

Unerringly, her gaze strayed to Michael's crotch.

Nothing out of the ordinary there.

Her gaze collided with his. She blushed and he flushed, taking his jacket from the back of his chair and draping it over his lap.

To hope the action would go unnoticed was to live in the desert and hope for snow.

"See!" Birdie crowed, pointing—actually *pointing*—at Michael's lap. "It's rising right now!"

Ashley stood so fast, she tipped her chair backward. It fell with a crash, but she didn't notice.

Or care.

Face flaming, she fled the bar and the outrageous couple she couldn't bring herself to dislike. She raced past laughing couples and kissing couples and fighting couples. She ran until she was out of breath and out of running space.

Which happened to be on the upper deck.

Breathing hard, she moved to the railing and gripped it with white-knuckled fingers, staring out over the darkened ocean. This cruise was either a nightmare or a fantasy.

She couldn't decide which.

Seeing Michael again filled her with mixed emotions. She still resented him, and the pain he'd caused her. Because of his uncontrolled libido, he'd wrecked their perfect marriage.

Okay, so maybe their marriage hadn't been perfect, but she'd *believed* they were happy. Right up until the moment she opened the hotel room door to find him in bed with another woman.

For the first time in a long, long time, Ashley replayed the ugly scene in her mind. She closed her eyes and swallowed a sob, fighting the pain. She'd believed herself beyond the ache. After two years of self-therapy, she *should* have been beyond it.

She was wrong. Seeing Michael again had resurrected not only the impossible attraction between them but the painful memories of why they had divorced.

He had been unfaithful.

She had been unforgiving.

Unfaithful and unforgiving equaled divorce.

She could never forget or forgive, and he couldn't turn back the clock and make it not happen.

Behind her, she sensed rather than saw Michael approach. He was quiet so long, she thought maybe she was wrong. Then he spoke, his voice quiet and serious.

"I don't think I've ever met anyone quite like Birdie and Bart." He came to stand beside her, his fingers curling around the railing next to her own.

Immediately, the rhythm of her heart increased and her breasts began to ache, as if he had some type of freaky control over her body.

"You might not believe this," he continued, "but I seriously don't think they realize how embarrassing they can be."

His hand closed over hers and she took a deep, steadying breath, waiting for him to continue.

"You have to admit, Ash, that the Scotts are eccentric people. Kim would love them."

The tension drained from her taut body, leaving her weak. She chuckled. "Yeah, you're right. Kim would love them." She forced herself to look at his face. "You're not embarrassed?"

"Should I be? I've never tried to deny the fact that you turn me on." He shrugged his broad shoulders. "So why should I try to deny it now, or become embarrassed over the fact?"

"Well, for starters, we've been divorced for two years."

"So?"

"And you've been seeing other people." .

"Just as you have."

"But I'm a woman. My reaction isn't so obvious—"

"It isn't?" His hot gaze touched her breasts for a brief moment. When he looked up at her again, she saw a flash of satisfaction in his brown eyes. "I can just look at you and your nipples respond as if I'd touched you."

She opened her mouth to lie, then quickly closed it. Denying the obvious would only make her look like a hypocrite. Instead, she angled her chin. "If I could change it, I would."

"So would I. The only thing we can do is try to ignore it and hope it goes away." He let go of her hand and raked his fingers through his hair, staring out to sea, his expression suddenly pensive. "I know you don't believe this, but I had no intention of cheating on Candy. It was the first time."

Ashley swallowed a bitter remark that would have revealed how much she cared. "I believe you." She didn't, but that didn't matter now. "I feel really bad about cheating on Tom, too. I love him, and I don't want it to happen again."

"So what do we do?" he asked.

"We can keep fighting it," she suggested, but even to her own ears she sounded weak. "We've got five more days and four more nights."

"Yeah," Michael said, then added dryly, "I'm going to need a new jacket."

Chapter Ten

Two A.M.

Ashley had never been more wide awake.

The king-size bed was huge, allowing Michael to keep a safe distance from her, yet she could still feel his body heat.

Smell his aftershave.

Feel every move he made. Hear every rustle of the sheet as he stirred restlessly.

And she knew he was as far from sleep as she was.

Maybe it was the clothes they were wearing. Michael had left on his jeans, and she had put on the one pair of jogging pants she'd brought, along with a T-shirt. She'd kept on her bra, too, just for the hell of it.

She was hot.

She suspected he was, too.

And it wasn't entirely due to the humidity in the room.

What was happening to them? Why couldn't they leave each other alone? After the hell he'd put her through, how could she even think about wanting him, let alone having sex?

Body chemistry. Deckland Jennings was writing a book about body chemistry, so it must be something big. Something important.

Something impossible. *That old rogue itch.*

"You awake?"

At Michael's whispered words, Ashley stiffened. She let out a slow, silent breath, trying to decide whether she wanted to 'fess up to being awake or pretend to be asleep.

Finally, she opted for honesty. "Yeah, I'm awake." It was pitch black in the room. She stared in the direction of the ceiling, her eyes burning.

"Wanna talk?"

"About what?"

"Anything. How are your parents?"

Ashley heard the underlying strain in his voice. Sounded just like her own. It was small comfort to know she wasn't in this hell alone. "Mom's gone back to school."

"Really?"

She smiled at the surprise in his voice. "Yeah. She wants to go back to work part-time, as a substitute teacher."

"Good for her. And your dad?"

"He's grumbling about it, but he knows Mom will do what she wants to do."

"Like you."

"Yeah. Like me." She turned onto her side but kept her distance. She couldn't see him, but she easily imagined him watching her with those hot, hot brown eyes. His chest would be bare with the exception of soft, curly hair that narrowed as it trailed along his stomach. . . .

There wasn't a bone in her body that didn't ache to reach out and touch him. "What about Sam? Is he doing okay?" Sam was Michael's stepdad and Kim's biological dad. Michael's mother had died of a heart attack shortly after their divorce.

"I think he's getting out more, seeing a few people."

"Really?" Ashley was glad for him. Sam had been a good stepfather to Michael and a good husband to Lilly, Michael and Kim's mother. "I'm glad. He deserves another chance to be happy."

Without hesitation, Michael said, "Yes, he does. Mom would have wanted him to find someone else."

She heard the covers rustle as he moved. Seconds later, she felt his hand on her face. He hooked her hair behind her ear—as he'd done a thousand times when they were dating and later, when they were married—then cupped her cheek. His skin was hot against her own.

Her heart started a heavy rhythm.

"It's not working, Ash. When I'm near you, my body has a will of its own."

She should have told him right then that it wasn't going to happen. She should have encouraged him to continue to fight it.

Instead, she hopped from the bed and felt her way around it to the bathroom. "This—this humidity is making me all hot and sweaty." Wrong words! "I'm going to take a shower." A cold one. A very long, very cold shower. If it worked for men, maybe it would work for women, too.

One of them had to try to maintain control!

Shaking inside, Ashley slammed the bathroom door, half-laughing, half-groaning as she stripped down and twisted the cold-water tap on to full force. She pulled back the shower curtain and stepped beneath the cold spray.

Only it wasn't cold. It was tepid at best. Dismayed, Ashley peered at the taps, double-checking to make sure she hadn't touched the hot water.

No, she hadn't.

Tepid water would *not* help, she discovered, stifling the urge to laugh hysterically. Her body still throbbed with need, and her mind remained cluttered with vivid, erotic images of Michael.

In her mind he was naked and aroused. Ready for her.

She felt as if she'd been on a rigid diet of no sex for two years and was suddenly faced with a feast in the form of Michael.

Facing the water, she thrust her head back and let the strong pressure pound her face and aching breasts. She would stay in here until she could think of something besides Michael and raw, orgasmic sex.

The rings on the shower curtain suddenly jangled as it was yanked aside.

She was no longer alone in the shower.

"It won't work," Michael growled into her ear as he hooked his arms around her waist and pulled her roughly against his hard body. He let go long enough to reach around her and turn the hot-water faucet slightly. "I've already tried it."

Then he grabbed the bar of soap and began to rub it over her breasts and stomach . . . working his way down to the part of her that throbbed the most.

His fingers were soapy and slick, his breath hot and fast in her ear.

Ashley moaned and spread her legs, letting her head drop back against his shoulder in total surrender.

She knew it was useless to fight it, especially when things had progressed this far.

123

His wonderful fingers moved faster and faster, until she was on the verge of crying out.

Then he stopped, leaving her trembling on the edge of her climax. He turned her around to face him. She opened her eyes, staring into his, recognizing the raw need mirrored there. Holding his gaze, she reached out and took the soap from his hand.

She began to work up a lather, watching him watch her with an intensity that rocked her world.

She was a sex goddess intent on enslaving him.

Michael was helpless to stop her.

He didn't even want to.

Her dusky nipples were rigid and begged to be suckled. He leaned forward, intending to do just that.

She pushed him away and glared at him.

"Don't you dare touch me," she hissed, her hands rubbing the soap back and forth, working up a thick, rich lather.

He nearly came right there on the spot, just watching her hands on the soap. Back and forth. Up and down. Stroking the bar of soap. The anticipation nearly drove him insane. *When was she going to use those hands on him?*

Finally, she dropped the soap in its holder and reached for him, closing her hands around his thick, hard length. Slowly, she slid her soapy hands down to the base, cupped his taut, heavy sac, then worked her way up again.

Michael's knees nearly buckled. He braced himself against the shower wall with one hand as her hands did an erotic dance along his shaft. Down. Then back up. Down again, lingering, cupping, stroking. Satin against silk.

Up again. He grew impossibly thicker, longer. Harder.

He dared to let go of his anchor and reach out to her, cupping her breasts, thumbing her nipples back and forth until she moaned. His fingers slipped down across her water-slick belly and into her, breaking her hold on his throbbing manhood.

He brought her closer, covering her mouth with his own and licking, sucking, biting her lips, her tongue, kissing her until she was crying with need and he was moaning with desire.

God, she was so sensuous, so sexy.

So right.

The second he thought the damning words, Michael broke free of her mouth. He caught her slender, curvy body and turned her, positioning her hands on the wall in front of her. Her long, wet hair streamed down her back.

Then, slowly, with his teeth clenched tight, he pulled her firm bottom against him and entered her from behind, thrusting deep and hard.

She came instantly, convulsing around him,

nearly shattering what was left of his control as she cried out his name.

Michael grabbed her waist before she collapsed, relentless in his quest to hear her scream his name again and again. He paced himself, his fingers delving into her wet curls and finding her still-throbbing, swollen nub.

Within seconds, she screamed again, this time more weakly, as if she didn't have the strength left to voice her pleasure.

She was tight and hot, squeezing him, urging him to his release. The water pounded over the elegant curve of her spine, spraying his chest and stomach, enhancing the sensuous pleasure he had always found in Ashley's body.

She was his wife, his life, his love.

She was *not* his wife.

With a mixture of anguish and pleasure, Michael thrust deep one last time, claiming her privately, if not publicly.

His arms closed around her, pulling her tight against his chest as pleasurable ripples continued to sweep over him. He buried his face in her neck, feeling the furious pounding of her pulse against his cheek.

From the moment he realized that he loved her, he had been faithful.

Nothing had changed.

Michael closed his eyes and sighed.

* * *

Sated, weak, and pleasantly sore, Ashley lay on her side of the bed, hugging a pillow to her chest, her back to Michael.

Unseen, tears streamed down her face.

She was terrified of Michael, of what he was capable of taking from her. Of the possibility that he could destroy her heart and her sanity a second time.

She couldn't go through it again. Couldn't love him with all her heart yet live in fear that she would walk in on another scene like the one that had shattered her.

And there were no options about loving Michael with all her heart. She knew that she couldn't love him just a little and hold the rest of her heart in reserve so that he couldn't break it all over again.

No, she didn't have a choice.

She could either refuse to love him, or love him totally and irrevocably.

With Michael, it was all or nothing.

Her breath hitched, and she smothered a sob into her pillow, praying Michael was asleep. How simple her life had been before this cruise. Safe and simple.

Without an all-consuming passion.

Without gut-wrenching emotion, the kind that made you feel as if someone was wringing your heart with his bare hands.

She wanted to get that security back. She did

not want to leap into another unstable, uncertain, nerve-racking relationship with Michael, no matter how good the sex.

Okay. No matter how awesome the sex. She would stop wasting energy denying that she and Michael were dynamite in bed, but she wasn't going to let it go to her head.

Or her heart, rather. Her head had more sense than her heart. So what if the sex was incredible? They probably weren't the first or last couple to be compatible in bed, but completely *in*compatible out of it.

She would stop fighting the attraction, too, for the rest of the cruise. It was not only a waste of energy, it was a waste of effort.

And at the end of the cruise, she would confess to Tom. If he still wanted to marry her, she would marry him and be through with Michael for good. Live a safe, simple, passionless, *painless* life with safe, dependable, faithful Tom.

Someone knocked softly on their cabin door. Ashley jerked upright, staring at the clock, which read four A.M. Who could be up at that hour? she wondered as she quickly slipped on her jogging pants.

"Michael?" She leaned over and touched his shoulder, shaking him lightly. "Michael?"

He groaned and turned his back to her, mumbling something about another thirty minutes of sleep.

Giving up, Ashley went to the cabin door and opened it a half inch, peering into the hall. She nearly screamed as she came face to face with Bart.

"Bart! You scared the daylights out of me," she scolded, opening the door wider. "What on earth are you—"

"It's Birdie," Bart said. "We need your help."

"What's wrong?" When the elderly man flushed instead of answering, Ashley's brow rose. This wasn't the Bart she knew; the man didn't have a bashful bone in his body. "Bart? Are you going to tell me, or are we going to stand here—"

"She—we were in the shower, and um, she fell. I just need a hand getting her out of the tub. She threw her back out, you see."

"Hmm. I see." Ashley struggled not to grin. She couldn't resist getting a little revenge for all the times they had embarrassed her. "You were both taking a shower at four in the morning?"

Bart's face turned a shade darker. "It was her idea. We heard you and Michael, you see—"

"Oh," Ashley inserted hastily, sorry she had asked. She suspected her own face now matched Bart's in color. Stepping into the hall, she pulled the door shut behind her and followed Bart into their cabin.

In the small bathroom, Birdie had the shower curtain pulled shut.

Ashley paused inside the bathroom door. "Birdie? Are you all right?"

There was a tiny moan from behind the curtain, then Birdie said, "If I were all right, Ashley, I wouldn't be sending Bart over to your cabin at this hour. I hope we didn't interrupt anything, although I don't know how you'd have the energy to keep going after all that screaming you did in the shower earlier."

The unmistakable envy in Birdie's voice went a long way toward easing Ashley's embarrassment over her frank talk. "You didn't interrupt anything. I was asleep." A tiny white lie. She didn't want Birdie asking questions about why she *couldn't* sleep.

Bart appeared in the doorway holding a towel. He stuck it behind the curtain. "Darling? Are you ready for us to move you to the bed?"

"I was ready an hour ago. A fat lot of good it did me."

Stifling a laugh, Ashley helped Bart carry Birdie to the bed. Then she helped her into her nightgown—which had been thrown on the floor—and sat beside her on the bed to make sure she was comfortable.

Birdie sent Bart in search of a heating pad, and the moment he was gone she focused on Ashley. "It wasn't Bart's fault, bless his heart. I keep forgetting that we aren't young anymore."

Even with her face free of makeup and her

blue hair in tiny sponge rollers, Birdie didn't look a day over fifty. The sparkle in her blue eyes added to her youthful appearance.

"You're only as old as you feel," Ashley reminded her.

But Birdie wasn't listening. With her gaze on the door, she asked Ashley, "Is Michael as good as he looks?" When Ashley blushed and tried to stand, Birdie grabbed her arm and pulled her back down. "Oh, never mind. I guess you wouldn't have been screaming if he wasn't any good. Don't mind me, dear; I'm just a dirty old busybody." Her eyes grew dreamy. "Bart used to be that good, back in his younger days. He'd be good to go two, three times a night."

"Birdie, I—"

"I used to worry, you know, that any woman would do when he got the itch."

"Look, I should—"

"But after a while, I realized that it was *me* Bart wanted. Only me." She blinked and smiled at Ashley, as if she had forgotten the younger woman was there. "I know that he's been faithful all these years, just like I know that Michael will remain faithful to you. Some men are one-woman men, and we've got ourselves a pair of those."

Ashley felt the blood drain from her face. She shook her head and tried to tug her hand free of Birdie's grip again. "I really need to get back to my cabin, Birdie." Before she did something she'd regret, like blurt out to Birdie that she was wrong, that Michael had already blown his pedestal all to hell and back.

Two years ago and counting.

Birdie held her in a remarkably strong grip, her brow furrowed. "What's wrong, dear? Did I say something to upset you?"

"No, no," Ashley said, trying to sound sincere. "You didn't. I'm just tired. If you're okay now, I think I'd like to go back to bed."

With a sly smile, Birdie let her go. "I don't blame you there, child. In your circumstances, I'd be anxious to get back to bed, too. There's nothing like good loving." She groaned and arched her back. "If Bart ever gets back with that heating pad, I should be good as new by lunch."

"I'll see you then." Ashley backed away, then turned and walked hastily out of the cabin.

One-woman man.

Michael?

Unfortunately, not.

Chapter Eleven

"They're having a miniature golf tournament today on the upper deck," Tanya informed Michael the moment he seated himself at the table. "The winning couple gets five hundred dollars in chips to use in the casino. Are you and Ashley interested? Deckland and I are going to give it a shot."

Michael hated golf. He'd much rather get down and dirty in a good rough-and-tumble game of football. He guessed that was out of the question on a cruise ship. "I don't think so, but thanks," he mumbled, hoping to discourage further conversation with the friendly blonde.

"Maybe when Ashley gets here, I can convince her to change your mind."

Tanya sounded very certain of herself, Michael noted. In fact, she was wearing that smug woman smile that Ashley used to wear when she was certain she could change his mind about something.

He couldn't resist an opportunity to knock it askew. "As a matter of fact, Ashley hates miniature golf." It was an outright lie, but the devil made him do it.

"Have a long night, Michael?"

Michael kept his gaze on the breakfast menu as Deckland attempted to use his manipulative talents to find out why Ashley's chair remained empty. He could feel the older man watching him and had to physically restrain himself from snarling. What was between his wife—his *ex*-wife—and this Harvard yuppie? The man was nice enough, but he wasn't Ashley's type.

Come to think of it, neither was Tom.

Casually, he said, "As a matter of fact, Ashley and I turned in early." What he didn't reveal was that he didn't have a clue where she was now. Her side of the bed had been empty when he awoke that morning.

He vaguely recalled Ashley's attempt to awaken him shortly after the hot shower incident, but he couldn't remember why. He clenched his teeth on a groan. Now, why did he have to go and remind himself of that steamy encounter?

Tanya yawned and tapped her fingers against the menu. Michael glanced at her, disgruntled anew to find that looking at her was like looking at Kim. She did absolutely nothing for him. Zip. *Nada.*

Now Ashley, on the other hand—

Deckland snapped his fingers, startling Michael.

"I think I know where Ashley is."

"You do?" Michael blurted out, then frowned to cover his blunder. He glued his gaze to the menu again. There weren't that many choices, but it gave him something to concentrate on. "Good for you, Detective Jennings."

His open sarcasm seemed to sail right over Deckland's head.

"She's off playing sleuth, isn't she? She's determined to find out the identity of the other lottery winner. She mentioned it to me yesterday, but I'd forgotten." He beamed at Michael, whose frown turned into a full-scale glower at the mention of Deckland's suspicious meeting with Ashley. "I'm right, aren't I?"

Michael hoped like hell he wasn't. "She's wasting her time," he said, with a hard look at the smiling psychologist, who couldn't possibly know the truth. "I'm certain that information is confidential, so unless the other winner wants it to be known, it remains confidential."

He could have bitten his fork in two when Deckland's smile grew wider.

"Oh, I think if she dug deep enough, she'd find out who he is."

"Maybe it's a she."

"Maybe. But I think it's a he."

Michael slammed down his menu. "Why?"

Deckland's smile wavered under the force of Michael's question. He looked puzzled as he explained, "Well, I just don't think a woman could keep it to herself."

Tanya protested, slapping at him with her menu. "Hey! Men gossip as much as women!"

"But men can keep secrets," Deckland argued in a good-natured way. "When they want to."

Reminding himself that Deckland was just guessing, he couldn't resist asking, "But why would he—if we're talking about a he—keep the joyous news to himself?"

Deckland's eyes narrowed slightly. "Good question." Then his Harvard smile returned in full force. "Maybe Ashley can ask him when she meets him. Ah, here's our waiter."

Caught with his mouth open as he readied a reply, Michael looked up at the cheerful waiter. "Nothing for me, thanks. I just remembered that I need to make a business call."

He left his breakfast companions without a backward glance. Maybe Tanya and Deckland would find something in common, Michael thought darkly as he navigated the crowded dining room. Deckland obviously needed a distraction. The man was obsessing over Ashley far too much for Michael's peace of mind.

Speaking of Ashley . . . he had to find her before she dug too deeply. Michael suppressed a shudder at the thought. No matter what it took, he had to keep her from discovering his embarrassing secret.

Even if it meant he had to spend every waking and sleeping hour with her.

Now, why didn't that idea make him want to jump overboard? "Body chemistry," Michael mumbled like a mantra. "Just body chemistry."

"I'm sorry, ma'am. Due to heightened security, we can't give out that information."

The *Funstar* was filled with frustratingly loyal people, Ashley was discovering. She gave the first mate her sweetest smile.

His expression remained stubbornly passive.

"I'm sure they wouldn't mind," she said. "I mean, they probably want to meet me as much as I want to meet them. After all, we both won the lottery using the same numbers."

"How do you know they're even on this ship?"

"Because the travel agency told me the other lottery winner had accepted the free cruise, too."

"Then why didn't *they* give you a name?"

Ashley clenched her jaw. She'd hoped he wouldn't ask that question. The truth was, the travel agency hadn't been allowed to give out that information, either. "Look, if you could just give me a list of everyone from Missouri—"

"Sorry, can't do it. I *like* my job." He seemed to soften slightly at her frustrated sigh. "But if I were looking for a lottery winner, I'd be watching for someone who has a lot of money to spend. Have you tried the casino?"

Great, she thought. He was suggesting she look in the one place she was trying to avoid! Mumbling a barely gracious, "Thanks," Ashley left. A quick glance at her watch told her that she had missed breakfast.

She had time to check on Birdie before gluing herself to Michael's side until the casino closed at midnight. What if she wasn't successful? How badly was Michael addicted? She should have phoned Kim again and told her that she knew, and demanded more information.

But then, she mused as she reached the Scotts' cabin, if she let on to Kim that she was worried about Michael, his sister would think she still cared, and redouble her efforts to get them together. And Kim definitely didn't need any encouragement!

She was just about to knock on the cabin door when she spotted Michael rounding the corner at the end of the hall. Her heart did a crazy flip at the sight of him, so big and lean and beautiful.

He smiled at her, and an old, familiar weakness flooded her knees. Her own smile was tremulous. "Good morning," she said. "I was about to check on Birdie before coming to find you."

Michael reached her. He lifted a casual hand and stroked her shoulder by way of greeting. He never just *touched* her, Ashley realized, bracing herself against the white heat that flashed low in her belly. He stroked, massaged, nuzzled, kissed, and nibbled.

"You tried to wake me this morning," he said, his smile rueful. "I remember now. Did something happen?"

The heat in her belly made a rapid ascent to her face. "They—she fell in the shower, and Bart needed help getting her to bed. She strained her back."

Michael's brows collided. "She was taking a shower in the middle of the night?"

Apparently, he didn't think it strange that she had been doing the same thing. It just hadn't crossed his mind that she and Birdie might have been taking showers for the same reasons, Ashley thought, growing hotter. "She—she wasn't alone, and they weren't just taking a shower."

This time Michael's brows disappeared into his hairline. His lips twitched. "You mean they were . . . ?"

Ashley nodded, hoping he would leave it at that. To her immense relief, the cabin door opened.

"I thought I heard voices," Bart said. He smiled at Ashley, but when his gaze landed on Michael, he expression turned uncharacteristically stern. "Do you have to be so damned creative? You're going to get me killed before this cruise is over."

If Ashley hadn't witnessed Michael's blush herself, she never would have believed it. She chuckled.

Michael slid his arm around Ashley's waist and slanted her a look that warned her there would be retribution later. "Can't help myself, Bart," he drawled, pulling her tightly against his side. "Ashley inspires me."

"Well," Bart grumbled, "*you* two inspire Birdie, who then seduces *me* into her schemes—"

"Ahem," Michael interrupted hastily. "You don't have to explain—I think we get the picture. Is Birdie okay?"

"Frustrated, but okay."

Ashley choked on a gasp. Michael's grip tightened almost painfully, as if he were trying to contain his laughter.

"The ship's doctor gave her a muscle relaxer, so she's out at the moment. He told her that if she stayed in bed all day, she might get to attend the pool party on the upper deck tonight."

"Tell her that we stopped in to check on her," Ashley said, shamefully relieved that she wouldn't have to face Birdie with Michael at her side. The woman invariably embarrassed her.

"I'll tell her when she awakens," Bart assured

her, his smile returning. "She's fond of you, you know."

"I'm fond of her, too." Ashley swallowed an unexpected lump, realizing that she spoke the truth. There was something about the eccentric couple that tugged at her heartstrings. Perhaps if Michael had remained faithful, he and she might have had the lasting, solid relationship the Scotts seemed to share.

The ugly reminder of why they had divorced made her stiffen and move from Michael's side. She sensed his confusion but wasn't ready to look at him just yet.

After the door closed and they were once again alone in the hall, Ashley felt unaccountably nervous. What now? She wanted to help Michael, keep him distracted enough to forget about gambling, but on the other hand, she didn't want him to think for a moment that she was developing feelings for him other than those of temporary friendship.

She licked her lips and forced herself to look at him.

He was staring at the path her tongue had taken as if mesmerized, his brown eyes darkening to almost black.

She recognized the signs. Her entire body recognized the latent desire simmering just beneath the surface. After last night, it was impossible to ignore. With one look, he could warm her from head to toe.

Set fire to her soul.

No, not her soul; just her body. Her soul remained untouched because it was much, much wiser than her foolish libido.

"So . . . what do we do now?" The moment she asked the question, she knew she'd blundered. Michael was staring at her as if she were a luscious dessert and he had a fork firmly in hand.

Taking her elbow, he pulled her across the hall to their cabin door. He pressed her against it, placing his hands on either side of her, trapping her. His face was inches from her own. His dark, liquid eyes bore into hers, his thick lashes lowered. Softly, he said, "I can think of a few things I'd like to do right now, but I think they're illegal in several states."

Curiosity—and Michael—would surely be her downfall. She licked her lips again. She had to; they had gone bone dry. His mouth was so close, and she wanted him to kiss her as only Michael could.

Until she was mindless. Whimpering. Begging.

"What—what things?" she asked, her voice a mere whisper.

He moved a bit closer, until his chest grazed her breasts. He moved an inch to the right, then an inch to the left, creating an irresistible friction.

Her nipples sprang erect and began to throb. It was embarrassing, really, how easily he could arouse her.

Instead of saying what she wanted to hear, he gave his head an exasperated shake. "Things that would get us thrown off the ship. I can't get enough of you, Ash. Dammit! I wish—"

He didn't finish. He didn't have to. More hurt than she cared to admit, Ashley filled in the blanks. "You wish you hadn't picked this particular ship? You wish you hadn't bumped into me? Am I cramping your style, Michael?"

His expression hardened. He dropped his arms and shoved his hands into his pockets, stepping back. "I see you're still an expert at jumping to conclusions."

Ashley felt like slapping him. After two years, he was still blaming her for his infidelity. "I've already told you, Michael, I'm not going to discuss the past with you." Gathering the shreds of her dignity, she tried to move around him. "I'm going to find the other lottery winner. Maybe *we* have something in common." She saw by the slight narrowing of his eyes that he hadn't missed her subtle barb.

As she walked away, she half expected him to stop her, but he didn't.

She told herself that she wasn't disappointed. But she was.

* * *

143

She had to be the most obstinate, narrow-minded, unforgiving woman in the world, Michael decided, watching her walk away. He should stop her, remind her again just what it was they had in common.

But he didn't.

Instead, he stood there in the hallway, hard and aching for her, for the chance to bury himself inside her, to show her again and again that she was *his*—

His fist hit their cabin door, causing it to shudder in its frame. The vibrations climbed up his arm and into his shoulder, making it throb. He welcomed the discomfort. He welcomed anything that could take his mind off his incredibly sexy, bullheaded ex-wife.

Why did he let her get under his skin? After two years, he should be immune to her taunts. Yet she'd just proved that she still had the power to drive him insane, taunt him into saying things that reminded them of their ugly divorce.

If Ashley found out he'd bought a lottery ticket using her numbers, she would have a new arsenal at her disposal.

And Michael couldn't let that happen. He wasn't going down again.

With a few choice curses, Michael went after her.

He caught up with her just as she reached the stairs leading to the upper deck. Swallowing his pride to protect his ego—and his heart—he called out to her, "Ashley, wait!"

She stopped in her tracks, her hand on the railing, her back rigid.

"They're having a golf tournament after lunch. That's why I was looking for you."

For several tense seconds, she didn't respond. Finally, she turned on the stairs to look at him. Her eyes looked suspiciously shiny, but Michael wasn't arrogant enough to think it was due to tears. Anger, yes, but not tears.

She lifted one perfectly arched brow and waited, looking so cool and ridiculously haughty, Michael felt himself biting back a grin. "I thought you might be my partner," he said.

The brow rose higher. "You hate miniature golf."

Michael shrugged and managed a rueful grin. "For five hundred dollars in prize money, I think I could swing a game or two without barfing."

"What about Tanya—"

"Tanya and Deckland are pairing up. Besides, I remember how good you were at the game." She flushed at his compliment, released the railing, and stepped closer. She was definitely more relaxed, Michael thought, inhaling her perfume and wishing he'd thought to grab his jacket. When she reached him, he held out his hand. "Truce?"

After a slight hesitation, she took it. "Truce,"

she agreed. She tugged her hand free and swept her hair behind her ear as she added, "Maybe I'll get the opportunity to talk to the other passengers. I'm dying to meet the other lottery winner."

Michael swallowed a groan in the nick of time.

Chapter Twelve

This was it.

Ashley took a deep breath and studied the distance between the ball and the mouth of the porpoise. If she made the shot, she and Michael would win.

If she missed, the prize would go to a young couple from California.

The miniature golf course, located on the upper deck just yards from the Olympic-size swimming pool, reminded Ashley of a theme park. The gaping mouths of sharks, dolphins, eels, and various other sea creatures delighted both young and old.

A crowd had gathered to watch the tournament, and Ashley could feel the eyes of a dozen people on her as she prepared to swing. Behind her, she knew the staff moved efficiently among the passengers, serving tart lemonade and iced tea, along with the usual array of colorful drinks decorated with tiny umbrellas and slices of fresh fruit.

"You're doing fine. Just relax, Ash. Think about where you're going to put the trophy."

Ashley bit back a rueful smile at Michael's serious-as-a-heart-attack tone; the award trophy was a brass-plated dolphin about three inches tall. As for the money, she didn't really need it. No, she would win for the sheer joy of winning.

She took another deep breath and lifted her swinging arm into position. It was a simple shot, but she'd learned the hard way that simple shots were sometimes the hardest.

"The hell with the trophy," Tanya said just as Ashley brought her arm down. "I'd be thinking about the five hundred in gambling chips."

Gambling chips? Ashley couldn't stop her downward swing in time, but she managed to put enough force behind it to ensure the ball would bounce. Gambling chips? Why hadn't Michael told her?

The ball ricocheted from the mouth of the porpoise and, like a boomerang, headed straight for Ashley.

She didn't have time to think.

She didn't have time to move.

The ball hit her in the forehead with a re-sounding *thunk*. Ashley staggered in dazed wonder; her hearing faded and her vision grew dim as she thought, *good grief, I've knocked myself out!*

Michael saw her begin to fold and was close enough to thrust his hands beneath her head before she hit the deck, somewhat cushioning her fall. At the sight of her pale, still face, his heart leaped into overdrive. "Get a doctor!" he bellowed, startling the passengers who had moved in to get a better view.

"What happened?"

"Did she get hit?"

"Is she suffering from heat stroke?"

"One minute she was swinging, the next minute she collapsed."

"Good God, Michael"—this from Deckland—"did the ball *hit* her?"

Tanya fell to her knees on the other side of Ashley, peering at her forehead. She glanced up, confirming Deckland's suspicion. "She's getting a lump the size of a golf ball."

Someone had the insensitivity to giggle.

Michael's head came up. Frowning, he scanned the crowd, daring the culprit to show himself. Fear fueled his anger. He almost wished that someone *would* come forward so that he could wring the culprit's neck.

The crowd fell silent beneath his burning gaze.

Moments stretched into an eternity for Michael. The sun beat hot against the back of his neck. Where was that damned doctor? If only he hadn't asked Ashley to participate, she wouldn't be lying unconscious on the deck. His reasons had been totally selfish. He'd wanted to keep her occupied so she wouldn't find out he was the other lottery winner.

"Move aside, please. Give the poor woman some air."

At the sound of the authoritative voice, Michael shaded his eyes with his hand, watching a gray-haired man approach. This was the ship's doctor? He looked eighty if he was a day!

The words were out before he could stop them. "You're kidding, right?"

The doctor's light blue gaze narrowed on Michael. "The husband, I presume?" When Michael nodded, he pointed to something in the far distance. "Can you see that stretch of reef?"

Shading his eyes again, Michael looked in the direction in which the doctor pointed. "I don't see anything." The man wasn't only ancient, he was senile! Ashley needed—

"Well, I do," the doctor said. "Can you hear a dull, pounding sound?"

Muffling an impatient curse, Michael shook his head.

"Well, *I* can. It's the waves pounding against that reef that *you* can't see. Now move aside so I can do my job. Never know when I might kick the bucket."

The latter, said with such droll sarcasm, generated a few snickers from the crowd, and a flush from Michael. He felt like an idiot—a *rude* idiot. Thrusting his hand through his hair, he knelt down beside the doctor on the deck. His apology was genuine. "I'm sorry. I'm not usually so rude; it's just that I was—"

"Never mind." The doctor waved his hand and bent to study Ashley's pale face. He turned her head from side to side, then lifted her lids to peer at her eyes. "Yep, just as I suspected."

Michael's heart lurched to a stop, then began to gallop. "What? What is it? Is she all right?"

The doctor looked at Michael. "She's out cold, but I don't think there will be any lasting damage. At the worst, she'll have one hell of a headache when she awakens." He picked out a couple of men from the crowd and waved them forward. "Let's get her to her cabin, shall we?"

"I'll carry her," Michael said, refusing to analyze his reasons for not wanting other men to touch her.

The doctor looked skeptical. "Are you sure? You still look a little shaky to me."

"I'm fine," Michael snapped. Ever so gently, he gathered Ashley in his arms and waded through the curious crowd. Like a couple of mother hens, Tanya and Deckland followed him.

"Watch her head on that door casing," Tanya warned.

"And keep her head elevated," Deckland added, racing ahead to open the door for Michael.

Carefully, Michael maneuvered the stairs, mindful of Deckland and Tanya breathing down his neck. Somewhere along the way, he thought a little jealously, Tanya and Deckland had forgotten that only days ago Ashley had been a complete stranger to them.

If he hadn't been so damned worried about Ashley, he might have found their concern amusing, if not touching. But then, Ashley had always had a way with people. It was one of the reasons she was so good at her job. Michael knew that often Ashley's clients became lasting friends. During their short marriage, he'd lost count of the number of weekend barbecues she had hosted in the backyard, inviting all and sundry.

He reached the landing and turned carefully with his burden, navigating the second set of stairs with the same ease and care as he had with the first. His lips curved as he recalled one particular backyard barbecue when Ashley had invited the entire staff from their local cable company—all because they had offered her prospective buyers free cable for a month.

Crazy in love with her, Michael had watched from his spot in front of the grill as she had flitted from one person to the next, leaving a smile or a laugh in her wake.

Those had been the days, he thought, surprised to find his eyes watering. Oh, how he had been looking forward to having children with her. She would be the best mother, he remembered thinking with absolute conviction. And because of her influence on him, he would be the absolute best daddy.

Finally they reached their cabin. Michael allowed Deckland to fish the cabin key from his pocket, then waited as Deckland unlocked the door. He stared down at Ashley's angelic face, fighting the urge to kiss her to see if she would magically awaken.

Who was he trying to fool? He wanted to kiss her, period.

Swinging the door open, Deckland turned and placed a bracing hand on Michael's shoulder. His voice was gentle as he said, "You heard the doctor, Michael. She's going to be fine."

Michael blinked rapidly, attempting to be sneaky about the lump he had to swallow before he could speak. "I know.

Tanya smoothed the hair from Ashley's cheek, her expression genuinely concerned as she gently probed the injured area. "The doctor said an ice pack would lesson the swelling. I'll find a steward and rustle one up."

"Thanks." His voice came out rougher than he

intended, but what the hell? Ashley was unconscious and couldn't witness his foolish reaction.

"I'll go with you," Deckland offered.

Michael was glad finally to be alone with Ashley. He placed her gently on the bed, then sat beside her to begin his vigil.

He wasn't moving until she opened her eyes, and if it didn't happen in the next ten minutes, he would call the nearest hospital and demand they send a medic helicopter. The fact that the doctor could apparently see and hear better than he could failed to impress Michael.

What if Sawbones Sam had missed something? What if there was a brain bleed or something? He'd watched enough "ER" to know that a dozen complications could arise from a knock like Ashley had endured. Why, just recently he'd seen on the news a story about a boy who'd been hit with a puck at a hockey game. Four days later, the boy slipped into a coma. He had lived, Michael recalled, but he had suffered irreparable brain damage.

God, it couldn't happen to Ashley! She was a light that never dimmed, spreading her warmth to others in a special way.

The thought made Michael suck in a sharp breath. He quickly assured himself that there was nothing wrong with admiring Ashley, as long as he wasn't foolish enough to love her again. Hell, they'd been married. Had been madly in love.

Or so he'd thought.

Yes, she had many, many admirable qualities, but she hadn't possessed the one quality that was essential to any good marriage.

Trust.

Michael picked up her limp hand and held it, watching her chest until he was certain it moved. He thought about the past two years, wondering if she still cooked burgers for strangers and left cookies in the mailbox for the mailman on cold, rainy days.

And despite himself, knowing the pain it would bring, he wondered if she made love with Tom the way she made love with him.

Just as he suspected, the image evoked a sharp, stabbing pain in his chest. He silently cursed his weakness, brutally reminding himself of the dark, crushing days and weeks following their breakup. Hell, *months*.

He had begged her to believe him. His friends—the very ones responsible for that night in the hotel—had sworn he was telling the truth. But Ashley had remained stoic, refusing to consider, even briefly, that he might have been an innocent pawn in a prank gone wrong.

Finally, Michael had come to terms with the fact that Ashley had *wanted* to believe he was guilty. She had wanted a way out of the marriage, and he had supplied the perfect excuse. That realization, more than anything else, had nearly destroyed him.

Then, blessedly, anger had moved in, pushing aside his grief. He'd welcomed it with open arms and had fed that anger over the past two years. It was his remedy for a broken heart, this anger.

As long as he remained angry, she couldn't hurt him.

But now . . . now Michael found himself with his guard down, and that just wouldn't do. Without trust, there could never be a relationship between himself and Ashley.

Sex. Body chemistry. Physical attraction. All of those he could handle—and shamelessly enjoy.

Love wasn't in the cards. At least, not with Ashley.

Her slim fingers tightened around his hand. Michael gave a start, his gaze flying to her face.

She was watching him.

For how long? Long enough to see the yearning on his face? Michael ground his teeth at the possibility. He forced a careless smile to his mouth. "Well, if it isn't sleeping beauty."

Her lovely mouth curved as she asked softly, "You were worried?"

And because Michael was feeling vulnerable and foolish and scared of those emotions, he said with studied flippancy, "Of course. Who wouldn't be?"

* * *

Okay. So this blunder she could blame on her head injury. If it happened again, she would have no choice but to blame it on sheer stupidity.

How could she think, for one moment, that Michael cared? Oh, sure, he *cared* cared. Cared like Deckland cared. Like Kim cared. Like Birdie would care. Like she cared about his gambling addiction.

And that, girlfriend, Ashley told herself sternly, *was all there was to his present concern.*

"And don't you forget it," she muttered beneath her breath.

Michael squeezed her hand, leaning forward. "Are you in pain?"

She shook her head, which made her into a great big liar. She winced and put a hand to her head, carefully outlining the golf-ball–size swelling. With a groan, she closed her eyes. How utterly embarrassing! She would never be able to face her dinner companions again. In fact, she briefly considered staying in her room for the remainder—

Michael was laughing.

Ashley tried to glower at him, but wrinkling her brow caused pain. Instead, she yanked her hand from his to emphasize her displeasure. "It's not funny, Michael. Aren't you upset that we didn't win? Now you can't gamble away five hundred dollars."

It was a risk, goading him into talking about his addiction, but Ashley was just irritated enough to do it. Let him try to deny that he had a problem with gambling.

She wasn't fooled a bit by his puzzled expression. And was that a tiny flash of hurt she saw in his eyes?

"You've forgotten," he said, "I don't like to gamble."

Stifling a disbelieving laugh, Ashley simply stared at him for a moment, waiting for him to come clean. She knew from past experience that Michael was an excellent liar. In fact, if she hadn't seen him with her very own eyes in that hotel room, she might have believed him when he'd claimed he was innocent.

But she *had* seen him, and there had been no mistaking what he had been doing.

Even now, after two years, it made her nauseous just thinking about it.

Ignoring her pounding head, she challenged him. "Are you saying that you haven't been gambling since the ship set sail?"

"Well, yeah, I've gambled a bit."

A bit? He called two thousand dollars *a bit*? Was business that good these days? Kim had probably told her a dozen times, but when Kim began talking about her wonderful brother, Ashley managed to concentrate on something else until her friend gave up and changed the subject.

Now she wished she had listened.

Forcing a laugh, she said, "There was a time when wild horses couldn't have dragged you into a casino. Next, you'll be telling me you started playing the lottery. And we all know *that* would never happen."

Michael smiled. "Right. We all know that would never happen."

He leaned forward and adjusted the pillows behind her head, his warm breath fanning her cheek. Ashley curled her fingers into the covers to keep them from reaching up and pulling his mouth to hers.

Being around Michael reminded her of dieting; the hunger pains were constant, always ready to tempt her willpower. Only her hunger pains had nothing to do with food and everything to do with the sexy man adjusting her pillows as if he truly cared.

"Tanya is bringing some ice. You should lie still."

"Yes, doctor."

"Don't be a smart-ass."

"Yes, doctor."

"If you say that again, I'm going to kiss you."

"Yes—" She swallowed the rest of it. He looked as disappointed as she felt, which most certainly should have alarmed her.

What was the use? She knew and he knew they lusted for one another like nobody's business. They could take up a whole chapter in Deckland's book about body chemistry.

Heck, maybe even the entire book!

Speaking of doctors . . . "Did a doctor look at my—"

"Yes," Michael interrupted with a growl. "And he looked old enough to be my great-grandfather."

At his tone, Ashley started to lift her eyebrows, but remembered in the nick of time that it probably wouldn't be wise. Just how hard had she hit that damned ball, anyway? "I take it you weren't impressed with him?"

"With the exorbitant prices they charge for these cruises, you'd think they could afford to hire a decent doctor, one who doesn't have one foot in the grave."

Ashley couldn't resist chiding him. "Michael! I didn't know you were so narrow-minded. 'With age comes experience—' "

"With age," Michael corrected, "comes forgetfulness, hearing loss, waning eyesight, muddled thinking—"

She held up her hand. "I get the picture."

"I've a mind to file a complaint. Surely they have a suggestion box on this ship, at least."

"Michael—"

"Maybe I should talk to the captain directly."

"Michael." She grabbed his hand and forced him to look at her. "I'm fine, really. I've got a headache—"

"I'll get you some aspirin." Abruptly, he pulled free of her hand and rose from the bed, as if he'd just realized he'd given away too much. He strode to the chest of drawers and began rummaging through the array of masculine items he'd brought. "I know I brought some aspirin along."

In puzzled silence, Ashley watched him, daring to speculate. Was it possible Michael cared a bit more than he wanted to admit?

And if that was true, did she want him to?

Chapter Thirteen

For the first hour and a half, Ashley couldn't deny that she enjoyed Michael's attentive care. With bittersweet nostalgia, she recalled the time she'd come down with a wicked virus circulating around town.

Michael had brought her chicken soup for her sore throat, hot water bottles when she felt chilled, aspirin when her head ached, and a dozen different magazines she hadn't had the strength to read. The only time he'd left her alone was when he'd thought of something else she might need. He had taken a week off from the club just to nurse her.

And he had driven her slowly crazy, just as he was doing now.

"Are you sure there isn't anything else I can get you? An Italian ice, maybe? I remember that you loved those."

Ashley adjusted the ice pack Tanya had brought her, closing her eyes in the hope that he wouldn't see how exasperated she was. "As a matter of fact, there *is* something you can get me."

He perked up, leaning over her eagerly. "What? You name it, baby."

"The ship's passenger list."

"Excuse me?"

"The list of all the passengers. You know, the roster." She nearly smiled at his dismayed look. "Well, you asked."

"You probably shouldn't be reading," he said seriously. "Not with that type of head injury."

Ashley silently ground her teeth. "I have a mild bump on the head. No nausea, no dizziness. No concussion."

"You're not a doctor."

"And neither are you," she countered, forgetting to hide her irritation. "Next, you'll be ordering me to stay in bed the rest of the night."

Michael frowned. "I thought that was understood."

"Michael!" At first, she thought he was kidding; then she realized he wasn't. "I'm not going to miss the pool party when there's nothing wrong with me."

Without a word, he rose and went into the bathroom, returning with a small mirror he'd

163

taken from her makeup case. He held it in front of her. "Take a look."

Ashley snatched the mirror from his hand and looked. "I see a red, round circle on my forehead." She gently probed the area. "And most of the swelling has gone down. I don't even think it will leave a bruise. In fact, I think a little makeup will take care of what's left."

"Maybe it's worse than you know. Maybe you're delusional."

She glared at him. "You're insane."

"And *you've* been knocked in the head by a speeding golf ball."

"Made of hard plastic."

"But solid through and through."

The mirror landed at the bottom of the bed, the action relieving a tiny bit of her frustration. "If you're not careful, I'll start to believe that you care." Ha! Now she would see him squirm—

"I never said I didn't. In fact, I remember telling you I did."

"And then you added, 'Who wouldn't?' " She didn't know why she was goading him this way. Hadn't she learned her lesson—over and over again?

Michael paced restlessly, his hands in his pockets. He came to stand by the bed, looking down at her. "What do you expect, Ash? I guess I could give you my heart and let you walk all over it, but you might fall into one of your old footprints and trip."

Her jaw dropped at his ridiculous metaphor. She couldn't believe he was still blaming her for something he had done! She gaped at him for a full thirty seconds before she managed to find her tongue. And then she had to speak slowly, carefully, to keep from screaming like a fishwife. "I hope and pray that Candy keeps a short leash on you, Michael. Does your intended know you have a tendency to stray?"

His eyes narrowed. "Candy doesn't have a mistrustful bone in her body, so she isn't prone to jumping to conclusions, like someone else I know."

Oh, she knew exactly whom he was talking about! "Then I pity Candy." She shrugged as if she didn't care. "Or maybe you think that what she doesn't know won't hurt her." She dropped the ice bag; her forehead felt frozen, like her heart. Why were they having this conversation? It was pointless and redundant and resurrected old hurts and past memories that neither of them cared to recall.

Michael seemed to realize this at the same instant she did. His gaze softened. "I'm sorry. You have a head injury, and here I am adding to your stress. Maybe I should leave and let you get some rest."

Ashley pounced on the suggestion. "I think

165

that's a good idea. We're both tired and our nerves are taut."

And Michael, with his amazing talent for making her forget that she was mad, reached out and drew his finger along her jawbone in a slow, sensuous caress.

Her nipples instantly hardened.

His deep voice was husky as he said, "When I'm around you, Ash, my entire *body* stays taut."

Her pulse leaped. She licked her lips and didn't dare look at him. "How—how can you feel this way after the argument we just had?"

His feathering finger traced a path from her neck to her taut nipple. "How can *you?*" he challenged softly.

She closed her eyes, fighting hard to keep her body still, to keep it from surging forward at his touch. "Maybe you should go," she whispered. Weakly. Pathetically. God, she was helpless when it came to Michael!

Which was exactly why she had refused to see him until their divorce was final. She knew what he could do to her, and the possibility was unthinkable. Though she might be able to forget his betrayal while she was in Michael's arms, there would always be the daylight hours when she would remember.

It would have destroyed their marriage eventually.

She had chosen to skip to the inevitable end.

The sudden click of the cabin door closing startled her. She opened her eyes, surprised, relieved, and shamelessly bereft to find him gone.

What a cruel twist of fate that they'd been thrown together, Ashley thought, searching for a grain of humor in the situation.

She found none.

Her gaze landed on Michael's cell phone on the dresser. Gingerly, she threw back the bedsheet and got to her feet. She waited a moment, and when nothing alarming happened, she walked to the dresser and picked up Michael's cell phone.

She dialed Kim's number. Her friend answered on the first ring.

"Don't tell me," Kim said in a breathless voice before Ashley could announce herself. "You lost a bundle trying to win my money back. I knew you would. I could have bet money that you would."

When she finally paused long enough for Ashley to get a word in, Ashley said, "Kim. It's me, not Michael."

Silence.

Suspicious silence.

"You're calling from Michael's cell phone," Kim stated unnecessarily.

"How did you know?"

Kim cleared her throat. "Um, because I've got my phone rigged for a certain ring if it's Michael." She laughed, but it sounded forced. "What *will* they think of next, huh?"

Ignoring the question, Ashley forced Kim to backtrack. "You said something about Michael losing a bundle trying to win your money back. Are you saying that Michael was gambling with *your* money?" A dozen questions tripped through her mind while she was waiting for Kim to answer. Had Michael borrowed money from Kim in order to gamble? Was his addiction that serious? Because the Michael she knew would never, in a million years, borrow money from his little sister. His pride wouldn't allow it.

"Please don't let on that you know," Kim said, snagging her attention again. "He'll be embarrassed. By the way, I saw Tom today."

Ashley was aware that Kim was once more trying to change the subject. This time she let her. "You did? Did you speak to him? Did he say that he missed me?" Now, why didn't her pulse accelerate when she thought about Tom?

She shook her head, disgusted with herself. She knew the reason why she was asking these questions—questions that hadn't occurred to her before this cruise—and the reason was kin to the woman on the other end of the line.

"Yeah, I spoke to him. I ran into him when I stopped in at Trudy's to have a drink with Cobalt. You remember Cobalt, don't you?"

She did, and wished that she didn't. Cobalt

often worked as bartender for Kim when she catered parties where liquor was served.

Cobalt . . . who was tall, dark, handsome, and gay.

And Trudy's was a popular gay bar. Ashley knew, because she had gone with Kim to Trudy's for Cobalt's birthday celebration.

Don't jump to conclusions, she told herself. *It's just what Michael would expect you to do.*

Tom was gay.

Ashley knew she wasn't being paranoid or jumping to conclusions. No, if she was guilty of anything, she was guilty of being terribly naive.

Tom had suggested they save lovemaking until after they were married.

Tom's overnight guest had answered the phone—from the loft bedroom where Tom slept.

And Tom was twenty-seven, yet he had never mentioned any old girlfriends, not even from high school.

Surprised to find her voice even, she asked Kim, "Was Tom with anyone?"

"Oh, yeah. He was with this really dishy guy named Lenny or Lester or something like that."

"Lindsey?" She heard Kim snap her fingers and knew what she was going to say before she said it.

"Yeah! Lindsey. That's the name. I was sitting with Cobalt, having a Merry Margarita and wondering why you'd never introduced me to this gorgeous guy when I realized he was gay."

Ashley's head throbbed and her eyes burned. Tom was gay. Her fiancé was gay. The man she might have married was gay. Why? Why would Tom pretend to be straight, going so far as to ask her to marry him? It didn't make sense. "Kim . . . how did you know that Lindsey was gay—aside from the fact that he was in a gay bar, I mean."

"I guess I realized it when Lindsey went to the dance floor with another man. Straight guys just don't do that."

"And that other man was Tom, wasn't it, Kim?"

The long silence that followed didn't surprise Ashley because she knew Kim would hate telling her, knowing how badly it would hurt. "Kim?" she prompted.

"Um, I didn't really notice—"

"Kim . . ."

"Okay, yes, it was Tom. God, Ash, I hate to be the one to give you that kind of news."

Ashley blinked the moisture from her eyes, determined not to waste her tears on someone as conniving and deceitful as Tom. Nevertheless, her voice wobbled as she said, "Better now than later, right? I would have gotten a nasty shock on my wedding night." Her laugh was hollow-sounding, even to her own ears.

"I'm sorry, girlfriend. I was planning to wait until you got back to tell you."

"It's not your fault, you goose." At that moment, Ashley would have given her lottery winnings to have Kim with her. She desperately needed the kind of solid, you're-too-good-for-him-anyway hug that only a best friend could give. Instead, she said, "If you talk to Michael, please don't mention this, okay? I'd like to tell him myself." She didn't plan to do anything of the sort, but Kim didn't have to know that.

"Okay."

"Promise?"

"I promise. Are you okay? I know that you think you love Tom, but—"

"No buts, Kim," Ashley interrupted to say sternly. "I did love Tom, and I don't love Michael, so don't get any ideas. Besides, he's still engaged to Candy."

"That isn't official," Kim argued.

Ashley groaned silently. She knew where this was heading, could hear the eagerness in Kim's voice.

"And Candy doesn't love Michael, anymore than he loves—"

Very quietly, Ashley folded the phone, breaking the connection. There wasn't any reason to listen when she knew exactly what Kim was about to say. The poor woman would never accept the sad truth, and now, with Tom out of the picture,

171

she would redouble her efforts to get Ashley and Michael back together.

She jumped as the phone in her hand began to vibrate. Without thinking, she opened it and put it to her ear. It would be Kim, of course, calling back to berate her for hanging up—

"Mike?"

Not Kim. Kim never called her brother anything but Michael.

"It's Candy."

Mystery solved, Ashley thought. She put a hand over her lurching stomach as she realized what she'd done.

She had answered Michael's phone. Now his girlfriend was waiting impatiently for him to speak.

The right thing to do would be to hang up immediately, before Candy realized she wasn't *Mike.*

She prepared to do just that, but when Candy began to talk again, she found herself shamelessly listening. She could always hang up afterward. . . .

"I guess you realize that after our little discussion, I won't be at the airport to pick you up when you get back to Kansas City. I'm flying to Vegas with a few friends." A lengthy pause, then: "Michael? I hear you breathing. Are you still angry with me?"

Ashley's only excuse for what she did next was

that the devil made her do it. The devil . . . and Michael's smug, taunting dig about Candy trusting him.

"This—this isn't Michael. It's Ashley. I, um, borrowed his phone." Which wasn't a lie. She *had* borrowed his phone—from a dresser that was in a room that housed a bed where they had made hot, steamy love several times.

The sudden surge of guilt didn't surprise Ashley. After all, this time *she* was the other woman, so to speak. Which made her no different from the naked woman she'd caught riding Michael in the hotel room.

The lurching in her stomach turned to outright nausea. Somewhere in the world there was a woman Ashley detested every bit as much as Candy should detest her.

If only she knew.

"Ashley? You mean, Ashley as in ex-wife Ashley?"

Candy sounded so amazed Ashley wanted to giggle. Hysterically, of course. She could always blame it on her head injury.

"Yes, that's the one." She forced a rueful laugh. "Bizarre, isn't it? That we ended up on the same ship?"

"Yeah," Candy responded after another shocked pause. "Bizarre."

Shocked, Ashley realized. But not suspicious or angry or jealous. She felt like gnashing her teeth in frustration. Candy was not only beautiful and limber, she was trusting.

Just as Michael claimed.

"Michael's told me all about you," Candy said, sounding genuinely friendly.

Ashley wanted to gag.

"I feel as if I already know you."

Oh, no. You don't know me at all, or you wouldn't be talking to me. I slept with your boyfriend.

More than once.

Reluctantly, Ashley said, "And Michael's told me a lot about you, too."

"Oh, I'll bet!"

What, exactly, did she mean by that? Biting the inside of her lip, Ashley said, "Congratulations on your engagement."

There was a long pause. Ashley thought she'd lost the connection when Candy finally laughed.

"Tell me you're joking."

Maybe there was some truth to Michael's suggestion that she was delusional, Ashley thought, trying not to frown. "Excuse me?"

"Tell me you're joking, that Michael didn't really tell you we were engaged."

"Well, he didn't exactly say—" Ashley stopped, remembering belatedly that Kim had told her he was thinking about popping the question. Was it possible he had changed his mind? Or . . . what if he hadn't gotten around to it yet, and she had just blown his surprise? If either possibility turned out to be true, she was in a heap of trouble.

Then Ashley realized that Candy didn't sound even slightly excited by the prospect of marrying Michael.

In fact, she sounded dismayed.

"Look, Ashley, just for the record, Michael and I aren't getting married. Ever. I made that fact more than clear to him when he invited me to go on the cruise."

Ashley was glad Candy couldn't see her gaping mouth. She snapped it closed, honestly speechless.

"God, I had no idea he was even *thinking* about marriage until he mentioned it!" Candy said, her voice growing more agitated by the minute. "I mean, he's gorgeous and sweet and wonderful, but I would never marry a man I wasn't physically attracted to."

Thumping her head to make certain she was awake wasn't an option for Ashley. She settled for pinching herself.

It hurt.

Before Ashley could remind Candy that this was their first conversation ever, and that maybe she should be confiding in someone else, say someone like her mother, Candy groaned.

"I mean, I was actually starting to think he was gay."

Ashley clapped a hand over her mouth to smother a gasp. She held it tight.

"Or maybe he just simply didn't like sex."

An image, starkly erotic, rose in Ashley's befuddled mind: Michael grabbing her hips as she braced her hands against the shower wall, his fingers sure to leave their mark on her willing flesh.

Of Michael, his hard, muscled body glistening with water drops, pounding into her as he called out her name at the moment of his violent release.

Of Michael, lying naked beside her in bed, fully aroused. "Give me your hand," he'd ordered.

Just the not-so-distant memory evoked an ache between her legs.

Michael . . . gay? She thought not. And neither did he dislike sex. Oh, no. Not at all. Quite the contrary.

"I probably shouldn't be telling you this," Candy said, far too late. "But I'm *so* curious, and I can't help wondering if you ran into the same problems with him when you guys were married."

Ashley's mouth was so dry she didn't know if she could speak. What would she say? What *could* she say to this dim-witted stripper who obviously didn't know squat about Michael?

She found herself feeling outraged on Michael's behalf. "Why did you go out with him for so long if you weren't interested in him romantically?" A question she couldn't wait to ask Tom, as well.

"Romantically?" Candy's throaty laugh held a hint of scorn, enough to make Ashley flush. "How old-fashioned! But to answer your question, I went out with Michael because he was fun and gorgeous. The girls at work were green with envy." She chuckled. "It was also the first time I'd had a platonic relationship with a man other than my father, and for a while that was kind of nice. I didn't have to worry about groping hands."

Groping hands? Ashley was simply stupefied. Or addled. Yes, she thought, pouncing on the excuse. She was addled from her head injury. She wasn't having this conversation with Michael's girlfriend at all; she was unconscious, or dreaming, or in a coma—

"Anyway, could you give him a message for me? I need to know if he's still planning on taking me to the Policeman's Ball a week from Saturday. I've already bought the dress."

"I don't think—"

"Thanks, Ashley. Michael said you were a special woman, and I can see that he was right. So glad we had a chance to chat!"

Ashley took the dead phone from her ear and stared at it. Despite her injury, she shook her head. In the space of a few minutes, she had discovered her fiancé was gay and that Michael's stripper girlfriend had no intention of marrying him.

Could her life get more bizarre?

She nearly dropped the phone when someone knocked on the door. Hastily, she replaced it on the dresser and went to answer the door.

A steward stood in the hall. He was holding a tray, and on the tray was a solitary can of whipped cream.

"You ordered a can of whipped cream?"

"No, I didn't." She couldn't speak for Michael, but she couldn't for the life of her imagine why he would—

"You're Mrs. Scott, aren't you?"

Ashley's face got hot. Now she suspected the reason for the whipped cream. "No. The Scotts are across the hall in stateroom six B."

She shut the door, then gently leaned her forehead against the cool wood.

And very, very carefully, she began to laugh.

Chapter Fourteen

Michael liked to think he wasn't a coward.

Oh, he feared the usual—plane crashes, snakes, and maybe getting old, but other than that, he liked to think he could face just about anything.

But there was one thing that terrified him: getting his heart broken again—by Ashley.

"You want another card?"

"Hit me." Michael waited for the dealer to turn up his final card.

When he lost, he ground his teeth. At the rate he was losing, he would match Kim's two thousand by the end of the night. Which gave him more reason to hate this no-brainer game. The idea that people actually became addicted to gambling blew Michael's mind.

Absently, Michael counted out another twenty dollars' worth of chips and pushed them forward. "I'm ready," he said, wondering if the aspirin had helped Ashley's headache, and if he was ever going to admit to himself that she still had the power to make him bleed.

Maybe he'd be better off, he mused, just admitting it, facing it, and dealing with the facts. Mentally, he went over those facts.

Fact one: He thought of Ashley constantly.

Fact two: He rarely thought of Candy at all, and he had believed that he was in love with her.

Fact three: He had to do something about fact one, and he had to do something immediately. Ashley had already burrowed beneath his skin. Now he had to make sure she didn't reach his heart.

Couldn't happen.

No way.

Never.

Bang her brains out. Care about what happened to her physically. Have a good time with her.

But don't love her. Loving Ashley was like shaking hands with Death.

"Damn," Michael whispered, and the dealer thought he was referring to the fact that he'd lost—again.

"Tough luck, buddy."

"I'm not your buddy," Michael growled, shoving another pile of chips forward. "Give me another."

"You'll have to wait a minute. I'm going on break and Rick will be filling in for me."

At the mention of the bartender, Michael snapped to attention. He lifted his gaze from the felt card table for the first time in an hour.

Rick with the bleached hair and aqua-colored eyes grinned back at him. "Hi, Michael. Having another rough night?"

Michael wasn't in the mood to share confidences with Rick, the bartender turned dealer. He hadn't forgotten that Rick's previous advice had backfired. Big time. "Why don't you just deal the cards?"

The bartender's grin didn't falter beneath Michael's hard-eyed stare. "Sure thing, Michael. Hey, I heard about your wife's accident."

"Ex-wife."

"Yeah. Hope she's okay."

"She is." With a faint surge of hope, Michael eyed the ace of spades laying face up in front of him. "Hit me again."

Rick flipped up a card. It was the jack of spades. "Looks like you've got this one." When he turned a king of diamonds next to his own six of hearts, he watched Michael rake the chips into his pile before he said, "Going to the pool party tonight?"

"Doubtful." Feeling lucky, Michael pushed fifty dollars in chips forward, hoping Rick would take the hint and shut up.

"We sure could use a judge for the wet T-shirt contest."

In the time before Ashley, the prospect would have delighted Michael. The realization that it did nothing for him now didn't improve Michael's black mood. "Not interested."

"Oh. Guess you'll want to stay in with your ex tonight, huh? Have a cozy evening and all. You two getting back together?"

Startled by the outrageous question, Michael knocked over a stack of chips. His first instinct was to laugh at the guy's blatant prying. Unfortunately, he was feeling a tad on the violent side tonight, thanks to Ashley. "No, we are not getting back together, not that it's any of your business."

Undaunted, Rick gave a careless shrug. "Okay, that's cool. But I think it's pretty neat that you won the lottery using the same numbers, you know?"

Michael froze in the act of raking his chips into the cloth pouch provided by the casino, hoping and praying he hadn't heard what he thought he'd heard.

"It reminds me of that movie, *Serendipity,*" Rick continued, shuffling the cards so fast Michael's eyes crossed. "You seen it? It's a chick flick, but I liked it. I mean, the way the guy in the movie came across that book with her name and phone number written in it the day before his wedding to someone else, and on the same day the girl came across a five-dollar bill he'd written *his* name and phone number on, well, that was pretty wild, wasn't it? Almost as wild as you playing the lottery for the first time using the same numbers as your ex-wife, and both of you winning. I mean, what were the odds of those numbers winning on that particular day? Blows my mind, man."

"How did you find out?" Michael managed to croak when the chatty bartender finally paused. Some of his chips had fallen to the floor, but at the moment he didn't care. What he cared about was how Rick had come by his information, and what he intended to do with it. Michael might have been a coward, but he wasn't stupid.

Rick shrugged, looking as cool as a cucumber. "Wasn't hard. At the beginning of the cruise, we all get a copy of the ship's roster so we can familiarize ourselves with the passengers. Your name had a star beside it, which means you're a VIP, which means you're loaded."

Hit by a sudden revelation, Michael rose and placed his hands on the table. He leaned forward until he was nose-to-nose with snoopy Rick. Very softly, he said, "Doesn't explain how you knew that I'd won the lottery, and that it was the first time I'd played the lottery . . . Rick." The instant flaring of Rick's pupils confirmed Michael's suspicions.

"Well, I . . ." Rick licked his lips and glanced nervously from left to right. Finally, he seemed to realize that short of calling security, he wasn't going to escape Michael's relentless gaze. "Um, I just assumed—"

"You know my meddling, conniving sister, Kim," Michael stated with conviction. He hadn't been exaggerating when he'd told Ashley that Kim had connections everywhere.

"Kim?" Rick pretended to think, but he wasn't fooling Michael. "The name does ring a bell, but I'm not sure—"

"What do you want?" Feeling suddenly weary, Michael straightened. "Just tell me what it will take to keep your mouth shut."

Rick tried to look repentant but failed. "Well, we *do* need an unbiased judge for the wet T-shirt contest for women, unless you'd rather judge the bare chest contest for men—"

"And if I do it, you'll keep your mouth shut about what you know?" When the bartender nodded, Michael forced himself to relax.

At least Rick had hit the nail right on the head about him being unbiased, Michael thought, gathering up his bag of chips and stalking away from the blackmailing bartender.

Because the only wet T-shirt he could imagine appealing to him was one with Ashley wearing it.

*　　*　　*

Wringing out the T-shirt in the bathroom sink, Ashley shook it and slipped it over her head, welcoming the cool feel of the wet material.

The cabin was uncomfortably warm. In fact, she was seriously considering filing a complaint about the faulty air-conditioning. This was a pleasure cruise—surely they didn't intend for her to suffer in a hot cabin?

At first, she had assumed it was her reaction to Michael that was causing the muggy atmosphere in the cabin. But Michael was gone, had been gone for more than two hours, and she was definitely too warm.

She looked at herself in the mirror, frowning at her red face. Had she forgotten to apply sunscreen this morning? It was highly likely, considering her muddled mind these days.

Her head ached, as well. Maybe she would just skip the pool party and go to bed early. Tomorrow the ship would be docking in St. Thomas, and she wanted to be fresh and ready. Missing a pool party would be a small price to pay for touring the island.

Besides, she didn't want to face Michael again tonight, not with the information she was carrying around. Candy should have stayed on the line long enough for Ashley to tell her straight out that she could do her own asking about the Policeman's Ball. She had no intention of doing her dirty work, and absolutely no intention of letting Michael know that she'd talked to Candy, or that Candy had told her far more than she wanted to know about their relationship—or lack thereof.

Poor Michael. She knew exactly how he felt, although he didn't know it and she had no plans to tell him that, either. To think that she had been planning a future with Tom, only to find out that he was gay!

Dressed in a pair of her ridiculously uncomfortable thong panties and the damp T-shirt, Ashley carefully lay down on top of the covers. She put a hand to her head and sighed. What a disaster this cruise was turning out to be, aside from the terrific sex with Michael.

And that, she admitted shamefully, almost made it worthwhile.

But on the other hand, wasn't it all for the best? She had discovered the truth about Tom before she married him and made a fool out of herself, and Michael had found out that Candy didn't love him.

Was he hurt? Was that the reason he was turning to her for sex? She knew what it was like to hurt . . . hadn't she died ten times over when she walked in on Michael and that—that woman? Michael might deserve to be dumped by Candy, to hurt the way she had hurt, but she discovered she found no satisfaction in his pain.

What did that mean? Was she getting over her

anger toward Michael? And if she was . . . well, she just couldn't. That would be too dangerous.

Just the prospect of Michael thinking she was beginning to care for him again made Ashley groan in agony. To repeat the past, to give him that power was unacceptable. She couldn't hide the fact that he turned her on, but she could and would hide the fact that she still loved him.

Loved him.

Loved him. Still. Had never really stopped, apparently, because it wasn't possible to love someone, stop loving him, then fall in love a second time. No, Ashley didn't believe that, even if she wanted to believe it. And she did. Desperately.

She put her fingers to her lips and bit down hard on the tips until tears sprang to her eyes. She had thrust him from her mind and had locked the door on her memories, but she had never truly stopped loving him. Seeing him with another woman had hurt, badly, but it hadn't killed her love for him.

He must never know that.

She turned on her side and let the tears fall onto her pillow. If Michael found out about Tom, he might feel sorry for her, feel as if he should pretend to care.

Or worse, he might think she was fair game.

But Ashley was done having her heart broken.

Sleep with him. Care about him. Participate in wild, unforgettable sex with him.

But *don't* love him.

With this firm decision made, she closed her eyes and tried to sleep.

Her T-shirt was wet and she wasn't wearing a bra. Her black thong panties left even more of her honey-kissed skin bare to his hungry gaze. Buttocks, tanned and firm, dared him to cup and fondle.

His intense gaze focused on the white shape of a butterfly on one smooth buttock. How had she managed to place a sticker in that position before tanning? he wondered, swallowing hard.

Michael took his hand from Ashley's shoulder and forced himself to step back. He filled his lungs with air, inadvertently inhaling her sweet, musky odor and the faint scent of her perfume.

God, she was beautiful.

And sexy beyond belief.

On unsteady legs, he moved to the stateroom's minibar, grabbed a miniature bottle of tequila, and downed the entire contents. Alcohol wasn't healthy and he rarely drank, but for once Michael wasn't interested in what was healthy.

He was interested in forgetting.

He grabbed another bottle and uncapped it as he let himself out of the cabin and away from temptation.

Rick didn't know it, but Michael had already picked the cream of the crop.

Hot Number

* * *

By the time the top ten contestants were lined up beside the pool and the final judges were called, Michael was seeing double. And that meant a lot of breasts.

From their poolside table, Bart, Birdie, and Deckland shouted out Tanya's name, stomping their feet and whistling wildly.

She had made the top ten.

Michael set his empty glass carefully on the judge's table and took his time looking over the last ten contestants.

Not a flutter, not even a twinge of sexual desire did he feel. Ten sets of perfect, perky breasts were revealed by wet T-shirts, and absolutely nothing stirred inside him—or elsewhere.

All he could think about was Ashley, alone in the cabin, wearing that sexy black thong and a damp T-shirt.

He focused his blurred gaze on Tanya, who smiled and winked at him. She was having a good time, Michael knew, and her flirting was harmless. Why wasn't he attracted to her? She was very pretty, and had a body that would make a monk cry.

Through an alcohol-induced fog, Michael willed himself to concentrate on Tanya, to forget, if even for a moment, about Ashley and how much he wished he were back in his cabin, gathering her into his arms.

Dammit!

Staggering slightly, Michael returned to the judge's table and marked his choice on a piece of paper. He added it to the hat Rick held out.

The crowd grew quiet as Rick slowly and carefully counted out the ballots.

Tanya won the contest.

Nursing another shot of mind-numbing tequila, Michael bided his time, waiting for the congratulatory crowd to thin. When it did, he made his unsteady way to Tanya.

Tonight, he would prove that Ashley wasn't the only woman in the world.

Chapter Fifteen

"Get lost."

The man flirting with Tanya gave Michael a startled look at his growled order. "She yours?" he asked, puffing out his chest. When Michael continued to glare at him, he lifted his hands and backed away. "Hey, dude, no hard feelings, right? I thought she was free."

When the guy had disappeared into the crowd, Tanya punched Michael in the arm. "Hey! Who are you, my big brother? I was finally making some headway and you scared him off!"

Michael shrugged and focused on the petite blonde. He curved his mouth in what he hoped was a sexy, flirty smile, and tried to balance himself on the swaying ship.

Only he wasn't certain the ship was actually swaying.

"That's because I want you to myself," he drawled.

Tanya's mouth dropped. Michael reached out and closed it, aware, even in his inebriated state, that Tanya was shocked by his actions. Hell, he was shocked by his actions, too, but his fear of getting involved with Ashley drove him onward. He feared he was going to go stark, raving mad if he didn't get her out of his mind.

"Michael? Have you been drinking?" she demanded, peering into his eyes. "You have, haven't you? Where's Ashley?"

"She's asleep." Michael sidled closer, using body language to convey what he couldn't seem to bring himself to say. Him, the ex-playboy, the lady's man. The guy who had once attracted women like bees to honey.

Or was it honey to bees? His mind was muddled; he couldn't think.

Tanya placed a pointy finger against his chest and shoved him back. Her eyes sparkled with growing outrage. "Michael! Have you lost your mind? You're a married man, or have you forgotten?"

"I'm not married," Michael stated. "Ashley and I are divorced." There, he'd said it. He'd told someone the truth for the first time since boarding the ship. Funny, he couldn't seem to remember why he'd lied to them in the first place. To protect Ashley's reputation? Or was it because he *liked* the idea of people believing them to be married?

That should have been his first warning signal.

"You're lying." Tanya shook her head, standing on tiptoe and looking over his shoulder, as if searching for someone to rescue her. "I don't know what's gotten into you, but you'd better go to your cabin before you say something you'll regret later."

But Michael wasn't ready to give up on proving that he could be attracted to a woman other than Ashley. His very sanity depended on it. Reaching out, he grabbed Tanya's arm, as much to steady himself as to stake his claim for anyone watching. "Let's go for a walk."

Tanya jerked out of his grasp, her eyes flashing. "I'm not going anywhere with you, you two-timer! I might be single and looking for love, but I happen to like Ashley, Michael."

"We've been divorced for two years," Michael slurred. "I swear it." On impulse—and driven by desperation—Michael leaned forward, intending to kiss Tanya just to prove to himself that he could feel something for another woman.

Before his lips could touch hers, she brought her knee up and into his groin with enough force to knock the breath from his lungs.

He bent over, gasping for air, and collided with her upraised knee. A very sharp, *hard* knee, he discovered.

"Oh, God, Michael!" Tanya cried, sounding horrified by what she'd done. "I didn't mean to hit you so hard, and I certainly didn't mean to catch you in the eye! Let me look—how badly does it hurt?"

Michael didn't know which body part hurt the most at that moment. He felt her tugging at the hand that covered his throbbing eye and let her inspect the damage. Bright spots danced behind his stinging eyelid, and the pain in his groin made him outright nauseous.

He was instantly sober.

"Does it hurt?" Tanya winced as *he* winced, and quickly dropped her hand from his eye. "Come with me. We'd better get some ice on that." Her gaze dropped briefly to his crotch. "And maybe on your, um, other injury, too."

"I'm sorry, Tanya—"

"Save it for later." Briskly, she steered him through the crowd and belowdeck to her cabin. She looked carefully in both directions before she unlocked the door and pulled him inside.

"Look, you've got every right to be mad," Michael said.

"You're damned right I do. Go sit on the bed while I fix an ice pack for that eye."

She was furious, and Michael didn't blame her. What had possessed him?

Ashley. That was what had possessed him. It was *her* fault. He was obsessed with his ex-wife and he was damned well going to put a stop to it.

Tanya placed a bulky towel filled with ice on his eye and urged him to hold it in place. She stood back with her hands on her hips, glaring at him. Any moment, Michael expected her to start tapping her foot.

He cleared his throat, feeling like a complete heel. "I apologize," he said sincerely. "I think I might have had too much to drink." A vast understatement, considering he usually avoided the strong stuff.

"That's no excuse for what you did—*tried* to do. You hit on me, Michael, and you're *married.*" Her eyes brimmed with tears. "Just when I was finally starting to believe in true love again, you had to go and burst my bubble."

Michael was lost. "What?"

"True love. The way you and Ashley feel for each other." She grimaced. "At least, I thought it was true love between you two—until tonight. Did you two have a fight? Is that why you're acting like a jerk?"

So much for thinking he couldn't feel any worse, Michael thought ruefully. He lowered the ice pack to his lap, stifling a groan of relief as the cold penetrated his throbbing groin. For a petite woman, Tanya wielded a powerful knee kick.

With genuine regret, Michael said, "I hate to

be the one to disillusion you, but Ashley and I really are divorced. It was an accident that we ended up in the same cabin."

Tanya stared at him long and hard. Finally, she sighed. "I guess you must be telling the truth. You know I could find out easily enough by asking Ashley." She sank onto the bed beside him, unknowingly jarring him.

He bit back a groan.

"Why the pretense? Why didn't you just tell us the truth at the beginning?"

Michael hesitated, debating just how much of himself he wanted to reveal to Tanya. But then, he supposed he owed her the truth after the way he'd acted toward her. Slowly, he said, "After the Scotts walked in on us . . . in the act, I didn't want them to think Ashley was—that she was—"

"Loose?" Tanya chuckled. "I guess that was before you got to know them and discovered there isn't an uptight bone in their bodies, right?"

He smiled. "Yeah. After that, I guess I just liked the idea of people thinking we were a couple again." He bit his tongue. He hadn't meant to be *that* truthful.

Damn that tequila!

Softly, and with an underlying sadness that made Michael's heart start to ache, Tanya asked, "What happened?"

He didn't pretend to misunderstand her question. "It's a long story. Sure you got time?"

"Well, Conan, since you ruined my chance of getting lucky for the night, I've got plenty of time. Lie back and relax. I'll get you another ice pack for your eye, since the one I gave you seems to be soothing your, um, other injury."

Michael shot her a rueful smile and obeyed, easing back on the bed. He stared at the ceiling, which seemed to be revolving. After a few moments Tanya returned with another ice-filled towel, and Michael placed it carefully on his eye. He waited for her to settle on the bed again.

The irony didn't escape him. He was stretched out on a bed with a beautiful, single woman and all he could think about was Ashley.

"Okay, I'm all ears. Just don't go to sleep on me. Ashley might be your ex, but any fool can see that she still loves you."

"Oh, you're dead wrong there," Michael said, wishing the knowledge didn't hurt. "She might have loved me once, but not anymore."

"Whatever. Now tell me the damned story before I go crazy."

And Michael did, reliving the nightmare all over again.

A beam of sunlight shining through the portal window awakened Ashley. She had her cheek buried in the pillow and knew before she opened her eyes that she had rolled to Michael's side of the bed.

The pillow smelled of Michael, a mixture of aftershave, shampoo, and soap.

She turned her head cautiously, relieved to discover nothing more than a vague ache remained to remind her of her humiliating injury. Slowly, she sat up and propped her back against the headboard of the bed, yawning and feeling remarkably refreshed.

How long had Michael been gone? she wondered, amazed that she had slept through the sound of the shower. She was normally a light sleeper, awake at the slightest sound. Her mouth curved as she realized that Michael must have been very, very quiet.

Considerate of him to let her sleep. But then, Michael had always been a gentleman.

It was his libido that was forever in question.

The sound of a foghorn startled Ashley out of her darkening thoughts.

Then she remembered.

Today they would dock at their first port of call, the beautiful island of St. Thomas, an adventure she had been anticipating ever since she'd read about the island on a travel Web site. According to her research, the shops and stores in Charlotte Amalie were not to be missed.

She had missed the pool party, but she wasn't about to miss their first port of call. Today she would double her sleuthing efforts to find the other lottery winner. It would be a shame to go through the entire cruise without meeting the person who had picked the very same numbers as she. She had a dozen questions to ask the winner. Had he or she picked the numbers at random? By computer? Or did the numbers actually have some significance, as they did to her?

Once in the shower, her thoughts turned to the heated argument she'd had with Michael before he'd stormed out. It seemed they were always fighting.

Unless they weren't having sex, that is.

Well, today she was determined to have a pleasant day browsing the shops in Charlotte Amalie, with or without Michael. If he chose to join her, she would do her utmost to avoid any subject that might spark an argument. She would prove to herself—and him—that they could eventually become friends.

Two years was a long time to live in the same town as enemies. They had gone from loving each other to hating each other.

Well, she had convinced herself she hated him, a self-defense tactic that had worked well for the past two years, while it remained unchallenged. Now she knew differently, but it changed nothing. Michael was still Michael. And with time and prayer, maybe she would eventually stop loving him.

Then she could get on with her life.

* * *

The breeze was warm and fragrant; the island exotic and beautiful, yet bustling with activity.

Ashley was enthralled.

A teenage boy dressed in blue-jean shorts tromped past her as she moved with the other passengers along the pier. He was carrying a wire cage filled with live lobsters, his feet as bare as his deeply tanned torso.

He flashed her a brilliant smile, and Ashley smiled back, envying the boy his freedom. What a wonderful life he must lead living on the island.

"Yoo hoo! Darling! Here we are!"

Ashley spotted Birdie, waving wildly at her from a few yards farther up the line. She saw Deckland, Tanya, and Bart, as well, but not Michael.

"Come on up here with us, dear!" Birdie yelled, and the passengers behind Birdie grimaced and covered their ears.

Biting back a grin, Ashley trotted along the line until she reached them. She felt a warm rush of affection as they gathered around her. After only a few days, these people felt like family.

"How are you? Let me see—"

"Don't push, Birdie! Can't you see the girl's got a bump on her head?" Bart scolded his wife with a smile.

"You're not dizzy, are you?" Deckland queried

with a worried frown. "I'm not a medical doctor, but I wonder if you should be out in this sun."

"She looks fine to me," Tanya said, taking her arm as the people behind them began to grumble. "We'd better walk faster. The natives are getting restless."

"Has anyone seen Michael?" Ashley asked when she was able to get a word in. To her astonishment, their little group immediately ground to a stop. Grumbling passengers flowed around them as the others continued to stare at her in a peculiar way.

"She doesn't know," Deckland said with an unhappy sigh.

Finally, Birdie folded her arms over her brightly flowered blouse and said, "Tell her, Tanya. She's a sensible girl—she'll believe you."

Ashley looked from one serious face to another, her curiosity growing. "Tell me what?" When Tanya wouldn't look her in the eye, her curiosity turned to dread. Her breath hitched. "Has something happened to Michael?"

Tanya quickly shook her head, but there were tears in her eyes. "No. It's just that he got drunk last night at the pool party and, um, he got hit in the groin and then the eye and—"

Birdie let out an exasperated sigh and pushed her aside. "You're not telling it right, Tanya. Let me explain it to her."

She took Ashley by the shoulders and moved

her aside. The others followed, as if they were all attached to the same string.

"It's like this, darling. Michael needed someone to talk to last night and Tanya just happened to be available. He never meant to fall asleep on Tanya's bed."

Bart leaned forward to add, "Nothing happened between them. Tanya wasn't even there with him. She spent the night in *our* room."

He braced a hand on his back and leaned forward. Ashley heard a loud cracking sound, followed by a groan.

"I slept on the floor, and she slept in the bed with Birdie," he concluded.

Michael hadn't gotten up early and left the cabin, as she had so naively assumed. He'd gotten drunk and spent the night in Tanya's cabin, where supposedly *nothing* had happened. Ashley felt sick inside, despite their attempts to justify his actions. Oh, she believed Bart and Birdie about Tanya spending the night in their cabin.

But what had happened before Tanya left Michael?

Keeping her voice neutral, she asked, "How did he get hurt?"

Apparently, her simple question had fallen on deaf ears.

"Bart? Birdie?" It wasn't easy looking at Tanya, but Ashley forced herself to focus on the petite, beautiful, sexy blonde. She had just begun to think she and Tanya could be friends, and it hurt to discover otherwise. "Tanya?"

Deckland shoved his hands in his pockets and stepped forward. "Please don't jump to conclusions, Ashley. It's obvious Michael loves you very much, despite being divorced—"

Ashley gasped. So Michael had told them. Or had he told Tanya? Before or *after* he slept with her? The implications were ominous. She shook her head, her throat tight with tears she was determined not to shed. "If Michael didn't do anything wrong, then why are you all standing in the middle of a crowded pier making excuses for him?"

They remained silent, looking at her with a mixture of pity and embarrassment. Ashley swallowed the lump in her throat and shouldered her bag. She forced a convincing smile to her lips. "Hey, don't look so serious! I'm glad our secret is out in the open. Did Michael by any chance tell you"—she looked pointedly at Tanya, who looked guilty as hell—"that both of us are engaged to other people? So, see?" She spread her trembling hands wide. "There's nothing to worry about. What Michael does is none of my business, and vice versa."

Thinking this would be an excellent time to join the other passengers—before she humiliated herself by bursting into tears—Ashley left them standing in a circle. Surely they would understand her need to be alone.

She had gone maybe ten feet when Tanya spoke.

"I hit him, Ashley. I kneed him in the groin. The black eye wasn't my fault, though. When he bent over, he accidentally hit my knee with his eye."

And her point was . . . ?

After a moment, Ashley resumed walking.

"He loves you, Ashley!" Tanya shouted after her. "You were all he could talk about!"

Knuckling a tear from her hot cheek, Ashley kept walking. It didn't take a genius to figure out why Tanya had kneed Michael in the groin.

There was only one reason Ashley could think of.

So maybe Tanya hadn't slept with Michael. Maybe the single sexpot was innocent and truly trustworthy.

But Michael wasn't.

Suddenly, she whirled around and stomped back to the whispering group. Deckland spotted her and elbowed Bart. Bart elbowed Birdie, and Birdie clamped a hand over Tanya's mouth.

"Swear to me that you won't tell Michael that I know about this," Ashley demanded.

"I swear."

"Of course."

"Me, too."

"Scout's honor."

"As far as I'm concerned," she clarified, "he left the cabin early this morning, while I was still asleep."

"Yes."

"Okay."

"Whatever you say, dear."

"Of course."

Ashley looked each one of them in the eye until she was satisfied they would keep their promise. Then she turned to Tanya again. Tanya looked miserable. Ashley softened slightly. After all, it wasn't Tanya's fault that Michael was a sexual predator. "Tanya, I believe your story. It's Michael I don't trust."

Instead of answering, Tanya groaned, as if she had been afraid Ashley would say those very words. "I know, he told me why you two divorced, which is why it's important that you believe—"

"Did he hit on you?" Ashley interrupted.

With obvious reluctance, Tanya nodded. "But he was only trying to prove—"

"It doesn't matter. We're divorced, remember?" When no one answered, Ashley said through clenched teeth, "Right?"

"Right."

"Yeah."

"Okay."

Bart had to nudge Birdie twice before she grudgingly said, "Of course. But—"

But Ashley was walking away again, and this time she didn't stop.

Chapter Sixteen

He found her at one of the many outdoor booths sprinkled among the shops and restaurants lining the boulevard. This one, he saw, sold fine jewelry and delicate porcelain figurines.

For a moment, Michael paused to watch Ashley, that old familiar ache filling his throat. She laughed at something the vendor said, tossing her head so that her hair fell over one shoulder.

Beneath the warm tropical sun, her glossy brown hair flickered with subtle highlights. He flexed his fingers, remembering with bittersweet nostalgia the many hundreds of times he had sifted through the satin strands.

Michael knew those highlights were natural, just as he knew that she worked out on a stair master several times a week to keep her calves firm and shapely.

His gaze dropped to skim the rest of her body.

She was wearing a short blue sundress that revealed the splendid length of her bare legs and the soft curve of her shoulders. It dipped low in the back, then flared over her pert behind, reminding Michael of the short, sassy outfit she'd worn as a cheerleader in high school.

She could probably still wear that outfit, he mused, his mouth watering. And look just as good, if not better. He shook his head, then winced. Too much alcohol, too little sleep.

At that moment, Ashley seemed to sense him watching her. She turned, her eyes widening at the sight of him. Her generous mouth curved into a bright, welcoming smile.

It was now or never, Michael thought with deep dread. Time to explain to her what had happened before someone else did. Would she believe him? More importantly, would she care?

And why was she smiling at him? He had expected a cold shoulder, at the least, for not coming back to the cabin last night.

"Michael! There you are!" She beckoned him exuberantly. "Come here; I want to show you something."

Michael took a deep breath and joined her at the booth, wondering what the hell was going on. Maybe the tequila he'd consumed had killed a few too many of his brain cells.

She held up a sparkling diamond wristwatch,

her expression almost reverent. "What do you think? Do you like it?"

He took his time examining the watch. He wasn't an expert, but the diamonds looked real. So did the thick gold band. "It's a fine watch, but it looks expensive."

She grinned at him, her eyes sparkling with excitement. "It *is* expensive. Just over five thousand, but I think it's worth it. So, you're being honest? This is something you would wear?"

Pleasure warred with guilt. Did she mean what he thought she meant? Was she actually considering buying the watch for *him*? Michael swallowed hard, feeling like the worst heel in the world. He didn't deserve it, and after he told her what he'd done, she would certainly agree.

"Of course I would wear it, but I have to tell—"

"Wonderful! If you would wear it, then Tom will like it, right? I think it will make a wonderful wedding present." She turned around and tapped the glass case in front of her with a long polished nail. "Along with these matching cuff links, of course. That's another three thousand, but my fiancé is worth it."

Fortunately, as she turned back to the vendor, she missed Michael's look of utter surprise, followed by a dark scowl as he realized she hadn't meant to buy the watch for him at all.

But for Tom. Her fiancé. Her *wonderful* fiancé.

"I'll take the watch and the cuff links," she told

the vendor cheerfully. To Michael, she said, "Did I keep you awake last night with my tossing and turning? I noticed you left early this morning."

She didn't know. *She didn't know!* Michael was so relieved, he felt like dancing. Or not. Thank God he hadn't gone on and humiliated himself by begging her forgiveness.

Eight thousand dollars for a wedding present. For Tom.

She had gotten him a barbecue grill.

Michael was certain he would choke before he could swallow the jealous lump in his throat. His smile felt as if it would crack his face as he said, "Let's hope that Tom can afford insurance."

"Oh, he can." Her smile was blinding. "After we get married, my money will be his money."

Right. The three aspirin he'd taken an hour earlier began to burn a hole in his stomach. And his headache was back.

"What did you buy for Candy?" Ashley asked as she handed the vendor her Visa card and took her purchases. She opened her shoulder bag and stuck the shopping sack inside, then firmly closed it again.

She was still smiling brightly when she looked at him again. "Michael? Did you hear me?"

Oh, he'd heard her all right. And he knew what he had to say. "As a matter of fact, I was hoping you would help me with that."

He watched her very closely, but her eyes

210

never flickered and her smile never wavered. Not even a tiny bit. She took her credit card from the vendor and slid it into a side pocket of her shoulder bag.

And smiled brightly at him again.

Michael ground his teeth. What was it about her smile that was bothering him? Was it a little too bright? A little too wide?

"Sure! What did you have in mind? A belly ring? Maybe a diamond-studded tongue ring? I hear those are great when you're—" She clamped a hand over her mouth and giggled, looking around to see if anyone was listening. "Sorry! I guess I got carried away."

Something wasn't right, Michael thought, narrowing his eyes behind his sunglasses. Ashley wasn't normally crude, and she most definitely wasn't crude in public. Whatever it was, Michael couldn't quite put his finger on it. She *seemed* sincere, right down to her not-so-subtle digs about Candy's body piercings.

Not that he was surprised she knew, considering Kim's penchant for keeping them both informed. After all, *he* knew personal things about Tom. For instance; he knew that Tom loved the opera and hated working up a sweat. The wimp. How could a vibrant, physical woman like Ashley be attracted to someone who thought picking up the newspaper was exercise?

The woman he had known loved good old-fashioned rock 'n' roll.

"Michael? Are you okay? You look a little pale."

Staring into her beautiful, unobtainable face, Michael heard himself saying, "I'm fine. I was just thinking about Candy's engagement ring. She wants something big and shiny."

Ashley let out a husky peal of laughter that drew the admiring stares of several men. "Of course she does! What woman wouldn't want something big and shiny?"

Again, her brilliant, sunny smile flashed up at him, and Michael felt that peculiar misgiving again.

"You should take a look at these." She took his hand and pulled him closer to the glass case, pointing at an impressive array of diamond rings. "See that one? The one with the cluster of diamonds around the huge one in the center?" She shrugged. "Of course, it's really expensive, so if you're thinking of something smaller—"

"I'll take it," Michael told the vendor. From the corner of his eye, he saw Ashley's eyes widen. The sight of her surprise gave him a blast of satisfaction that nearly made him forget his hangover.

"Those earrings would go well with the ring," Ashley suggested.

"I'll take those, too." Out of sheer perversity, he pointed to a glittering diamond necklace.

"Add the necklace. Wouldn't want to break up a family, would we?" Beside him, Ashley gasped.

"Michael, that's—that's over ten thousand dollars! Are you sure—"

"I'm sure." And then, with a sincerity that equaled hers, he added, "Candy's worth every penny, and then some."

"Hmm," she murmured, taking his elbow after he concluded his purchases. They began to stroll between the long row of booths. "You must have won a bundle at the casino last night."

Michael shrugged. "As a matter of fact, I lost. I don't think I'm going to win back Kim's money." And then, in an undertone, he added, "Crazy nut, insisting I bet it all on one hand. She knows I hate to gamble." He felt Ashley jerk, as if in surprise, which confused him. His aversion to gambling shouldn't have surprised her.

"What? *Kim* made you bet her money on one hand? The two thousand?"

It was Michael's turn to be surprised. "She told you about the two thousand? She made me promise not to say anything to anyone. She didn't want anyone else thinking she was crazy, like Granddad."

"Michael!" Ashley protested. "She's your sister and my best friend."

"Exactly. And that's why I can call her crazy."

"She's not crazy. Eccentric, maybe. But not crazy."

Suddenly, she squealed like a schoolgirl and began to drag him to a booth.

"Look at these paintings, Michael! Aren't they gorgeous? And they're by a local artist, which makes them even more priceless."

Michael eyed the oil painting depicting a nutbrown child chasing a giant sea turtle crawling along a white sandy beach. Beyond the beach stretched a blue lagoon lined with palm trees so authentic-looking he could almost see them swaying in the tropical breeze.

His brows rose as he caught sight of the price tag. "Priceless isn't the word for it. Highway robbery, maybe. They probably bought them from the artist for peanuts."

"Oh, who cares? Tom would *love* to have one. Or two."

"Why not make it a dozen?" Michael asked with thinly veiled sarcasm.

Ashley gave his arm a playful slap. "We don't have that much room in our cabin, silly."

The rest of the day continued in the same bizarre manner. By the time they returned to the ship, Michael could barely see over the armful of packages he carried.

Presents for Tom and Candy. After all, his pride had taken a beating. He couldn't very well stand by and let Ashley shower Tom with expensive presents without doing the same for Candy, could he?

No, he couldn't.

He just hoped Kim liked everything he'd bought for Candy.

Ashley's mud pack couldn't disguise her steady flow of tears. In fact, the muddy rivulets running down her cheeks were so noticeable, the tiny Asian man applying a clear coat to her toes tried to get her to talk about it.

"Jon good listener," he volunteered.

She couldn't see him, but she could hear the pity in his voice. She sniffed and shook her head, and a chunk of mud went flying from her chin. There was a splat, then a surprised grunt.

Mortified, Ashley cautiously turned her head until the unfortunate woman filing her nails came into view. Her name tag read BLAIR. "I'm sorry, Blair," she whispered. "I just can't seem to stop crying."

The manicurist gave her a pitying smile and patted her arm. "Dat's okay, honey. You just go ahead and cry, mon. If you feel you want to talk about it, Jon and I are listening."

Jon indicated his willingness again by squeezing her toes.

"Men," Blair said in a disgusted voice. "Dey sometimes need to be smacked around."

Despite her bleak mood, Ashley nearly laughed at Blair's statement. Ashley could easily imagine the tall, broad-shouldered Blair smacking her husband around.

Blair thrust Ashley's fingertips into a warm liquid and slapped her hands against her knees. "Let dat soak. Relax."

Ashley cracked one eye just in time to see Blair haul Jon to his feet and literally yank him out of the room.

She was left alone with her thoughts, and they weren't pretty.

Oh, how foolish she felt! Michael didn't have a gambling problem at all. Not that he deserved her concern if he did. And instead of coming forward with the truth about last night, he had been *relieved* when she had acted as if she hadn't known he'd been gone.

Nothing about him had changed; he still couldn't be trusted. The one time she had given him the benefit of the doubt, he had made a fool of her.

Served her right for forgetting, even for an instant, that Michael was bad news.

Another chunk of mud slipped from her face and plopped to the floor. Ashley couldn't bring herself to care. How was she going to get through the rest of the cruise without letting Michael know how much he'd hurt her—again? Could she continue the farce?

She didn't see how. The first time he touched her and she resisted, he would know something was wrong, and it wouldn't take him long to figure out the truth. After that, he would also figure out that he'd hurt her, and he would have to realize that she cared a lot more than she should.

And then he would gloat.

Oh, it was all a big mess. She wished she had never gotten on the damned ship. As for Kim . . . maybe Kim would finally see once and for all that she and Michael were all wrong for each other, and stop trying to throw them together.

The only light at the end of the tunnel, as far as Ashley could see, was the fact that she no longer felt compelled to spend every waking moment with Michael.

He didn't have a gambling problem.

So what had Kim meant about the money? Michael had spent a lot of money buying presents for a nonexistent girlfriend. Not the actions of a man heading for bankruptcy. And why was Michael lying to her about Candy, anyway? Was it for the very same reason she lied to him about Tom?

Despite the fact that she was doing it to keep Michael at an emotional distance, the possibility that Michael was using Candy for the same reason actually hurt. Was the thought of loving her that abhorrent to Michael? And why the hell should she care anyway?

Nothing in this world could convince her that Michael was capable of loving her unconditionally, and most importantly, faithfully.

In high school, already half in love with him, she had watched him go through the entire senior class of girls, one by one. Amazingly, the girls seemed to remain fond of him after he moved on to the next one.

In college, it had been the same.

When he finally noticed that she was no longer Kim's little friend, but a woman in her own right, she had been wary, and who wouldn't have been? It had taken him two months to convince her to go out with him, six months to convince her to consider marrying him, and another six months to get her in front of a preacher.

She'd never lost her reservations about Michael settling down with one woman, not completely. Always, the fear had been at the back of her mind, waiting for an opportunity to make her nuts.

The constant reminders hadn't helped. The way his buddies always teased him and talked about his past, as if he had been the stud of all studs and they couldn't get over how much he'd changed.

The phone calls from old girlfriends to wish him a happy birthday. Harmless . . . but annoying. With an attractive man like Michael, her jealousy had never lacked for fuel, although she thought she had kept it under control. Sometimes it had showed, and when that happened, Michael had teased her until she felt foolish.

Finally, there had come a time in their marriage when she'd started feeling more secure and confident. Her flashes of doubt and jealousy became rare, almost nonexistent.

That was when Ashley had been the happiest.

And that was when Michael had done the unforgivable, ending it all in a heartbeat of time. Their beautiful life together—their beautiful love—shattered in an instant of betrayal.

Afterward, Ashley had had her moments when she thought, "What if he's telling the truth?" But then she would close her eyes and bring up the torturous image of the blonde bimbo sitting on top of Michael, riding him and moaning with pleasure.

The blonde had been blocking her view of Michael's face, and Ashley had been glad. She might have died right there on the spot if she had had to witness Michael's expression of pleasure at the hands of another woman.

As it was, she had barely made it to the restroom down the hall before she began to retch uncontrollably. Oh, the pain! The pain had been deep and wrenching. She thought it would never stop, that her heart would just give up and stop beating.

It felt like grief, and Ashley supposed that in

a sense it had been. If she had found Michael dead, she didn't think she could have hurt any worse.

The disadvantage of loving someone as wildly as she had loved Michael became very clear to her over the following weeks and months.

She lost sleep. She lost weight. And for a while, she lost her will to give a damn about anything.

But eventually her grief faded and numbness set in. After that ran its course, caution took its place. If she was cautious, she could avoid another man like Michael, another marriage like theirs, another consuming love with the power to destroy.

Tom would have fit the bill.

Perhaps it was just as well, Ashley mused as her tears stopped and the mud dried on her face, that most people didn't meet their true soul mates.

They were the lucky ones. *They* wouldn't have to go through life feeling as if a part of them was missing.

Ashley nearly shrieked as a shadow fell over her face.

"Mrs. Kavanagh?"

She squinted at the freckled-face man through one mud-caked eye. Briefly, she considered correcting him, then decided it wasn't worth the effort. "That's me."

"Are you ready for your body waxing?"

Swallowing hard, Ashley nodded. After the body waxing, there was the sauna, then the hairdresser, then a leisurely shopping spree in the dozen or so boutiques on the ship, followed by a few drinks at the bar.

Had she left anything out? Anything that would keep her away from the cabin and Michael until she absolutely had to go back?

Maybe she'd get her belly-button pierced. . . .

Chapter Seventeen

Standing in the doorway of the ship's gym, Michael surveyed the equipment with a critical eye. He was surprised to find everything state of the art.

He wasn't surprised to find the room empty at this time of night. The casino and lounges on the ship would be a far greater attraction for vacationers than working up a sweat on the Bowflex.

But Michael couldn't think of a better way to work out his frustration than pumping iron, or rowing as if his life depended on it. Even the stair master looked more appealing than any curvy blonde he could imagine.

His rueful smile went unnoticed as he made his way to the complicated workout machine in one corner of the room. He was a sorry sight all right, mooning over his ex-wife while she fantasized about her fiancé.

He settled on the seat of the Bowflex and pulled the weighted handles forward, touching his chest and holding the position to the count of ten.

Did she dream of Tom when they made love? he wondered. It was the first time the possibility had occurred to Michael, and he silently cursed his conceit. It was obvious she was nuts about Tom, so why wouldn't she pretend he was Tom? If Tom had been on the ship, he and Ashley might never have exchanged more than a few stiff, polite words.

Michael closed his eyes and tried to concentrate on his workout. It felt good to feel his muscles tighten and his heartbeat increase to a rapid, healthy rate.

Something Ashley could do with one smile, one flirty sweep of her lashes. A sassy crooking of her little finger.

It was no use. As hard as he tried, he couldn't *not* think about Ashley. Three nights and four days in her company and he was hopelessly hooked. Again.

Thinking about the past was a waste of time, Michael knew, but he couldn't help doing just that. What if he'd never gone to that bachelor party? What if his friends had never convinced that stripper to climb into bed with him? What if they had, and Ashley hadn't walked in?

He knew without a doubt that he wouldn't have taken advantage of what the stripper had offered. He knew it, but Ashley hadn't believed him. She had gone back home, packed her things, and moved in with her parents until the divorce was final.

She had refused to speak to him. Oh, she had listened to his buddies, but she hadn't believed them. In a fit of desperation, Michael had gone back to Aspen, found the stripper, and convinced her to return with him and explain to Ashley that the entire incident had been a joke.

Ashley had refused to talk to the woman.

It was at that point that Michael realized Ashley was sadly lacking a basic ingredient for maintaining a good marriage. He had given up, allowing anger to soothe his shattered heart. Never again, he had decided, would he allow a woman to have that kind of power over him.

Yet here he was, pushing his body to the limit in the hope of forgetting how wonderful Ashley had felt in his arms these last few nights. He'd forgotten what the sound of her laughter could do to his insides. He'd forgotten what a punch her smile carried.

He'd forgotten, dammit, how much he had loved her.

Loved her still.

His cell phone rang. Michael let out an explosive breath and reached for the phone, flipping it open as he brought it to his ear. Breathlessly, he said, "Hello?"

"Michael? It's Kim. How are things going? Are you having a good time? Did you buy me a souvenir?"

Michael thought about the fortune in jewelry he'd hidden in his chest drawer. Souvenir? More like a few years' worth of birthday and Christmas presents rolled into one glittering package. "Yeah, I bought you something very special. Not that you deserve it," he added dourly. He could very easily picture Kim pouting at his tone.

"Now, Michael. Can you honestly say you're having a terrible time?"

"Hmm. Let's see if this gives you a hint. I'm in the gym working out."

"You're working out on a cruise ship?" Kim squeaked in disbelief. "Michael! You're supposed to be having fun! Go lie in the sun, or take a dip in the pool. By the way, where's Ashley?"

Before Michael could think, he said, "Probably back in the cabin, admiring the five-thousand-dollar watch she bought for Tom."

Kim was silent for several moments. "Oh, I doubt that," she said rather smugly.

"Come again?" What was his meddling little sister up to now? Michael wondered.

"I promised not to tell."

"Kim . . ."

"But I *can* make a suggestion," she said, ignoring his warning tone. "Why don't you go have a drink at the bar?"

"Because I drank enough last night to drown a fish," Michael snarled. "And I'm not in the mood for your games."

Once again, Kim ignored him. "Ask for Rick's Remedy. He'll tell you what you need to know."

This time Kim was the one to hang up. Michael let out a stream of curses that made him glad he was alone in the gym. "One of these days," he muttered. He stood and wiped the sweat from his brow with a towel, then slipped his T-shirt over his head. He stomped from the gym and headed in the direction of the bar.

How deep was he going to sink before the ship docked in Ft. Lauderdale? He couldn't believe he was actually seeking the company of a man who had flagrantly blackmailed him. If he had the slightest bit of sense, he would ignore Kim's pitiful—and totally useless—attempts to mend fences between him and Ashley.

But then, he'd never claimed to have much sense where Ashley was concerned. It was one of the reasons he found himself in his current situation, mooning over his ex-wife again.

How foolish could a man get?

Rick looked up as Michael slid onto a bar stool and slapped his hand onto the bar. He glowered at the grinning bartender. "Give me your remedy, or whatever the hell it is I'm supposed to say."

With his customary shrug, Rick began mixing various liquids at a speed Michael could scarcely follow. Grudgingly, Michael admitted that the man was good at his job. Too bad he had a nasty habit of blackmailing people.

Rick set the drink before Michael with a flourish. Michael eyed it with suspicion before taking a sip.

"Oh, and I'm supposed to tell you that Tom is gay," Rick announced just as Michael filled his mouth with the too sweet concoction.

Michael blew the liquid onto the bar, gasping for air. Rick leaned over and pounded him on the back until tears ran down Michael's cheeks.

Finally, when he could breathe again, he demanded, "Come again?" He wanted to be absolutely certain he'd heard Rick correctly.

"Tom's gay. Likes men. Goes with the same sex. Gets turned on—"

"I get the picture," Michael inserted hastily. "How do you know? I mean, how does *Kim* know?"

"Believe me, she knows. She would never tell you something that important without proof." He began mopping up the mess Michael had made.

"It isn't important," Michael said, knowing he

227

was lying through his teeth. If it wasn't important, why did he feel this ridiculous elation? "Does Ashley know?"

Rick nodded. "Indeed she does." He glanced around, then leaned across the bar. "Kim says she wasn't that beat up about it, either."

Michael's mouth went dry at the implications. He gave his head a slight shake, warning himself not to get too excited. "When did Ashley find out?"

"Yesterday evening."

Before they docked. Before Ashley bought those outrageous wedding gifts for Tom. What was she trying to prove? Why did she want him to believe she was happily engaged? Was she using Tom for the same reason he was using Candy—as a safeguard?

The possibility intrigued Michael more than he cared to admit.

Hiding in her cabin wasn't an option, not as long as she shared it with Michael. Besides, if she didn't show up for dinner, someone might get careless and let Michael know that she knew where he had spent the night.

And she wasn't ready for him to know.

So Ashley arrived at the table dressed to kill and wearing a painted-on smile that hurt her mouth.

To her relief, she saw that Michael had yet to

join them. She slipped into her chair and pretended not to notice the sudden silence. Smiling brightly at one and all, she clasped her hands in front of her and said, "So, what's new?"

"I've got a nice surprise for you," Deckland announced. He handed her a thin stack of papers stapled together in the left-hand corner. "See if that doesn't cheer you."

Ashley stared at the list of names in growing excitement. "It's—it's the passenger list! How did you get this?"

Deckland smiled mysteriously. "I can't reveal my sources, I'm afraid. Just don't go flashing it around, okay?"

Not about to look a gift horse in the mouth, Ashley tucked the list beside her plate, anticipating the moment when she was alone in the cabin and could look it over at her leisure. Deckland had no idea what a lifesaver he was, she thought, flashing him a grateful smile. She needed all the distraction she could get to keep her mind off Michael.

"Hey, gorgeous!" a deep voice murmured in her ear, sending a shiver down her spine. "You look good enough to eat."

Speak of the devil and here he was, looking mouthwatering in jeans and a pullover white polo shirt that emphasized his golden tan. There wasn't a man alive who could top Michael in a pair of butt-hugging jeans, Ashley admitted, dragging her gaze back to her salad. And why did he sound so cheerful? No doubt because he believed he had gotten away with his despicable attempt to hit on poor Tanya.

Ashley shot a glance at Tanya, not surprised to find the woman looking everywhere but at Michael. When her gaze met Ashley's, Ashley winked to show that there were no hard feelings as far as she was concerned. Tanya relaxed visibly but continued to avoid Michael's gaze.

Michael, on the other hand, talked and joked with everyone at the table as if everything in his life was just peachy. The rat.

Dinner seemed to go on forever. Finally, Ashley excused herself and rose from the table, muttering something about a headache and the need to lie down. She hoped that Michael got the hint and stayed away from the cabin. If she had to spend much more time with him, she might be too tempted to blast him with her contempt to hold back.

"Don't forget your passenger list," Deckland said, nodding at the folded paper beside her plate.

Ashley grabbed it, smiling at Deckland. "I wasn't about to forget it, but thanks." She froze as Michael's fingers curled around her wrist.

"Passenger list?" he echoed.

"Yes, the passenger list." She couldn't help

sounding a little smug as she added, "Deckland was sweet enough to get it for me."

"Oh, he was, was he?" Michael asked softly, his narrowed gaze flicking between Deckland and Ashley. "That was enterprising of him, wasn't it?"

Exasperated by his absurd show of jealousy, Ashley pulled her wrist free. "You can drop the act, Michael. I told them we were divorced." She forced herself to laugh at his startled expression, as if everything in *her* life was just peachy. "Now we're free to do as we please."

The moment Ashley was out of earshot, Michael folded his arms and glared at his dinner companions.

Each and every one of them looked as guilty as hell.

"She knows," he stated, daring them to deny it. "And she's furious."

Birdie sighed and nodded.

Bart cleared his throat. "I'm afraid you're right, Michael."

A dinner roll bounced off his right shoulder, drawing his attention to Tanya's flushed expression. Ashley wasn't the only one who was furious, he realized.

"I told her that you loved her, but she didn't believe me," Tanya said.

Michael stiffened. "You what?"

"Yes, she told her," Birdie said. "And that girl just kept on walking."

"Let's get something straight," Michael growled. "I don't love Ashley. We were married once, and I might have loved her then, but that's in the past. I *care* about her, of course—"

"Hogwash," Bart said with a dismissive wave.

"It isn't hogwash." Michael wanted to smash something. He kept his arms firmly folded so that he wouldn't be tempted to do it. "How could I love her? As you can see, she lives to believe the worst about me."

Tanya lifted a sarcastic brow, making him flush. "I wonder why, Michael. You've certainly done nothing to deserve her mistrust, have you?"

"You know why I hit on you. I explained all that."

"To Tanya," Birdie inserted gently. "But you didn't explain it to Ashley."

"And I'm not going to." They had no idea what they were asking, Michael fumed. To try to explain to Ashley why he had hit on Tanya would be to open himself up to ridicule and outright disbelief.

She hadn't believed him two years ago, and she wouldn't believe him now. He knew it. *They* just didn't know it. No, he wouldn't go there again. Ha! He'd be crazy to even think of putting himself through that kind of hell. Besides, he couldn't explain without admitting that he still loved her.

"Well, I think you should," Deckland said. "And I'm giving you my professional advice. You two obviously have something that's rare and wonderful. It would be a shame to waste it."

Michael had had enough. "With due respect to all of you, you don't really know Ashley. When she sets her mind to believing something, nothing will change it."

"Nobody is that narrow-minded," Birdie said.

Rising, Michael looked grimly at Birdie. He hated to disillusion her, but he didn't see any other choice. "You're wrong about that, Birdie. Unfortunately, you're dead wrong."

"You could at least try!" Tanya called after his retreating back. "You coward!"

And that was something Michael couldn't deny. As far as Ashley was concerned, he *was* a coward, and he didn't care who knew it. Better a coward than a fool, he decided as he made his way to the upper deck for a quick workout in the swimming pool.

Thank God those busybodies didn't know the one thing he was determined to keep from Ashley. But if he didn't get that list from her, she would find out for herself, and that was a possibility Michael refused to contemplate.

He stepped into a changing room and stripped down to the swimming trunks he wore beneath his clothes. Tonight, after Ashley had gone to sleep, he would hide the list from her. With luck, she wouldn't have a chance to look at it before then. She would never suspect him of taking it.

Deckland would probably give her another list, he mused, snatching up a towel from the stack on the bench. He had his suspicions about Mr. Jennings. Maybe it was time he paid the helpful writer a visit.

In the meantime, he had a dose of frustration to work off before he returned to the cabin and Ashley. Just being near her at dinner had made him hungry for the touch of her skin, for the taste of her mouth, for the incredible satisfaction he found in her arms.

Michael dived cleanly into the water, coming up on the other side. He grabbed the edge of the pool and placed his forehead on the fiberglass surface. There were other people in the pool, but they might as well have been mannequins for all that he noticed them.

His heart pounded, but it wasn't from the physical exertion. No, he feared it would take more than a mere swim to exorcise the ghost of Ashley. . . .

Chapter Eighteen

The lamp was on beside the bed.

Michael crept to the nightstand and slowly pulled the passenger list out from beneath Ashley's cabin key.

Ashley moaned in her sleep, a fitful sound that made Michael freeze.

After a long, tense moment while she settled down again, he tiptoed to the bathroom and quietly closed the door.

He held the list up to the low glow of the light over the sink, scanning the contents as he flipped the pages. Ashley had made it easy for him; with a pink marker, she had highlighted the passengers from their home state.

Seventeen in all, including himself and Ashley.

Five passengers—other than himself and Ashley—boasted stars beside their names. VIPs, Rick had explained, to alert the staff of passengers with money to burn. Michael thought it highly unlikely Ashley would know the reason for the stars, but he couldn't take any chances.

If she asked the right people, she might find out.

Michael folded the list and tapped it against his chin, considering the best hiding place. If he left the bathroom with it, he would risk Ashley waking up before he could hide it.

But the bathroom was small, and his choices were limited.

After some debate, Michael slid the folded list beneath the stack of towels on a shelf above the sink. It would have to do until Ashley left the cabin the next day. Then he would find a better hiding place, or take it with him and drop it into a trash receptacle on deck.

Feeling immensely relieved, he got undressed and slipped into bed beside Ashley.

She lay facing him, curled on her side with one arm flung above her pillow and the other tucked beneath her chin.

Wearing a T-shirt and those damned sexy thong panties.

Hot pink this time.

Within seconds, he was fully, painfully aroused.

Michael let out a long, frustrated sigh as silently as he could and tried to concentrate on something that would take his mind off the sleeping sex goddess beside him.

Tom. But no, Tom was no longer in the picture. No longer a buffer, a reason to feel guilty for making love to Ashley.

Not that he remembered feeling guilty, Michael admitted truthfully. He'd been married to Ashley. She'd been his before she'd been Tom's. A primitive way of thinking, perhaps, but then, he'd never claimed to be all that civilized where Ashley was concerned.

Or gentlemanly. Or rational. Or strong on willpower.

Take now, for instance. He was seriously considering seducing Ashley while she slept. If he played his cards right, she would be beyond resisting him before she became fully awake. It was a game they'd often played. Would she remember?

A soft sigh slipped from her lips as she stirred on the bed. Her hand landed on his stomach, an inch above his erection.

Michael jumped, his stomach clenching in reaction.

Slowly, she uncurled her fingers until her hand lay flat on his taut belly. Her palm was hot against his cool skin.

But her breathing remained slow and shallow, reminding Michael that she was still asleep.

To hell with it, he thought, sliding out from under her hand. He moved to the end of the bed, then knelt at her feet. With infinite care, he lifted her foot and brought it to his mouth. He began to suckle her toes.

Once upon a time, it had driven her wild.

She moaned and stirred restlessly, proving to him that nothing had changed.

Michael swallowed his own moan as she lifted her other foot and placed it against his throbbing shaft. On purpose? Accidentally? Who cared?

Slowly, she curled her toes around him, then drew her foot down the length of him.

His breathing already ragged, Michael worked his way along her leg, nibbling and kissing, using his free hand to stroke her other leg. Her skin was satin; her scent intoxicating.

Closer and closer he came to her pink-covered mound. He hooked a finger in the waistband of her panties and slowly pulled them down, exposing her tasty little flower to his hot, eager mouth.

When he touched his tongue to her, she cried out and rose up in the bed, gripping his head.

She was wide awake now, he realized.

"Michael? What are you doing!"

Her voice was husky with sleep . . . and desire. The knowledge inflamed Michael. He smiled in the dark, confident that she couldn't see him.

"If you want me to stop, just say so," he whispered. And before she could answer, he dipped his head again, thrusting his tongue hard against her.

Her fingers tangled in his hair, pulling, then kneading, pulling, then kneading. As if she couldn't decide if she wanted him to stop or continue.

Michael was prepared to make her forget any indecision. He slipped two fingers into her wet, slick warmth, then thrust his tongue at her trembling nub until she writhed beneath him.

Her muscles contracted around him.

He grabbed her hips and rocked against her, using his tongue to drive her beyond the point of sanity. She was so sweet, so willing . . . so *his*. Right now she *was* his, and no other's. When they were together like this, nothing else seemed to matter.

Ashley went rigid, pulling at his hair, attempting to dislodge his mouth. "I want you inside me," she demanded, breathing hard. "Now."

It was an order Michael couldn't refuse. "Yes, baby. I'm coming."

She gripped his forearms, halting his forward movement. "Don't you dare! Not yet."

He chuckled at her crude joke . . . only it didn't seem crude to Michael. Nothing Ashley could say, when they were together like this, could sound crude.

Sexy and funny, maybe.

Exciting, yes.

Enormously arousing, you bet.

"Baby, I won't be doing that until I've heard you scream," he promised, his voice thick with suppressed need. He just hoped he could keep that promise.

"The Scotts—"

"Are probably sound asleep," he concluded, settling his mouth over hers with a sigh of pure pleasure. He kissed her until her nipples rasped hard and urgently against his chest and his bones felt soft and buttery. It was amazing, he thought, what kissing Ashley could do to him. He could never kiss her without becoming aroused, which had proved to be frustrating and awkward at times.

This not being one of those times, of course.

Catching her by surprise, Michael grabbed her hands and thrust them above her head. There was just enough moonlight shining through the portal to pick up the sheen of desire in her eyes. "Tell me that you missed this," he urged, bringing the tip of his shaft to her opening. He could feel her quivering . . . *there,* and his body shuddered in response.

"No," she hissed, but she was smiling a slow, sexy smile that knocked another inch into his arousal.

Michael continued to tease her, inching closer, then drawing back. He was near the explosion point himself, but he couldn't resist making her squirm. "Say it," he demanded huskily. He lowered his mouth and captured a hard, thrusting nipple. His teeth scraped lightly against it; then his lips suckled until she was moaning and twisting beneath him.

She thrust her hips forward in an attempt to capture him.

He chuckled and dodged her sneaky attack. "Oh, no you don't, baby. Not until I say so."

"Say so," she ordered.

"Not until you admit you're my slave."

"I'm your slave. Now *do it!*"

He was still chuckling as he slid into her, but his chuckle quickly turned into a strangled gasp of pleasure.

And that was when the knock came at the door.

"What the—"

They froze, staring at each other in the dark, not daring to breathe.

The knock came again, this time more urgently.

With a muffled oath, Michael rose from the bed and moved silently to the door. He used the door to cover his naked state as he cracked it an inch and peered into the gap.

Bart was standing in the hall, grinning like a fool.

"What is it, Bart?" Michael demanded. He

didn't care how ungracious he sounded. The man had no idea what he had interrupted—

"I thought you might like to borrow this," Bart said, thrusting the cold object into the gap. "Poor Birdie fell asleep before I could figure out how to operate the damned thing." He rolled his eyes. "Give me an old-fashioned tub of Cool Whip any day!"

Michael automatically took the can of whipped cream and shut the door.

He was stunned for all of two seconds.

Then the absolute bizarreness of the conversation struck him.

He began to laugh.

Michael's sudden burst of laughter brought Ashley to her senses.

She snatched the covers over her body, mentally lashing herself for her weakness. How could she forget that just last night he had made a pass at Tanya? Had she no pride at all where Michael was concerned?

How easy he must think her!

Shame spread over her naked skin, heating it with a different kind of warmth. She fell back onto the pillow and closed her eyes, totally disgusted with herself *and* with Michael. She had been so determined to resist him . . . and he had tricked her, sneaking up on her while sleep fogged her brain.

He was insufferable. A womanizer. A breaker of hearts.

And she was a fool.

Again.

"Can you believe that guy?" Michael said, still chuckling as he approached the bed.

Ashley braced herself to resist the husky, sexy sound of his voice.

"He gave me a can of whipped cream. Apparently, he heard us making love—"

"Having sex," she inserted in a brittle voice. "We were about to have sex, not make love, Michael." Although her eyes were closed and the room was dark anyway, she knew he had frozen in his tracks.

"You cooled off in a hurry," he observed.

The bed dipped beneath his weight. Cotton sheets rustled as he moved closer.

But he didn't touch her.

Ashley was intensely grateful. Despite her horror, despite her shame, her body was still taut as a bowstring, aching for him in a big way.

She hadn't exactly cooled off, but she *had* come to her senses.

"This is about last night, isn't it?" he asked softly, but with an edge to his voice that matched hers. "The deal with Tanya?"

"Deal?" She gave a short bark of laughter. "I think it was more like an attack, wasn't it? That *is* how you got the black eye, right?"

"I was drunk."

"It's none of my business, but if it *was* my business, I'd say that was a sorry excuse." She heard him sigh. For a long moment, he didn't speak.

"I was desperate."

"Has anyone ever told you that you're over-sexed, Michael?"

"Not that kind of desperate."

He shifted, and she stiffened. But he didn't touch her. She almost wished that he would, so she could give his other eye a shiner.

"I'm probably a fool for asking you this," Michael said. "But doesn't this . . . this intense attraction between us scare you just a little bit?"

Ashley frowned. Of all the excuses he could invent, he had to give one that she could almost believe.

Because it *did* scare her . . . just a little bit.

She chewed her bottom lip, carefully selecting her words. With Michael, she had to always be on guard. "So you're trying to say that you hit on Tanya because you're scared of the way we—" God, had she really almost said *the way we feel?* She hastily amended her words. "Because of this physical attraction between us?"

Michael's voice was dry. "At the risk of over-feeding your ego, yes, that's what I meant. When you're around, I seem to have a one-track mind."

He reached out, unerringly finding her hand in the dark. Before she was aware of his actions, he placed her hand on his rock-hard arousal. Fire and satin.

She jerked her hand back, sucking in a sharp breath.

"That doesn't happen around Tanya," Michael concluded. He didn't sound too happy about it, either.

Ashley let herself consider for a moment that maybe they shared the same feelings about this body chemistry between them.

As if he could read her mind, he said, "I wouldn't have slept with her, Ash." There was a pregnant pause before he added reluctantly, "I didn't want to."

Absurdly, considering the circumstances, his reluctance stung. "It's none of my business who you sleep with."

"I got that the first time you mentioned it. Do you believe me?"

"Does it matter?"

"If I hurt you, then *yes*, it matters!"

Of all the words in the English language that Michael could have used, he'd picked the very one that held the power to send Ashley into a furious spate of denial.

"Oh, no. Let's get something straight here, Michael. You didn't hurt me. You *can't* hurt me. Not again. Ever." She had to struggle to keep her voice level. "So if you have some sadistic plan stewing in your little brain to see how badly you

245

can hurt me, let me save you the time and energy. *It isn't going to happen!*"

She didn't know how she could have been any clearer. Now, if he would just believe her.

He sounded convincingly weary as he said, "I don't have a plan."

"Good."

"Fine."

"Good night, then." Ashley ignored her yearnings and turned her back to him.

"Good night."

She felt the bed move, and realized that he had done the same. A single tear slipped from the corner of her eye. She brushed it away, still furious that he'd had the gall to think he had hurt her.

Because she thought she'd done a great job of hiding it.

Chapter Nineteen

Just as dawn crept into the cabin, Michael came awake. He eased out of bed, forgoing his morning shower in the hope of escaping before Ashley awakened and found the passenger list missing.

He didn't think she would suspect him, but he wasn't taking any chances.

Topside, a few sleepy-eyed waiters served coffee and doughnuts to a dozen or so early bird passengers gathered to catch the spectacular sunrise over the ocean. They conversed in low tones, as if the sun was a living thing that could be startled.

As Michael took a cup of black coffee to the railing, he had to admit that the sunrise was definitely worth watching. Like a slow-moving fog, the fiery sun spread a blanket of golden light over the ocean, creeping along until it had painted the ship with the same golden hue. Michael sipped his coffee, enjoying the warm, salty breeze and the hushed beauty of the morning.

For all of thirty seconds.

"Morning, Michael," Deckland said, joining him at the railing with coffee mug in hand. He, too, spoke softly, as if there were some unspoken rule.

Michael allowed a smile to kick up the corners of his mouth. Deckland was just the guy he needed to see. Now that he was fairly certain he knew Deckland's business on the ship and with Ashley, he no longer felt hostile toward the man.

But his exasperation toward Kim . . . well, that was another matter entirely. He could cheerfully wring her neck.

"Morning, Deckland," Michael said politely. He sighed, as if life couldn't get any better, dropping his bombshell as casually as he might comment on the beautiful sunset. "So, how long have you known my sister?"

His question startled Deckland into spilling his coffee. He recovered quickly, but not quickly enough to fool Michael.

"Your sister? I don't believe I *do* know her."

Michael shot him a cheerful grin. "Sure you do. Petite, blond-haired. Mid-twenties. Lives to drive her brother crazy by meddling in his love life." He paused, staring at Deckland, whose gaze remained stubbornly on the sunrise. "Does that description ring a bell?"

Deckland, apparently, knew when to fold. "How did you know?"

"I didn't really suspect anything until you handed Ashley that passenger list. I would think something like that would be hard to come by."

The writer's mouth twisted in a rueful smile. "Kim definitely owes me one. I had to blackmail the ship's first mate to get that list." As if he suddenly realized he'd said too much, he clamped his mouth closed.

But he was too late. Michael pounced gleefully. "Hmm. Something like that could cost the man his job, wouldn't you say? If word got out, that is." When Deckland paled, he knew that he'd hit the jackpot. He gently pressed his point. "Did you make a copy of that list?"

Deckland nodded.

"Then I suggest you get rid of it," Michael said. "No sense costing a man his job." He wasn't making an idle threat, and Deckland seemed to sense this.

"I'll get rid of it, but—"

"I don't need a session, Doc."

"I wasn't going to offer you one. I was just going to ask you a simple question."

With an inward groan, Michael said, "What?"

"If Ashley finds out you're the other lottery winner, what's the worst that could happen?"

Michael didn't hesitate. "She'll think that I care."

"And that's so terrible?"

"You have no idea," Michael said with feeling.

In her search for the passenger list, Ashley discovered something that made her forget, for the moment, the missing list.

The diamond watch and cufflinks she'd bought were gone.

She stared at the empty drawer of her nightstand, silently berating herself for putting the expensive jewelry in such a vulnerable place. Michael had always complained that she was too trusting.

Methodically, she went over every inch of the room again. The only place she hadn't looked was in the drawer where Michael kept his underclothes and personal items.

There would be no reason for the items to be in there, she told herself, sinking onto the edge of the bed. When? When had someone had the opportunity to come in and steal them?

But then, there had been any number of times she and Michael had been gone from the cabin since returning to the ship with the jewelry.

And she had just gotten out of the shower.

Ashley shivered at the thought of a stranger prowling around the cabin while she took a shower. How would someone have gotten in?

Could Michael have been careless enough to leave the cabin door unlocked when he left this morning?

She got up and walked to the door, twisting the knob to see if it was locked.

At the same instant, the doorknob was jerked out of her grasp. She gasped and jumped back, hugging the damp towel.

It was Michael. He looked startled to find her so close to the door. "Ashley?" Noting her pale face, he frowned and closed the door. "What is it?"

"I—I was looking for the passenger list—" Was that guilt she saw flare for an instant in his eyes? She stopped abruptly, considering, for the first time, that Michael might have taken the jewelry. Why hadn't it occurred to her? It was just the kind of spiteful stunt he might pull. In fact, he'd probably thrown them overboard!

The possibility grew as Michael appeared to have difficulty looking her in the eye. "Michael," she began slowly, "did you do something with Tom's watch and cufflinks?"

Michael's jaw dropped, forcing Ashley to reconsider her suspicions. He looked genuinely shocked by her question . . . when she was certain that only moments ago, he'd looked guilty.

"Are you out of your mind?" he asked angrily. "You think I would steal from you?"

"Well, maybe not steal, per se. Maybe throw

them overboard, so that I couldn't give them to Tom—"

"That would imply that I was jealous," Michael cut in softly, in a furious tone. "Besides, why would I go to all that trouble when I know that there *is* no Tom?"

Ashley failed to stifle a gasp of surprise. She tried, desperately, to deny his accusation. He couldn't know, not unless Kim had told him. And Kim had promised! "What do you mean, there is no Tom? Of course there's a Tom! He's my fiancé—"

"And he's gay."

"He's not!" Ashley wished she wore more than a towel, because she could feel an all-over body blush coming on as she told the lie. "Why—why would you say that?" *How could he know?* Kim had promised, and Ashley couldn't believe that she would break that promise.

"The bartender told me."

For a moment, Ashley's mind went blank. "How—how would a bartender know?"

Michael's smile was grim. "His name is Rick, and he's a friend of Kim's." Her shock must have shown, for he nodded. "Yeah, that's the guy. I see you've met him."

"Yes, but—" She sighed and shook her head. "I just can't see Kim breaking a promise." Then, realizing what she'd revealed, she bit her lip, praying he hadn't noticed. No sense in arousing his curiosity about why she'd made Kim promise not to tell Michael about Tom.

"Kim has a sneaky way of getting around those promises she makes," Michael said with a mixture of exasperation and affection. "She doesn't consider herself breaking a promise when she gets someone else to do the telling."

Ashley grimaced, thinking about the long talk she was going to have with Kim about splitting hairs—right after the talk she had with her about Michael. She hitched up her towel and returned to the real subject at hand. "If you didn't take them, then that means . . . someone else did."

"Have you looked everywhere?"

She jerked her head in the direction of the chest of drawers where he kept his clothes and personal items. "Everywhere but there."

"I'll check. Maybe the maid moved them."

Ashley thought it highly unlikely, but she kept silent and hopeful as Michael carefully looked through all three drawers. He was frowning by the time he finished.

"Nope. Not in there." His frown deepened as he added, "We've definitely been robbed."

"You mean—"

"Yes, the engagement ring, necklace—all gone. Unless *you* took them thinking that *I* had taken yours."

She shook her head vehemently. "No, I didn't

touch them. Why would I? I know that they're not for Candy."

It was Michael's turn to look surprised. "Rick?"

"No. She—Candy called you on your cell phone. Before I could think, I answered it. I'd been talking to Kim, so when it rang immediately afterward—"

"It doesn't matter. What did she want?"

"She wanted to know if you were still taking her to the Policeman's Ball."

Michael's chuckle was dry. "That sounds like her. Dump a guy, then expect him to keep a date when it's convenient for her."

"She dumped you?" Although Candy had said as much, Ashley realized she hadn't truly believed her. She couldn't imagine anyone dumping Michael. Women loved him . . . as she well knew.

"Don't look so surprised," Michael drawled. "You dumped me, remember?"

"I—"

"Never mind. Why don't you get dressed and I'll tell you all about it over breakfast." He paused, his gaze moving with increasing warmth over her towel-clad figure. "We'll eat in another dining room—away from our meddling friends."

Ashley ignored the excited leap of her heart at the prospect of dining with Michael. Alone. "What about the jewelry?"

"We'll report the theft after breakfast."

"Maybe that's why they took the passenger list," Ashley said, mostly to herself. "They plan on robbing someone else and wanted to familiarize themselves with the passengers."

It was a long moment before Michael answered.

"Yeah, maybe."

Michael watched as Ashley spread cream cheese on a toasted bagel and daintily sank her teeth into it. He was very glad for the concealment of the table, because just watching her eat turned him on.

It also jarred his memory of a time when he'd served her breakfast in bed. A rainy Saturday, he recalled. But they hadn't cared about the weather, and breakfast had been forgotten until hours later when they realized they were ravenous. And was it any wonder after three hot, steamy bouts of lovemaking?

Every time with Ashley was like the first for him. He felt the same intense excitement, the same zing of anticipation.

"Do I have something on my teeth?" Ashley asked, pausing with the bagel inches from her luscious mouth.

"Um, no. I was just thinking." Wrong answer. He knew it the moment it came out of his mouth.

"About what?"

"About Kim," he lied. "I think it's time she concentrated on her own love life. Maybe then she'd keep her pert little nose out of ours."

Ashley smiled, and this time she *did* have something on her teeth. Michael suppressed a grin and said nothing.

"Too bad we don't have the connections she has," Ashley said. "We could ship her to a deserted island with about a dozen single men."

Her smile turned impish. God, she was gorgeous, even with a piece of bagel stuck between her teeth! And he still loved her.

"Hand selected, of course," she added, dusting her hands together as she finished her bagel. "Now, let's get down to business. Is there anyone else on this ship under Kim's spell?"

After a slight hesitation, Michael shook his head. However unfair, warning her about Deckland wasn't an option, because Deckland had given her a clue to finding out something Michael definitely didn't want her to find out.

Discovering that he still loved Ashley made him more determined than ever to hide his secret; loving Ashley and trusting Ashley were two completely separate things.

"Not that I'm aware of," he said, keeping his expression carefully neutral. "But I do know that she arranged the cabin mix-up, and I wouldn't be at all surprised if she dropped a bug in Candy's ear about the Policeman's Ball so that

Candy would call me—knowing you had my cell phone."

Ashley wiped her mouth and steepled her hands in front of her, looking pensive. "That's pretty calculating, Michael. I know Kim meddles sometimes—" She stopped abruptly when Michael lifted an incredulous brow. "Okay, so she meddles a lot."

"Even *that's* an understatement, darlin'. From the day our divorce became final, she's made it her life's work to mend the break between us."

Her gaze dropped. She picked at the corner of her napkin as she said, "I know. I've talked until I'm hoarse, but she just doesn't understand that some things can't be mended."

"Like us," Michael murmured, watching her. Wondering why she wouldn't look at him. Did she hate him that much? he wondered with a sharp pang of despair.

"Yeah, like us." Suddenly, she brightened. "Hey, maybe this cruise was her final attempt before she gave up. You have to admit, she went to a lot of trouble to get us together." She grabbed her juice glass and took a drink.

Michael had to drag his gaze from her moistened lips.

"You were going to tell me about Candy," she prompted.

"Yes, as long as you were going to tell me about Tom."

She grimaced. "It's not a pretty story, but you've got a deal. You first."

"There's not really much to tell. We went out for six months, and I thought everything was going along fine. When I proposed to her the day Kim called to offer me this free cruise, Candy laughed at me." He winced inwardly at the lie. Kim hadn't offered the cruise, of course. But he couldn't tell her the truth.

Ashley covered her mouth to stifle a horrified laugh. "Oops. Sorry! It's just that I can't imagine a woman *laughing* at you . . . for anything."

She was blushing, Michael observed. His own smile was rueful. "She said she thought I knew we were just friends."

"And you didn't have a clue? Not one?"

Michael frowned, thinking hard. Finally, he shrugged. "No, I didn't. We went out several times a week. Her friends thought we were a couple, I'm sure of it." His lips twisted. "I guess it's true what they say about the man being the last to know."

"Sounds like *my* story. Tom and I were a couple to everyone and to each other . . . only I turned out to be of the wrong gender."

"Have you talked to him since you found out?"

"No." She heaved a great sigh. "I've just got one question I want to ask him, and I'm waiting until I cool down before I ask it."

"What's that?"

"Why? I want to know what his plans were when he proposed to me. Was I supposed to be a smoke screen for his alternate lifestyle? Did the jerk actually think I would stay married to him once I found out?"

Michael felt his heart stop. "So you and he— you never—"

"No." She was blushing again. "We never did. I guess that should have been a big clue for me. After all, Tom *is* a man."

A fierce, dangerous relief flooded him. Later, Michael would blame that relief for his next reckless question. "Have you slept with anyone at all since . . . me?"

Her jaw dropped. She snapped it closed, anger darkening her eyes. "Of course I've slept with other men."

But Michael saw the lie in her eyes, and his heart started beating again. Pounding. Joyously. Foolishly. Instead of challenging her, he let it go. He knew first hand about pride, didn't he? Which made him extremely ready for *her* reckless question.

"How about you?"

He made a face, as if he couldn't believe she would ask such a question. "It's different for a man, Ashley."

She snorted and looked away, but not before he saw the pain in her eyes.

The sight of that pain stopped his heart

again—this time with shock. She hated him, didn't she? So why would his careless lie hurt her? If he had told her the truth, chances were she wouldn't have believed him anyway.

When she turned back to him, she wore a bright smile very similar to the one she'd worn on the island, the same smile that had sharpened his instincts.

"So," she said with a false brightness that matched her false smile, "we're both aware of Kim's elaborate plan to mix oil and water. Now we can be on our guard against further plotting."

"Right."

"You've told me everything you know, and I've told you everything I know."

This time Michael's, "Right," came out a little slower. Lies never came easy to him; this one was no exception.

"Now we can concentrate on finding out who stole our jewelry. Got any suspicions?"

Michael considered her question. Slowly, he said, "I would think it must be someone who knew we'd bought the jewelry. If I was a thief, I wouldn't take a chance on sneaking into some-one's cabin unless I had a good idea of what I would find."

"Good thinking. Hmm. That could be anyone from the ship, couldn't it? I mean, a lot of peo-ple went to shore that day."

"I was thinking of someone a little closer," Michael suggested.

Ashley's eyes went wide. "Michael! You're not thinking it could be Deckland or Tanya, or the Scotts?"

He didn't like to think it, no, but he had to admit they would be his first suspects if he was heading an impartial investigation. Grimly, he explained his reasoning. "They know a lot about us, and their cabins are close to ours. They can see us come and go."

She put her hands over her face and shook her head, as if the idea was too awful to contemplate. Finally, she pulled her hands away. "Michael, if it's okay with you, I'd rather we kept this to ourselves for a little while longer. If one of our dinner companions—friends—stole the jewelry, I would like to know their reasons before we turn them in."

"You want to play detective?" Michael asked, surprised and, yes, pleased at the prospect. If it meant spending more time with Ashley . . . precious little time, considering the fact that they only had two days to go before the cruise ended, then he was definitely agreeable. "Okay, as long as you're open to the possibility that it could be one of them."

"Good. Have any ideas as to how to begin?"

"As a matter of fact . . ." Michael lowered his voice and leaned closer. Ashley did the same. As he explained his plan to her, he realized that for the first time since they'd bumped into one another in the cabin, they were having a civilized conversation that didn't center on sex or the past.

He wasn't certain if he should feel relief or trepidation.

Chapter Twenty

"Are you sure you won't join us?" Birdie pressed.

The elderly woman had been pestering Ashley for the past fifteen minutes, and Ashley was beginning to think she'd never leave. She had asked the same question at least five times.

Ashley sniffled and brought another tissue to her streaming eyes. Amazing, she thought, what a little pepper sauce could accomplish. "I'm sure, Birdie. After the fight I had with Michael, I just couldn't stand all that revelry. You're such a sweetheart for offering to let me stay in your cabin."

Birdie picked up a list from a small table by the porthole. She squinted as she looked at it. "But the hotel's serving an authentic Mexican buffet, and Marvin the Magician's going to do a show—"

"I couldn't."

"Well," Birdie sighed, "I guess there's no changing your mind for now. I gotta tell you, though, that after two nights on this ship, I'm looking forward to sleeping in a bed that doesn't move."

"You mean *four* nights." With another miserable-sounding sniff, Ashley added perversely, "I hadn't noticed the movement." Maybe because she and Michael had been moving the bed a lot on their own.

Birdie, wearing a black satin teddy and nothing more, planted her hands on her hips, her expression one of deep concern. "Honey, I hate leaving you here all alone."

Ashley swallowed a frustrated sigh. The woman was impossibly stubborn. "I'll be fine, I promise. Maybe—maybe I'll join you later at the hotel." To her great relief, Birdie gave up and finished dressing. After she was dressed, she chatted as she consulted the list in her hand, then tossed items haphazardly into a small suitcase.

With a jangle, a pair of gold-plated handcuffs landed on top of the bag. Ashley prudently pretended not to notice as Birdie indifferently shoved them inside the bag.

"Tomorrow Tanya and I plan to spend the day shopping while the men go fishing," Birdie said. "We don't have to be back on the ship until six o'clock tomorrow evening, you know. Plenty of time for you to change your mind and join us."

A few moments later, Birdie planted a moist kiss on Ashley's cheek and left her alone in the cabin.

Ashley stretched out on the bed and counted slowly to a hundred. If Birdie had forgotten something, she wanted to give the unsuspecting woman plenty of time to come back.

Finally, Ashley rolled off the bed and began her search of the cabin. As she methodically looked through every drawer and closet, she wondered how Michael was faring. Did he feel like a snoop, as she did?

She pulled open a drawer, glanced inside, started to shut it, then did a double-take. Although she was alone, she felt herself blush.

Inside the drawer was an assortment of sex toys: some she didn't even recognize, and a few that made her brows shoot upward.

No doubt about it—if there had ever been a doubt—the Scotts were as kinky as they came.

She winced at her choice of words and slammed the drawer shut.

That did it. The Scotts might be a lot of unusual things, but she couldn't believe they were thieves.

Her work here was done.

"So you're saying she never actually let you tell your side of the story?" Deckland asked incredulously. "Ashley doesn't strike me as the type to hang a man without at least giving him a fair trial."

Michael shrugged, but he clenched his jaw tight as he stared at the melting ice in his empty glass. "She was the one-woman jury and the judge, all right. I'm surprised my sister didn't fill you in on all the sordid details," he added with dry sarcasm.

"Come on, Michael. Ease up on Kim. She cares about both of you, you know."

"She just doesn't know when to give up. Ashley and I are a lost cause."

Deckland eyed him speculatively. "Maybe she sees what I see."

"There's nothing to see . . . other than a physical attraction," Michael stated firmly. "And our recent fight proves that nothing has changed, as if I didn't already know it." He shook his empty glass, considered having another drink, then decided he needed to keep his wits about him. Deckland was no dummy. So far, he had succeeded in convincing the doctor that he and Ashley had had a terrible fight, resulting in Ashley throwing him out of the cabin. He didn't want to pour it on too thick.

Propping his hip against the minibar, Deckland said, "Maybe you should just admit you're guilty and beg her forgiveness."

Michael nearly choked. "You're kidding, right? Why would I admit to something that I didn't do? No. That's not ever going to happen. If she can't believe in me . . . well, it's a moot point, anyway."

"You have to admit that the evidence was damning."

Softly, Michael asked, "You think I'm lying?"

Deckland shook his head, frowning. "No, I'm just trying to put myself in Ashley's shoes. She saw you in bed with another woman. Then your friends—friends you've known for years—all vow you're innocent. Tell me, Michael: If you *had* been guilty, would your friends have lied for you if you asked them to?"

Although Michael suspected he knew where Deckland was heading, he answered truthfully, "Yeah. Probably."

"Then how can you blame Ashley for not believing them?"

"I don't," Michael growled, not entirely truthfully. "I blame her for not believing *me.*" How the hell had they gotten onto this subject?

"Did you suggest a marriage counselor?"

Michael's short bark of laughter held no humor. "I never got the opportunity. She wouldn't speak to me, remember?"

"What about the last few days—"

"No. Any time the subject comes up"—he'd lost count of the number of times it had—"she clams up or gets mad. She's not any closer to listening to me now than she was then. I've long since come to the conclusion that Ashley wanted out of the marriage. She was just waiting for an excuse."

"You don't really believe that."

It hadn't been easy to convince himself, but he eventually had. "Yes, I do. Otherwise she would have given me the opportunity to tell my side of the story, instead of running to her mother and filing for a divorce."

Michael's eyes burned. He blinked hard, deciding it was time to implement his plan. He'd already said more on the taboo subject of Ashley and their divorce than he'd intended. "Would you mind if I used your cabin while you're gone? I think it would be a good idea to give Ashley some space."

Deckland shrugged. "Help yourself."

To Michael's relief, Deckland glanced at his watch, looking alarmed.

"Didn't realize the time. I'm supposed to meet the others at the hotel for a drink before dinner. Sure you won't join us?"

"Maybe later." He managed a convincing, tired sigh. "I just need to crash for a few hours."

The psychologist folded his laptop, slipped it into a carrying case, and grabbed up a small overnight bag. "All right, then. Hope I'll see you later. Lock up on your way out."

"Will do. I'll probably join you guys for the show."

After Deckland had gone, Michael forced himself to wait a good ten minutes before he began his search of the cabin for the jewels. He felt a little like MacGyver and a lot like a snoop.

When he came across Deckland's notebook, he couldn't resist flipping through the pages. He came to the last entry and paused to read the contents. *Interview with Ashley Kavanagh, divorced white female. Subject states her ex-husband is the only man she's sexually attracted to.*

The entry reinforced Michael's belief that Ashley had been lying about multiple sleeping partners. Michael allowed himself a slow, satisfied smile.

Then he reminded his inflating ego that it didn't matter whether Ashley went two years or ten without sleeping with another man. She was no longer his to covet and never would be again.

The brutal realization stabbed a hole in his ego, deflating it in three seconds flat.

"I think we're barking up the wrong trees, Mi—" Ashley swallowed the rest of her words as she paused in the doorway of their cabin.

Michael was standing in the middle of the bed, his hands braced on the ceiling. To her further mystification, he gestured for her to shut the door, then put a finger to his lips.

Ashley obeyed, watching with a puzzled frown as Michael used a pocket knife to unscrew the vent cover. She wasn't really surprised to discover there was something wrong with the vent, but she was surprised at his secrecy.

Until Michael carefully withdrew an object from the vent shaft and held it up for her inspection.

She sucked in a slow gasp, coming closer.

It was some type of wireless videocamera, she realized.

Silently, she waited as Michael turned the recorder in his hand until he found a switch. He clicked it off, then jumped off the bed.

Ashley put a hand to her mouth, feeling a slow heat move into her face. Her voice was nothing but a mortified whisper as she stated the obvious. "Someone was . . . was taping us in bed."

"Not necessarily in bed," Michael corrected. He put his hand over the lens and moved it around. "Whoever did this probably has the power to move the viewer to any position in the room."

"Who, Michael?" Regaining her voice, Ashley pointed a trembling finger at the camera. "Who did this?" She recalled how she had given the room a haphazard check for videorecorders when she had first arrived, thinking Michael might be attempting to sabotage her relationship with Tom.

But she hadn't really believed Michael would

stoop that low. To think that *someone* had . . . well, she felt violated.

And furious.

Judging by Michael's grim expression, she wasn't alone.

"When I was in Deckland's room, I noticed that he had a very sophisticated laptop computer," Michael said.

But Ashley had her own suspects. "The Scotts always seemed to know when we were—when we were—"

"True. Did you find anything unusual in their cabin?"

Ashley thought about the drawer filled with sex toys, blushed, and shook her head. "Why would anyone tape us?"

"You won the lottery, Ash," Michael reminded her bluntly. "And you agreed to go public with it. That makes you a prime target for professional con artists, burglars, and thieves."

"If what you're saying is true, why didn't they remove the camera when they took our jewelry?"

Michael shrugged. "Maybe they didn't have time."

She wasn't satisfied with his answer. Walking to the baggage closet, she removed a small suitcase and placed it on the bed. She unzipped a pocket in the liner and withdrew a wad of cash. "Why didn't they take this? There's about two thousand dollars here."

His brows rose, and there was a hint of censure in his eyes as he chided, "You shouldn't be carrying that much cash around, Ash."

"I'm not stupid, Michael. I haven't been waving it around."

"Which is probably why the thief didn't know about it," Michael pointed out mildly. "And why haven't we mentioned Tanya lately? She's as much a suspect as the Scotts and Jennings."

The idea that any of their new friends would invade their privacy and steal from them made Ashley nauseous. She put the cash back in the suitcase, snapped it closed, and shoved it into the closet.

"Do you think that's a good idea?" Michael asked.

"Whoever it is will realize when they can't access the video camera that we've discovered it. I don't think they'll be back, do you?"

"You've got a point."

Ashley shivered, hugging her arms. "This cruise is turning into a nightmare," she mumbled.

Michael closed the distance between them, taking her into his arms. Ashley melted against him without even a token sign of resistance. God, it felt good to be in his arms, she thought, laying her head on his shoulder.

She sighed and said, "If it's one of our friends,

I hope they have a good reason for doing what they did."

"There isn't a good reason for stealing."

She tipped back her head, searching the unrelenting lines of his face. Against her belly, she could feel him hardening and tried not to think about it. "You don't think there's a difference between a man stealing a loaf of bread to feed his starving children and a man robbing a convenience store to buy drugs?"

He hesitated, then gave his head a rueful shake. "I fell right into that one, didn't I?"

Ashley smiled. "Yes, you did. Besides, I don't think it's anyone we know."

"I hope you're right, but I still think we should search Tanya's cabin. It would only be fair."

"You're right, but how? We don't have a key."

With a wolfish grin, Michael reached into his pocket and held up a key attached to a plastic dolphin.

"How did you get that?" Before he could answer, Ashley shook her head. "On second thought, never mind. I probably don't want to know."

"Actually, it's not a big mystery. I bumped into her in the corridor. She took one look at my scowling face and handed me her key."

"That was big of—"

"And told me to give it to *you*," Michael finished with a laugh at Ashley's chagrined expression.

"Well, that's probably a good sign that she had nothing to do with this."

"Or maybe that's what she wants us to think." Michael ran a teasing finger along her jaw, pausing on her parted lips. "We knew when we started searching that it was unlikely the thief would leave the jewelry on the ship for us to find. The most we can hope for is to find other clues."

Ashley could feel her nipples growing taut. She licked her lips, prudently stepping out of his tempting arms. "We'd better get going, then, before someone decides to come back for something."

Michael's eyes had darkened. His gaze swept slowly over her, making her shiver. "Yeah, we'd better go before it's too late."

But Ashley had the distinct impression he meant something quite different from her.

Chapter Twenty-one

One thing was very obvious about Tanya, Michael discovered the moment they entered her cabin.

She was definitely not a neat freak.

Funny, he didn't remember the cabin being so untidy the night he'd crashed in her bed. But then, he'd been smashed.

Clothes, shoes, purses, and underwear were strewn everywhere. The bed, the chest of drawers, the floor, the nightstand, and even the bathroom floor were a mess. There wasn't an inch of carpet or floor in sight. As a result, they couldn't take a step without walking on clothing.

Ashley started to nudge a shoe from her path, but Michael stopped her.

"Don't. As crazy as it might sound, Tanya just might notice if we move anything."

Reluctantly, Ashley left the shoe where it lay.

Michael suppressed a grin when she took off her own shoes instead, and proceeded into the room in her bare feet.

"I don't feel right about this," she muttered, heading in the direction of the built-in armoire.

From the nightstand, Michael said, "If you find yourself feeling guilty, remember the video-camera."

"I didn't even know they made them that tiny."

"Haven't you seen *Mission Impossible?*"

"Not recently."

Something in her voice snagged his attention. He caught her gaze, and hot tension flared between them. Michael felt himself growing hard and suppressed a groan. He jerked his gaze back to the task at hand, knowing that she had remembered, as he had remembered—belatedly— the last time she'd watched that particular movie. She had fallen asleep in his arms.

He had carried her to bed.

She'd woken up in a very interesting position.

"Find anything?" Ashley asked after a moment.

At the husky note in her voice, Michael's fingers tightened involuntarily around the sketch-book he held. "She's an artist."

"I'm not surprised. She strikes me as a highly intelligent person."

Her voice came closer. Michael tensed.

"Let me see."

Before she could reach around him—possibly

touching him in the process—Michael turned and thrust the sketchbook into her hands. Briskly, he sidestepped her as he said, "I'll check the bathroom."

"Good idea. Oh, she's a fashion designer. Why am I not surprised? I wonder why she doesn't talk about it. She's good. Very good."

Inside the bathroom, Michael turned on the water and splashed his face with it. He grabbed a hand towel, his gaze sweeping the room as he dried his face. *Concentrate,* he urged himself.

On anything but Ashley. Her smile. Her scent. Her voice, with that sexy little lilt. Her touch. She was slowly driving him insane with need.

He didn't understand. They'd made love plenty of times since boarding the ship. Why, then, did he ache as if he hadn't had her for years? And it wasn't just physical. Michael might not admit this fact to Ashley, but he couldn't lie to himself. He wanted Ashley with his body *and* his soul.

She made him complete. Made him feel like a man. Made him feel a joy such as he had never known with any other woman. Without her he was only a shadow of his true self.

She was his soul mate, dammit, and it was unnatural for them to be apart.

Michael gripped the sink and closed his eyes, willing himself to regain control. Little by little, he felt his body start to relax. The pain lingered, but he knew there wasn't much he could do about it. He'd lived with that pain since the night she'd found him in bed with another woman.

When he opened his eyes again, it was to find Ashley next to him, staring at him in the mirror with wide, bemused eyes.

"Michael, are you—"

He used one hand to slam the door, shutting them inside the tiny bathroom.

She gasped.

With his free hand, he cupped her jaw and held her still as he devoured her mouth with a hunger he suddenly couldn't control. It was a balm to his pain, to his anguish over having lost the most precious thing in the world to him.

She kissed him back with the same mindless fervor, as if she knew his thoughts and agreed. Michael knew he was kidding himself, and the knowledge cut through him like a knife. To her he was nothing more than a means of finding sexual satisfaction.

Her fingers tangled in his hair. She pulled away to catch her breath. "Michael," she panted, and it was sweet music to his ears. "Have you forgotten where we are?"

His mouth traced a hot path along her jaw, down her neck, and to the tops of her heaving breasts. He could hear her heart pounding. "Yes. No. I don't care."

"What—what if Tanya comes back?"

"Then she'll think we're making up," he muttered, taking her mouth again. Feverishly, he ran his hands along her thighs, pushing her dress to her waist. In one smooth movement, he tore her panties from her and tossed them behind him.

The flesh he grabbed was firm, yet warm and pliant.

She gasped as he lifted her onto the edge of the sink. It was just the right height, he thought, as he unfastened his pants and freed his pulsing arousal.

And she was wet and ready, he discovered, spreading her legs and testing her with his fingers. Hot, wet, and pulsing with anticipation. Ready for *him*, her soul mate, even if she didn't realize it.

Her husband, even if she *had* forgotten.

"Do it, Michael," she whispered, catching his bottom lip and sucking until he growled with pleasure. Her hands moved across his back . . . down to his buttocks.

She grabbed him and pulled him forward.

The moment he filled her, Ashley felt that old familiar feeling of rightness. This man was where he belonged. Inside her. Loving her. Planting his seed. Shattering her sanity.

Michael was the reason she wanted no other man.

Michael was the reason she couldn't love another man.

Michael was . . . everything to her, yet nothing she could have.

She bit back a cry, clutching his rock-hard buttocks with each stroke that brought them closer to an explosion that would topple them from the clouds.

And Ashley knew, as Michael loved her hard and fast, that if he had chosen that moment to ask her forgiveness, she would have given it.

But he remained silent, loving her with his mouth, his hands, and his body. Loving her as only Michael could do.

Loving the sheer hell out of her, yet holding his heart in reserve.

Vaguely, through a thick fog of lust, Ashley heard the sharp sound of something cracking. The hard surface beneath her butt shifted . . . but how could that be? She was sitting on a sink, which was bolted solidly to the wall.

Then Michael's pace increased, demanding all of her attention as she felt the glorious release build inside her. He caught her mouth, kissing her deep, his hot tongue taking possession and demanding a duel. His fingers dug into the flesh of her hips; she reciprocated by kneading the firm muscles of his pumping buttocks.

She broke from his mouth and sank her teeth into his neck, lightly, erotically, biting and sucking, tasting him. His breath blasted her ear, kicking her heart into overdrive.

"Hold on to me," he rasped against her ear. "I think I'm going to break apart."

But it wasn't Michael that broke apart. The very instant he threw back his head and roared her name, at the very instant that Ashley felt her inner muscles spasm around him, there was another sound.

A loud ripping, grating sound coming from the wall behind her.

The sink beneath her shifted ominously again. Ashley tried to focus on the strange phenomenon, but she was being sucked under a current of pure pleasure.

The sink shifted again, and Ashley, in the throes of an earth-shattering orgasm, finally found the presence of mind to alert Michael. She locked her arms around his neck and gasped out through a series of moans and screams, "Michael, the sink—"

As if he had been aware of the impending catastrophe all along, he lifted her up and swung her around to the opposite wall just as the sink came crashing to the floor. The impact snapped the plastic pipes as if they were matches. Water shot toward the ceiling and rained down over their heads.

Within seconds, they were soaked.

Ashley spotted a stack of washcloths on the

shelf above the bathtub. Still breathing hard, she wiggled free of Michael's arms and grabbed a handful of the cloths, stuffing the ends into the spewing pipes. It stopped the gushing, but water continued to gurgle from the pipes, flooding the floor.

Michael took her arm and stepped over the sink, slipping through the door and pulling her with him.

"Michael . . . we can't just leave it," she protested, rearranging her dress.

He pulled her, stumbling through the clothes-littered floor without pause, throwing over his shoulder, "What reason could we give them for being in Tanya's cabin?"

Ashley found that she didn't have the breath left to answer. She was literally dragged down the fortunately deserted hall to their cabin door.

"Michael, what—"

He opened the door and pulled her inside. Leaning against it, he wiped at his dripping face and stared at her.

To Ashley's amazement, he began to laugh.

"Michael! We just destroyed a bathroom because of our—our animalistic urges. I don't find it funny!"

But Michael, apparently, did. He continued to laugh, his gaze skimming her body. He pointed at her as he gasped out, "You—you look like a drowned rat—"

His laughter halted abruptly.

Ashley frowned and followed his gaze to her feet.

Her *bare* feet.

"I left my . . . shoes in Tanya's cabin," she said unnecessarily.

Sobering swiftly, Michael said, "Yes, you did." He folded his arms over his rock-hard chest. "Okay, here's the plan. Tanya gave me her key to give to you. You took her up on her offer and went to her cabin. You got something in your eye and climbed onto the sink to get a closer look."

"Oh, that's just great. Send *me* back to face the music."

Michael's brow rose at her injured tone. "You have a better plan?"

"Yes. How about *you* go." She folded her arms and eyed his two-hundred-pound frame. "It would sound more believable coming from you, Michael."

"And what about your shoes? How would I explain their presence in Tanya's cabin?"

Ashley's smile was impish. "Um, you were wearing them?" His instant scowl made her laugh outright. "How do we get ourselves into these messes?" she asked.

His eyes darkened as they drifted over her body. Her dress was plastered to her skin, outlining her pebbled nipples, her taut belly, and the gentle flare of her hips. "Because you're irresistible," he said, and sounded as if he meant it.

She rolled her eyes, not daring to take him seriously. "Try again." Wearing a determined expression, he shoved away from the door and started in her direction. She quickly threw up a hand in surrender, laughing. "Okay, okay! I believe you. Now go before the water floods the entire deck!"

His laugh held a knowing quality that was pure Michael as he turned back to the door. Just as he reached for the knob, someone knocked.

They froze. Ashley sidled up behind him, pressing against his back as she whispered fearfully, "Maybe someone saw us leaving the scene of the accident."

Michael turned his head slightly to whisper back, "If they did, you were already there and I came to talk to you after our fight. We ended up in the bathroom . . . making up."

Ashley shook her head so violently her wet hair slapped him in the neck. "No way, Michael! I'm not going to humiliate myself by confessing what really happened. Anything but that!"

"Chicken."

"Damned right," she whispered. "It's bad enough that some creep has been recording our every move inside this cabin. I'm not about to tell the staff that we broke a sink making out on it."

She saw the corners of his lips tip upward, and her heart gave a funny little leap.

The knock came again, followed by Deckland's urgent voice. "Michael? Ashley? Are you in there?"

Since she was plastered against him, she felt him sag with her. Her eyes widened as Michael reached for the door. "Michael, don't! I'm—"

The door swung open before she could finish. Deckland stood in the doorway. Hovering behind him, Ashley could see a white-faced Bart and an equally pale Tanya.

Birdie was nowhere in sight, which immediately struck Ashley as odd. She rarely saw one member of the couple without the other.

Deckland stepped into the cabin, forcing Michael and Ashley to move back and let them in. Ashley stayed hidden behind Michael, mentally preparing an explanation for their soggy state.

When they were all crowded inside, Deckland closed the door, his grim expression chilling Ashley to the bone. Suddenly, she knew that what he had to say wasn't going to be pleasant, and that it had nothing to do with Tanya's mangled plumbing.

The others didn't even seem to notice that she and Michael were dripping on the carpet.

"We have some really disturbing news to share with you," Deckland said, glancing in Bart's direction.

Ashley followed his lead. Bart looked as if he were on the verge of going into shock. He was so pale he looked gray. With a shaking hand, he shoved a lock of white hair from his brow. His bloodshot eyes filled with tears.

"Birdie's been taken," he said in a quavering voice.

"Taken?" Michael repeated. "What do you mean, she was *taken*? By whom?"

In the grip of a horrifying premonition, Ashley forgot to hide behind Michael. She stepped up to Bart and took his trembling hand. "Tell us, Bart. What's happened to Birdie?"

"She's—she's been kidnapped!"

Chapter Twenty-two

"Who would . . ." Ashley's voice trailed away. She looked at Michael, wondering if he was thinking what she was thinking.

The missing jewelry.

The small videocamera in the vent shaft.

And now Birdie had been kidnapped.

Slowly, she turned back to Bart, wincing at his pallor. She led him to the bed and gave him a gentle push. Without taking her eyes from him, she instructed Michael to get him a shot of whiskey from the minibar. "Tell us everything, Bart. And take your time."

The old man's hands were shaking so hard, the small amount of whiskey in the bottom of the glass leaped and danced along the sides. He brought it to his mouth, taking a fortifying gulp.

Whiskey dripped from his chin, but he didn't

seem to notice. Ashley took the end of her wet dress and wiped it away.

"One minute she was behind me and the next she was gone," Bart whispered, staring into space. He looked so lost and forlorn. "I searched and searched—came all the way back to the ship looking for her. Calling her name." He shook his head and a fat tear rolled down his lined cheek. "I was in the process of looking in every shop when this kid came up to me and gave me a note, said a man had paid him to deliver it."

Michael, who had come to stand beside Ashley, asked urgently, "Did the kid give you a description of this guy?"

Bart shook his head. Another tear rolled down to join the first. "When I tried to ask him questions, he just turned tail and ran." He sniffed and hung his head, his voice breaking. "I don't have that kind of cash. He—he said he'd kill her."

"Let me see the note," Michael ordered. When Bart handed him the crumpled piece of paper, he held it so that Ashley could read it with him.

"They want ten thousand dollars," Ashley said, stunned. "And they want it by noon tomorrow." She clutched Michael's arm, staring into his grim face. "Michael, do you think this is the same person who stole our jewelry?"

"What? What's this about stolen jewelry?" Deckland asked, coming forward.

Ashley quickly explained about the videocamera and the missing jewelry. In light of this new development, it was obvious their friends were no longer suspects. "Michael thinks it's someone who knows I won the lottery," she concluded with a shiver. "To plant the videocamera, the thief would have had to know about me before the ship set sail."

"But if it's the same people, why would the thief give the ransom note to Bart instead of you?"

Deckland had a point, Ashley mused. "Well, if they've been observing us . . . then they've noticed that we've become friends. They probably knew Bart would come to us."

"That's a little iffy, don't you think?" Tanya asked.

"I wouldn't have," Bart inserted quickly, sounding both embarrassed and desperate. "If I had the money, I wouldn't have bothered anyone."

"Nonsense, Bart. We're your friends, and Birdie's life is at stake." Ashley emphasized her sincerity by patting his shoulder.

Bart took a deep, shuddering breath. "What am I going to do?"

"I suggested he go to the local police," Deckland said.

"No!" Bart sounded frantic. "He said no police. He'll kill her, I know it!"

"He's right," Tanya said. "We can't take that

chance, not until we get Birdie back. I've got about a thousand dollars in cash." She shuddered and hugged herself. "God, this sounds like a bad movie."

"Amen," Ashley muttered. "I've got two thousand and some change. There's an ATM machine in the casino. I should be able to get another four hundred. I think that's the most they'll give me in one day."

"You can have what I've got," Deckland said. "Which is about six hundred in cash. The rest of my money is plastic."

"I've got the rest."

Michael's quiet announcement floored Ashley. She was speechless for a moment. "You—you mean, after the lecture you gave me about having that much cash, you've got six thousand dollars on you?"

He actually had the grace to blush. "I wanted to be prepared. Besides, I'm a man. There's a difference—"

"Don't even go there, buddy," Tanya warned.

And then Ashley remembered that he'd been expecting Candy to join him. The reminder left a bitter taste in her mouth, but it explained why Michael had brought along so much cash.

Even so, she would have felt a lot better if Michael had been the one doing the dumping. But this wasn't about her feelings, she reminded herself.

She mustered an encouraging smile for Bart's benefit. "So you've got your money. Soon we'll have Birdie back safe and sound."

"I—I don't know how I can ever repay all of you," Bart said, his voice breaking. "When we get back home, we can take a second mortgage on our house—"

"No," Michael said, his voice flat and final. "At least, don't mortgage your house on my account. I won't miss the money."

"Neither will I," Ashley added, although she did wonder about Michael's generosity. Was his business doing that well, then? When they were married, he'd made a decent income from his health clubs, but nothing mind-boggling. Not the kind of money that would allow him to carry around six thousand dollars as if it were pocket change.

Kim's hint came back to her. *"It's about money, and that's all I can say."*

"Count me out, too," Tanya said, although she sounded less convincing.

Deckland added his assurance that Bart didn't have to worry about paying him back. "Now that we've gotten that out of the way, who's going to take the money to the drop-off spot?"

"I am," Bart said, sounding stronger by the minute. "I have to. I don't want to take any chances. And afterward, I'm not going to the authorities, either."

"Why not?" Michael asked, voicing a question Ashley was certain they all wanted to ask.

"Because we don't know who the abductor is. He—he might be someone on the ship, and if we report this, he might decide to hurt Birdie." Bart hesitated, glancing slowly around at the grim faces surrounding him before he added, "Or come after one of us."

"He's making sense," Tanya said. "Maybe we should just pay the money, get Birdie back, and forget about it."

Ashley knew without looking that Michael didn't agree.

"I don't like the idea of this slimeball getting away with it," he growled. "That will just encourage him to do it again and again."

Bart staggered to his feet. Ashley reached out to steady him, truly concerned for his health. He wasn't a young man.

She hated to think how frightened Birdie must be. God, what kind of sicko would kidnap an old woman?

"We're talking about my wife," Bart said. "I'm not taking any chances with her. She's too precious to me."

"Of course she is." Ashley shot Michael a quelling look. He scowled back at her, but remained silent on the subject. She turned back to Bart. "We should concentrate on getting the money together. Then we should probably go ashore and act natural. If he's—if he's watching, it's important for him to see that we didn't go to the authorities."

"Much as I hate to admit it," Deckland said, "I think Ashley's right. We don't know who he is. He could be a steward, or someone who works in the casino. He could be anybody."

"Shut up, Deckland," Tanya said, shivering again. "You're giving me the creeps. By the way, mind if I share a room with you tonight?"

Deckland eased the tension by slanting her a mocking leer. "It would be my pleasure."

Tanya's eyes narrowed in warning. "Don't get any ideas, buster, or you'll get what—" She broke off abruptly, biting her lip. She darted an apologetic glance at Ashley. "Sorry, Ash. I didn't mean to bring that up."

"It's okay." Ashley was surprised to discover that she meant it. It *was* okay, because she believed Michael when he insisted he wouldn't have slept with Tanya.

She was either losing her mind or learning to trust him.

She didn't know which possibility frightened her more.

"Let's gather the money and take it with us," Michael said, stalking to the closet. "Just in case we're dealing with two slimeballs instead of one." He withdrew a suitcase and set it on the bed.

When he popped the lock, the lid sprang open, showing an empty suitcase.

As Ashley watched, he lifted out the bottom liner, revealing neat stacks of cash.

"Clever," Deckland observed.

Tanya came closer, whistling low. "I don't think I've ever seen that much cash at one time."

"I don't know how I can ever thank you enough," Bart began in a humble voice.

He didn't get far.

"Don't mention it."

"No problem."

"Forget it."

Ashley patted his arm, touched by his humbleness. "Bart, we all know you would do the same for us, so please, stop worrying about thanking us."

While Michael stuffed the money in an empty duffel bag, Ashley retrieved her stash of cash and added it to the bag. "We can stop at Deckland's cabin along the way."

"Then mine," Tanya said.

Michael cleared his throat and stared hard at Ashley. She blinked; then her eyes widened as she remembered. "Er, you might feel safer sending Michael in," she suggested, her face heating up as erotic memories assaulted her. She didn't think she'd ever be able to brush her teeth over a sink without remembering.

Tanya wasn't inclined to argue. "Good idea. I

wasn't looking forward to going in there alone anyway."

Deckland's cabin was to the left and Tanya's to the right, which was also the way out. They waited outside as Deckland retrieved his money, then continued on to Tanya's cabin. Michael took her key. When he opened the door, he quickly stepped inside and shut it behind him.

Ashley let out a slow breath of relief. So far the water hadn't reached the hall, but she knew they would have to get word to someone or the entire lower deck would soon be flooded. But how? How could they alert the staff without alerting the others?

By the time Michael emerged, she still hadn't arrived at a solution. She tried to catch his eye, but he appeared to be too preoccupied to notice. They came to the end of the hall and turned the corner, starting up the short flight of stairs leading to the upper deck.

Michael suddenly stopped. The entire group stopped with him. It was as if they were all attached at the hips, Ashley thought, grabbing the guardrail to keep from bumping into Deckland.

"I left my cell phone in my room," Michael announced, giving Ashley a meaningful look. "We might need it."

She read the silent message he sent her, her shoulders sagging in relief. He had figured out a way of reporting the water leak without alerting the others. "We'll wait here," she said before anyone else had a chance to speak. As antsy as they all were, Ashley wouldn't have been surprised if everyone insisted on walking back with Michael. She was reminded of a group of teenagers prowling through a haunted house.

The moment he disappeared from sight, a big, burly steward appeared at the top of the stairs. He came to an abrupt halt, frowning at the tight-knit group clogging the stairs.

Tanya lifted her big, frightened eyes and muffled a shriek with her hand at the sight of him. Bart turned a few shades paler and flattened his body against the wall next to Tanya. Deckland moved in front of Tanya and Bart, apparently feeling the need to take over Michael's unofficial role as leader.

Which left Ashley alone on the opposite side of the stairwell. Alone and unhappy. She glanced in the direction Michael had taken, then looked at the steward again. They were all being hopelessly paranoid, she suspected.

The suspicion didn't help slow the erratic pounding of her heart.

She mustered a polite smile. "We're, um, waiting for a friend," she explained to the steward, who was now staring at them with narrow-eyed suspicion. Was it any wonder? Ashley thought, looking from Tanya's terrified face to Bart's pale expression to Deckland's belligerent stance.

They all looked ridiculously guilty.

The steward slowly descended the stairs, keeping his eye on Deckland. Ashley held her breath, willing him to be on his way without delay. If he started asking questions . . .

After the steward disappeared around the corner, the group expelled a communal breath of relief. For several long moments, no one spoke.

Then everyone tried speaking at once, eager to justify their foolish reactions to the steward. If the situation hadn't been so dire, Ashley would have found the moment comical.

"He could have been the kidnapper," Deckland said, daring to glare at the empty space where the steward was last seen.

Tanya, with a hand to her racing heart, let out a shaky laugh. "He looked like a pirate, didn't he? A mean one."

"Did you see the way he looked at us?" Bart asked. "As if he knew what we were up to."

"You all look guilty as hell," Michael said, startling them into round-eyed silence.

Ashley had never been so happy to see him in her life. There had always been something about Michael that made her feel safe.

"Thank God you're back!" Tanya said with heartfelt sincerity.

Apparently, Ashley thought, surprised at her lack of jealousy, she wasn't alone in the feeling.

Chapter Twenty-three

Michael swallowed the question three times before he gave up and asked Ashley, "Why aren't you eating?"

With a visible start, she looked up at him, her eyes storm dark. "I can't stop thinking about Birdie. She was really looking forward to this Mexican buffet."

"And the magic show," Tanya added glumly. She pointed her fork in the direction of the bar, where Bart sat on a stool nursing a drink. From their position in the center of the dining room, they could see into the dim bar through the wide, arched doorway. "Poor Bart. He's lost without her, isn't he?"

Ashley's lovely eyes suddenly gleamed with unshed tears. Michael resisted the urge to scoot his chair around and offer her a comforting arm.

Hell, he wanted to pull her onto his lap and shield her from the entire world.

He settled for pressing his foot against her own beneath the table. At the contact, she shot him an enigmatic look but didn't shy away from his comforting touch.

"I'll bet Birdie and Bart regret taking this particular cruise," Tanya continued, pushing her food around on her plate with the same lackluster motion that Ashley had used. "I just hope Birdie's okay. I hate to think of her being manhandled by some swarthy, bearded fellow with rotting teeth and an ugly scar across his cheek."

If they thought she was being overly dramatic, nobody commented on the fact.

Deckland sighed and pushed his plate aside. "There's a good chance the kidnapper won't harm a blue hair on her head," he said.

Tanya shot him a suspicious glance. "Are you just saying that to ease our minds?"

"No. My comment is based on statistics."

Michael silently applauded Deckland. Maybe the doctor wasn't such a bad guy after all, he mused, staring at Ashley to see if Deckland's professional assurance had eased the worried look in her eyes.

It hadn't.

He frowned, wishing he had his hands wrapped around the kidnapper's neck. He'd take great pleasure in twisting the life out of him.

When the meal was finished, they moved to a table in the bar and continued their vigil. Deckland joined Bart at the bar to check on the older man's state of mind. The band began to play a slow, sultry tune, giving Michael an idea.

He rose and grabbed Ashley's hand. Her eyes widened when she realized his intent.

"No, Michael. I couldn't."

"You can, and you will." He tugged on her hand again, and she reluctantly came to her feet. Pulling her soft body firmly against him, he moved with her to the tiny dance floor. Several other couples joined them.

With his mouth close to her ear, he whispered, "If Birdie was here, she'd be stomping her feet and cheering us on and you know it."

"And making crude comments about your anatomy."

Sighing, she relaxed against him, laying her head on his shoulder. Michael could feel the warmth of her body seep into him as they swayed to the sultry beat of "Black Velvet." For once, he ignored his instant arousal. It wasn't something he could control, anyway.

"Ashley—"

"Michael—"

She lifted her head and looked at him. Time seemed to stand still as they gazed into each other's eyes and swayed together. Slowly, Michael touched his mouth to hers in a kiss that was as sweet as it was brief. He had to swallow several times to get rid of the suspicious lump in his throat. "You first."

"I was just going to say thank you."

He lifted an inquiring brow.

She blushed and ducked her head. "For helping Bart. That was a lot of money to just give away."

Michael stumbled. Was she suspicious? he wondered. Or just fishing? Striving for casualness, he shrugged, as if her compliment made him uncomfortable. "A woman's life versus six thousand dollars. Hmm. Nope. No contest."

"But she's virtually a stranger."

"How about you? You didn't hesitate to hand over your money."

"But *I* won the lottery. It wasn't like I had earned it, the way you have."

For one insane moment, Michael considered blurting out the truth.

The moment came and went as he imagined her taunting laughter, her smug smile. It was only difficult to imagine, he assured himself, because she was in his arms and looking at him as if she might actually care.

Tomorrow was another day, and the day after that, they would be sailing home to resume their separate lives. She hadn't mentioned love, and he hadn't either.

Lust.

Passion.

Body chemistry.

Physical attraction.

Everything but love. He loved her, and he ached to tell her so.

But he was a coward. That fact and pride kept words of love locked inside him. If she wanted to talk about their future, she would have to initiate the conversation, starting with a sincere apology for not believing in him. He didn't think he could ever put the horrible past behind him unless Ashley believed he was innocent.

"Michael? You look so serious. Is something wrong?"

He jerked his attention to the here and now. "No. Nothing's wrong." He forced out the lie, because he knew that he had to. "I've made a few lucrative investments." She looked disappointed with the brevity of his answer. Was she thinking about the long, lively discussions they used to have about their careers? he wondered.

"Oh. That's good." She fiddled idly with the top button of his shirt, causing his body to harden in response to the innocent action. "For a moment I thought you were going to tell me that you joined the Mafia."

"Very funny." He kissed the top of her head, and she sighed and pressed her face against his chest as if they hadn't spent the last two years avoiding each other.

Her hot breath fanned the ever present embers of his desire. Not that it took much, he mused ruefully, wondering how he was going to live the rest of his life without her.

Right now his future looked pretty bleak.

Ashley toweled her hair dry in the bathroom and slipped one of her sexy nighties over her head. A pale, shimmering pink with spaghetti straps and a plunging neckline, it was like all the others she'd packed; it revealed more than it covered.

The hem came to the top of her thighs, hardly covering the matching thong panties and leaving her tanned bottom bare. What in the world had she been thinking? Taking a deep breath, she opened the door and stepped from the bathroom.

Michael was in bed, propped against the pillows with the sheet pulled to his waist.

The rest of him was deliciously bare.

He took one look at her and groaned. "Dammit, Ash! Don't you have one single piece of clothing that doesn't scream 'Take me'?"

Despite the fact that his growled statement turned her bones to mush, her chin rose a notch. She glanced pointedly at his bare chest, swallowing quietly at the sight of his bronzed skin dusted with dark, curling hair.

The line of hair tapered down across his wash-board belly, disappearing beneath the sheet.

"At least I'm *wearing* something. And no, I don't. I bought an entire new wardrobe just for this cruise."

He patted the bed beside him, an unmistakable gleam in his eyes. "At least it wasn't wasted on what's-his-name."

Ashley grimaced. "Did you have to mention *him?*"

"Sorry." He crooked his finger, since she had yet to move from the bathroom doorway. "Come here."

"Why?" Her heart beat faster. She knew why, of course, but she didn't want to appear too obvious. But Michael surprised her with his husky, low-voiced answer.

"I want to hold you."

She went very still. Holding implied tenderness and caring, not passion and lust. Her gaze dropped to the bulge in the sheet by his hips. The sight of his arousal strangely reassured her. "You—you just want to hold me?"

He flashed her a crooked grin. "Don't sound so skeptical, Ash. You've had an upsetting day. Did you really think I would take advantage of you?"

Once again she glanced at his arousal.

"Hey, don't hold it against me," he said softly, teasingly. "There are certain parts of me that are obviously not connected to my brain. Just ignore it."

Ignore it? Ashley stifled a laugh at the thought. What normal woman could ignore anything about Michael? Slowly, she approached the bed and slipped beneath the sheets.

He pulled her firmly against his side, urging her to snuggle her head against his shoulder. He let out a soft, contented sigh while Ashley's heart did a triple somersault.

She was staring right at the silken, talented body part he suggested she ignore.

She tried closing her eyes, but it didn't work.

Even with her eyes firmly closed, she could still see the hard length of him outlined by the sheet. Her thighs quivered. Was she truly oversexed? Why couldn't she ignore it, as he suggested? Did she have no shame?

"You're trembling," he observed, sounding concerned. "Are you cold?"

Cold? Not by a long shot. Oh, no, she was far from cold. Hot to the point of melting would be closer to the truth.

"And your heart's beating a mile a minute. Are you sure you're okay?"

When would he get a clue? Ashley wondered, feeling her nipples spring to attention. Could he feel them poking him? How could he not?

She blew out a frustrated breath—but slowly, quietly.

Ashley slammed her eyelids closed and tried to leave his arms for safer ground. He tightened his hold, sounding so innocently puzzled Ashley wanted to punch him.

"Hey, where do you think you're going? What's wrong?" She tried to avoid his hand, but he managed to grasp her chin and tilt her face so that he could see her expression.

She kept her gaze stubbornly lowered.

"Ash?"

His soft query made her shudder. "For a sharp businessman, you're remarkably dense some-times. This is one of those times."

"I don't get it."

"I know." She clenched her jaw, letting her breath hiss out between her teeth. "Why don't we just turn out the lights and go to sleep?"

"Is that what you want to do?"

He was either teasing her or he was truly as dense as she claimed. "Of course."

"Then . . ." Michael paused a beat, as if he'd suddenly realized something. "Oh."

She jumped as he placed the tip of his finger squarely on top of an aching nipple. Very slowly, he brushed his finger back and forth.

Fanning the flames.

Ashley bit her lip to keep from moaning. Her face felt fiery as she tried to guess what he was thinking without having to actually look for her-self. If she looked . . . and found him grinning that cocky grin of his, she didn't think she could handle it.

Very softly, he asked, "Why didn't you tell me, Ash? I'm lying here, aching like hell for you, but determined to be a gentleman. And if I'm finally understanding you correctly, you want me as badly as I want you."

"Yes." What was the point of lying? Besides, she didn't want to take the chance that he might believe her if she lied.

"Aw, honey," he whispered, his mouth brushing hers. His tongue came out and moistened her lips, then slipped between her teeth, teasing her with rapid strokes similar to what she hoped he'd be doing to her very shortly.

If there had been such a thing as pro lovers, Michael would have been an All Star.

With the lights on, Michael undressed her, kissing and stroking his way to her navel . . . then lower still, until she was crying and begging him to stop . . . or go faster.

She couldn't make up her mind.

Finally, he released her from the mind-boggling pleasure of his tongue and teeth, laying her gently beneath him. Hovering over her, he stared into her desire-glazed eyes, his own bright and intense as he lifted her legs over his shoulders and brought his erection to her moist center.

He bent his head and suckled one breast at a

time, until she was panting and arching upward. Then he looked at her again.

"This time," he ground out, as if the mere act of speaking pained him, "we're going to take it slow and sweet."

Ashley smiled into his taut, determined face, knew his control was shaky at best, and very softly, she said, "Liar."

Smiling at her challenge, he supported himself with his arms as he sank into her, inch by incredible inch. Ashley bit her lip and tried to squirm closer, but he dodged her attempts to capture all of him.

"You are going to regret you called me that," he promised, sinking in to the hilt, then slowly, torturously withdrawing. He sank into her again—and did that swivel dance with his hips.

Her smile abruptly faded. "No fair!" she gasped, arching against him as her insides caught fire and began to spasm. "Don't—don't do that!"

"Don't?"

"No, don't—yes, do! Ahh, Michael!"

"That's it, baby," he panted, increasing his pace as he watched her. "Come for me, darling. I want to see your face light up with wonder."

The sheer beauty of his voice, filled with raw passion and joyous anticipation, sent Ashley tumbling over the edge. She arched her entire body into his, pushing him deep, suspended in time for a brief moment as they exploded together, the force of her orgasm temporarily shattering her sanity.

Very slowly, her sanity returned. Something warm and wet trickled down her cheek. Ashley brought up her hand, quickly wiping away the tears she hadn't known were going to fall.

Her body felt gloriously renewed from the inside out, yet her heart felt hollow and sad. How could two people be this good together yet be so wrong for each other?

Chapter Twenty-four

Michael was awakened the next morning by someone pounding on the door.

"Just a minute!" he shouted, dancing around the room as he tried to put his pants on and losing his balance. Behind him, he heard Ashley yawn.

When he opened the door, Tanya came rushing in, followed by Deckland. Michael frowned and looked out into the hall. "Where's Bart?"

"We can't find him," Tanya announced. "And his bed hasn't been slept in."

Ashley sat up in bed, holding the covers up to her chin. To Michael's eyes, she looked warm and sexy and adorably sleepy. He fought the urge to push Deckland out into the hall and slam the door until Ashley got dressed.

"What's that?" Ashley asked, knuckling her eyes. "Bart's bed hasn't been slept in?"

"He's missing," Deckland confirmed, shoving his hands into his pants pockets. "We coaxed the desk clerk into opening his door—"

"We told him that Bart had a bad heart," Tanya finished.

"Does he?" Michael looked from one dumbfounded face to the other.

"Does who what?" Tanya asked.

"Does Bart have a bad heart?" Michael repeated, feeling as if he'd fallen into a rabbit hole. Apparently, the stress of the situation was wearing on them all. Nobody was making any sense.

Tanya waved an impatient hand. "Oh, that. Not that I know of, but the desk clerk believed us and unlocked his door. He wasn't there."

That much Michael had gathered. "Where could he be?"

"We were hoping you might have some idea," Deckland said, politely keeping his gaze averted from the bed.

Michael rubbed a hand over his whisker-rough chin, forcing himself to concentrate. "The drop-off time is noon. Maybe the kidnapper changed his mind and contacted Bart."

"I don't think Bart would just leave without telling us," Ashley said.

Tanya and Deckland agreed.

"He probably couldn't sleep," Tanya said. "And is it any wonder? For all we know, Birdie

311

had to sleep on the ground last night, or in a lice-infested hut—"

"This is Barbados, Two thousand three," Deckland reminded her irritably. "They don't sleep in huts anymore."

"Oh, well." Tanya shot him a sour look. "Still, you don't know what kind of conditions she's having to deal with. I doubt her kidnapper is concerned about her comfort." She shuddered visibly. "I don't know if I can last another three hours."

"We've got to find Bart."

Everyone turned to look at Ashley, including Deckland, which made Michael stiffen and scowl. He didn't want the man—any man—looking at Ashley half dressed.

"Why don't we meet downstairs for breakfast?"

"I couldn't eat a thing." Tanya put a hand over her stomach. "For all we know, Birdie could be having to eat—"

"Oh, please," Deckland interrupted before Tanya could launch into another dramatic description. "Let's go downstairs so Ashley can—so they can get dressed and join us."

When they had gone, Michael shut the door and turned to Ashley. "If Bart shows up before noon, I'm going to follow him," he stated, bracing himself for an argument.

She surprised him. "I think that's a good idea. And I'm going with you."

"No, you're not."

"Yes, I am."

"No—"

"Michael—you can't stop me," she inserted firmly. She threw the covers aside, revealing a long length of honey-kissed leg and a mouth-watering amount of her perky bottom in her hasty dash to the bathroom.

The door slammed, ending the peep show. From the other side, she warned him, "And if you try to sneak off without me, I'll never speak to you again."

Since Michael didn't like that possibility, he decided she could go with him.

Bart's wild Hawaiian shirt was hopelessly wrinkled and he needed a shave. His eyes resembled the tomato juice Tanya had ordered with her toast.

"I couldn't sleep, so I've just been walking up and down the sidewalks in front of the shops," he explained, casting Ashley a grateful look when she handed him a cup of steaming coffee. "I didn't mean to throw everyone into a panic."

"Oh, no. You didn't."

"Not at all."

"That's okay."

Ashley listened to their lies, placing a hand on her hip. "Well, you scared me," she admitted.

After an hour-long search of the shopping

area, the group had returned to the hotel res-
taurant. Twenty minutes later, in walked Bart,
wearing the longest face in history. Ashley could
have sworn he'd aged ten years.

"Do you think you could eat something, Bart?"
she asked, ready to signal a waiter if he so much
as hesitated to answer.

"Oh, no. I couldn't. Well, maybe a little something."

He cast her a tentative smile that melted her
heart. She quickly snagged the waiter's attention
and ordered a man-size breakfast for Bart. After
all, the man had to keep up his strength. She
glanced at her watch, saw they had only an hour
to go, and tried to quiet the butterflies in her
stomach.

The others didn't know that she and Michael
planned to follow Bart to the drop-off point. She
was unclear what Michael intended to do when
they got there, but anything had to be better
than standing around waiting for Bart to return.

What if he never did?

What if they never saw the Scotts again, and
they had to get back on the ship and sail away
without ever knowing what had happened to
them? She would go stark, raving mad!

Despite his haggard appearance, Bart ate like
a hungry man, seemingly unaware of his ship-
mates watching him with varying degrees of surprise.

Nobody had been able to eat more than a few bites of toast or bagel before Bart arrived on the scene.

Maybe he was the kind of person who had a tendency to eat when under stress, Ashley mused, as Bart swallowed the last bite of jelly-smeared toast.

He drained his coffee and slapped down the mug. "Let's go get the money," he stated, rising.

Everyone followed suit.

Bridgetown's Broad Street was rumored to be a shopper's dream, but for Ashley, everything was a blur.

She had to skip to keep up with Michael's long strides. She was out of breath within minutes, while Michael looked as if he could go ten miles at the same killing pace.

Finally, she huffed out, "Michael! Will you please slow down?" The heck with the shops, she just wanted to breathe!

"We'll lose Bart if we do," he said without breaking stride. "Do you want to lose him?"

"No." She cast a glance over her shoulder just in time to see Deckland yank Tanya into a shop doorway. "But you might want to know that we're being followed."

"Tanya and Deckland?"

"Yes," she said breathlessly. "You knew?"

"Well, I knew they didn't believe you when you

315

said we were going to go upstairs to take a nap. You should have come up with a better excuse."

"I couldn't *think* of a better excuse." Just ahead, Bart, with duffel bag in hand, turned the corner and disappeared out of sight. Ashley's lungs burned, but damned if she was going to complain again. "He acts as if he knows where he's going."

"He probably walked the route this morning just to be sure. I know *I* would have." At the end of the intersection, Michael stuck out his arm to halt her forward stride. "Wait. We don't want him to see us. Might make him nervous."

"As if he isn't nervous enough. Do you see him?"

Michael peered cautiously around the corner of the building. "Yes. Come on." He dropped his arm and resumed his killing pace.

Ashley would have let out a breath of relief when she, too, spotted Bart up ahead, but she didn't have any breath to let out. She glanced over her shoulder to see if Deckland and Tanya were following, and saw half of Deckland's face peering around the corner of the building.

He would make a lousy detective, she thought, shaking her head. Up ahead, Bart began to slow down. They did the same—and boy, was she glad.

Bart turned into an open doorway and disappeared again.

"He's gone into that hotel," Michael said without slowing down. "You keep walking. I'll follow him inside."

"Michael—"

"Don't argue, Ashley. I can't stand the thought of you getting hurt."

His words temporarily robbed her of speech. She swallowed a lump before she said, "I feel the same way, which is why—"

"No." He grabbed her elbow and pulled her into the alley beside the hotel. "Stay here and wait for Deckland and Tanya. Keep out of sight until you see me come back out, understand?"

Mutely, she nodded. The moment he disappeared into the building, she followed, pausing long enough at the door to signal Deckland and Tanya to follow her. She wasn't about to let Michael go without her. Why, that creep might have a gun! If Michael was going to get himself shot, she wanted to be there to rescue him.

Terror seized her heart at the possibility, and doubts assailed her. What were they thinking? They should have gone to the local police, or at least reported the kidnapping to ship security. They were amateurs—

Michael paused at the desk. Ashley hastily darted behind a cluster of potted palm trees in the foyer. She nearly shrieked when a hand landed on her shoulder.

Heart in her mouth, she whirled around, re-

317

lieved to find that it was only Tanya. Deckland, looking grim but determined, stood behind her.

"You scared the life out of me!" she hissed, immediately turning back to see which direction Michael had taken. She was lucky to catch the bottom of his loafer disappearing out of sight around a corner.

"We should wait here," Deckland said. Both women shot him a scornful look that made him flush. "Well, we don't want to jeopardize Birdie's life, do we?"

Tanya grabbed her arm. "Look!" she whispered, pointing, yet at the same time dragging Ashley deeper behind the palm trees. "There's Bart with Birdie!"

Ashley's mouth went dry. "But—but where's Michael?"

"Possibly trying to keep out of sight?" Deckland suggested with veiled sarcasm. "Like *we* should be."

As one, they shuffled around the concealing foliage as Bart and Birdie approached them, continuing to inch around and out of sight until the couple reached the gleaming glass hotel doors. Bart, Ashley mused after a quick glance at the couple, looked grim but strong. Birdie looked none the worse for her adventure. In fact, she looked relieved that it was over.

Ashley started to step out from behind the

palms and call out to them, but Deckland yanked her roughly back.

"What are you doing? *He* could be watching!"

"You guys!" Tanya whispered frantically, her round-eyed gaze fixed on something over Ashley's shoulder. "There's—there's a man coming, and he's carrying a duffel bag just like the one Michael put the money in."

"She's right," Deckland said, keeping his voice low. "It looks like the same duffel bag."

Unable to take her eyes off the tall, thin man approaching their hideout on his way to the door, Ashley could do nothing but watch helplessly as he marched to freedom. With dark, thinning hair, dark eyes, and swarthy skin, he looked every inch the ruthless kidnapper.

And he had a jagged scar along his left cheek.

What would Michael do? Where was he when she needed him most? Ashley worried her bottom lip, trying to think. If they didn't do something, in another moment the man would be out the door and on his merry way with their money and a kidnapping charge he would never have to face.

"We should stop him," she told her companions. If she had known Tanya would take her so literally, she might have reconsidered her rash words.

Before they could realize Tanya's reckless intent, she went dashing into the foyer toward the man, coming to a sliding, clumsy halt in front of him. Dazed, Ashley thought for one crazy moment that she meant to curtsey.

Instead, Tanya smiled sweetly into the man's startled face and brought her knee up and into his groin.

He howled and doubled over, dropping the duffel bag. Tanya snatched it up and ran back to them, her expression a mixture of elation and almost comical terror.

"I've got it! I've got it!"

The man was on his knees, moaning, both hands covering his groin. Ashley dragged her stunned gaze from the man to the duffel bag Tanya held in her triumphant hands.

She did a double-take on the bag.

Slowly, she put her hands over her face and moaned.

It wasn't Michael's bag. Michael's bag was black. This bag was navy blue. Same shape. Similar in color.

Not Michael's bag. Not the money. Not the kidnapper.

"Ashley? What is it?" Tanya tried to pry Ashley's fingers from her face, but Ashley held firm.

She wanted to disappear before Michael found out that they had not only followed him into the hotel but had also tackled the wrong—

"What's going on here?"

It was Michael, and he was helping the poor

man to his feet. He had spotted them clustered behind the potted palms.

"Michael!"

The excited triumph in Tanya's voice moved Ashley to action. She grabbed Tanya's arm, halting her in midstride.

Tanya scrambled to hold her footing on the slickly polished floor, slapping at Ashley's bruising hold. "Ashley! Let go! Don't you see that Michael's—"

"It's not him!" Ashley hissed, holding on to her arm. "I mean, that's not Michael's duffel bag."

"What? What do you mean it's not—"

"It's not," Ashley repeated, wishing she was wrong. Oh, how she wished she was wrong! "Michael's duffel bag is black. This one's navy blue."

Finally, realization dawned. Tanya's eyes grew big, then bigger, until Ashley felt certain they would swallow her face.

"Oh. My. God. You—" Tanya swallowed hard, and shook her head, her face flaming to match Ashley's. "You mean I tackled the wrong man?"

Ashley winced. "Yes. You tackled the wrong man." Beside her, Deckland swore softly, then quickly apologized like the gentleman he was.

Tanya looked at the moaning man, then at Michael's frowning, exasperated face. She turned back to Ashley. "But we all thought—"

"Yes, we did." Ashley turned to give Deckland

321

a flinty look, daring him to deny it. "Didn't we, Deckland? We *all* thought he was the guy. The kidnapper."

For a moment, it looked as though Deckland would defect, but in the end he gave a short, resigned nod. "Yes, we made the mistake together."

"Oh." Tanya's eyes watered. She put a hand to her mouth and spoke between her fingers. "Oh, oh." Holding the duffel bag, she walked back to the man and held it out. Her mortified, apologetic expression would have made the devil hesitate.

"I'm *so* sorry," she began. "I thought you—"

"Stay away from me!" the man shrieked, throwing one hand in front of his groin. He used the other to snatch his bag from her fingers.

Ashley had never seen a man limp so fast.

When he had gone, Ashley sighed and said, "Let's get this over with, shall we?" She took Deckland's arm in a firm grip—just on the off chance the coward was thinking of bolting—and led him to where Michael and Tanya stood.

After all, he couldn't eat them, right? He wasn't the big, bad wolf. Just her ex-husband.

Okay. An extremely angry ex-husband.

Chapter Twenty-five

"You could have been killed," Michael said, his heart stuttering at the thought. He couldn't decide if he wanted to kiss her senseless or bend her over his knee. To think that she might have actually run into the real kidnapper—

"The same applies to you, Michael." Ashley's chin came up several notches. "Anyway, nobody was hurt, so let's just drop it, okay?"

Oh, so she wanted to drop it, did she? When he had a few new gray hairs as a result? When he wasn't at all certain he hadn't suffered a mild heart attack when he discovered the reckless stunt they'd pulled?

He thought not.

"What if he'd had a gun?" he persisted. For good measure, he turned his angry, quelling gaze to Deckland. "And is this how you protect the ladies?"

"Hey, I'm the one who brought him down," Tanya put in. She shrank back when Michael whirled on her.

"Yes, you did. Had he been the real kidnapper, you would have been the first to die."

"Oh, get over it," Ashley snapped, coming between Michael and a white-faced Tanya. Her confident look said that she knew Michael's bark was bigger than his bite, even if Tanya didn't. "We're wasting time on something that might have happened but didn't," she emphasized for his benefit. "What did you find out?"

With a sigh, Michael dug into his back pocket and pulled out a set of handcuffs. "The window was open and the room was empty. He got away, obviously. I found these."

Ashley gasped, staring at the gold-plated handcuffs. "That creep! He handcuffed her with her own handcuffs! I saw her put those in her overnight bag—"

"What?" Tanya sounded totally bewildered. "What would Birdie be doing with handcuffs?"

"Do you really need to be told?" Deckland whispered in her ear, but loud enough for the others to hear.

For the second time that day, Tanya's face flamed. "Oh, now I get it. But aren't they a little too old—"

"You have no idea," Ashley muttered, but Michael noted that she was staring at the handcuffs, frowning.

Before Michael could question her further, Tanya spoke.

"They couldn't belong to the Scotts, Ashley. Birdie's bags were in the hotel room with Bart's. I saw them when we were looking for him this morning."

"Right. You're absolutely right, Tanya," Ashley said, a little too strenuously for Michael's peace of mind. "Let's get back to the hotel and get our bags before our ship sails without us. I feel the need for a drink."

It was the second clue that something was wrong. Ashley wasn't a drinker, unless she had taken up the habit since their divorce. Michael had to admit, however, that after their harrowing adventure, even a teetotaler might consider a stiff drink or two.

Getting back on the ship proved to be a little more complicated than they'd expected.

Since Michael was leading the way—and it was Michael who set off the metal detector—everyone in his group had to be throughly searched.

A moment too late, Ashley realized what the security guys would find when they went through their bags.

Or Michael's bag, to be exact.

When the security clerk confirmed her fears

by dangling the handcuffs in the air, she gave serious thought to jumping ship.

The dozen or so passengers crowded behind them got an eyeful.

"These belong to you?" the security guard trilled in a high, squeaky voice that grated on Ashley's nerves. The snicker that followed made her want to sic Tanya on him.

When Michael unexpectedly popped off, "No, they belong to your mother," Ashley had to press her face into his back to muffle her spontaneous laughter.

Behind her, Tanya did the same to *her* back.

Deckland, however, began to laugh and couldn't seem to stop. The more he laughed, the redder the security guard became.

"Hey, man. That wasn't funny."

The laughter spread from Deckland to the man standing behind him to the woman standing behind him and on down the line, until the dozen passengers who could see and hear the security officer were all laughing or chuckling.

Without cracking a smile, Michael shrugged. "You asked me."

The red-faced security officer slapped the handcuffs back into Michael's bag and waved the entire group on through.

Tanya continued to giggle. When they were out of earshot, she said, "I thought he was going to have a stroke!"

"Yeah. Did you see his face?" Deckland wiped tears from his eyes, clapping Michael on the back. "I have to say, Michael, you managed to surprise me."

Ashley linked her arm through his and gazed up at him, batting her eyelashes. "My hero," she purred sweetly.

"Knock it off," Michael growled, encompassing them all with a fierce scowl.

They quickly sobered, but the moment he turned his back on Deckland and Tanya again, they burst into laughter. Ashley suspected their response was a delayed reaction to their adventurous morning.

She quickened her steps at the reminder, anxious to see for herself that Birdie had suffered no ill effects from her kidnapping. She also had a question or two to ask her about those handcuffs. . . .

By the time they reached the corridor to their cabins, the group had sobered to the point of silence. Bart was waiting outside his door.

He met them halfway, just in front of Tanya's cabin. He angled his head at the door, keeping his voice low. "Can we talk in there?"

Tanya opened her mouth, but before she could answer, Ashley hurriedly spoke up. "Deckland's cabin is the biggest. Why don't we meet there?"

327

"I second that motion," Deckland said. "I've got a fully stocked bar, too."

"Amen," Michael muttered, and Ashley knew he wasn't referring to Deckland's mention of liquor.

She met his gaze for an instant, her cheeks flushing at the memory of their heated encounter in Tanya's bathroom. He lifted an amused brow before breaking eye contact.

Together, they walked to Deckland's cabin and waited for him to unlock the door. They piled inside, Tanya and Deckland heading for the bar, Bart seating himself at the small table in front of the portal, while Michael and Ashley remained standing.

Bart waited until Deckland handed him a drink before he said, "I want to thank you all again for your help." He cleared his throat, took a sip of his whiskey, then continued. "Birdie's resting after her ordeal."

"Of course," Tanya murmured sympathetically.

"But we had a chance to talk," Bart said. "We both agreed that it would be best to put this nasty incident behind us, just pretend it never happened."

When Michael took her hand, Ashley didn't resist.

"Birdie said she was treated fairly, but she

doesn't want to talk about it to anyone. She hopes you'll respect her wishes."

"We understand."

"Of course."

"Whatever she wants."

As Ashley suspected, Michael wasn't so agreeable. "Will you at least report the incident when you get back to Ft. Lauderdale?"

Bart rolled his shoulders in a helpless shrug. He looked tired and beaten. "What good do you think it would do? We don't have any idea who the culprit was. The money's gone and Birdie's safe. That's all that's important to me."

Ashley squeezed Michael's hand, hoping he'd take the hint and leave the subject alone. She agreed with Michael that an attempt to punish the man should be made, but ultimately, it was Bart and Birdie's decision.

"Don't worry, Bart," she told him quietly. "We all understand perfectly. Consider the incident forgotten . . . right, Michael?" She gave his hand another subtle squeeze, urging him to agree.

He did, but with obvious reluctance. "Against my better judgment, I guess I'll have to let it drop."

Bart's shoulders slumped in relief. "Thank you. Thank you all. I will never forget your kindness."

* * *

The moment Michael got Ashley alone in their cabin, he began to drill her.

"When I showed you the handcuffs, you had a funny look on your face. Why?"

Ashley's gaze slid from his. She moved to the bed and began to unpack her overnight bag. "Um, I just got confused, Michael. That's all."

"Because you thought they belonged to Birdie."

"I thought so, yes."

He moved to the opposite side of the bed so that he could see her expression. Very softly, he asked, "And what do you think now, Ash?"

She sighed and threw the laundry she had gathered onto the bed. She began to pace the room as she spoke, her jerky movements revealing her agitation. "When I went to Birdie's cabin before she left for shore, she was packing an overnight bag. I saw her put a pair of gold-plated handcuffs into her bag." Ashley threw up her hands and looked at Michael. "It could be nothing more than an odd coincidence."

"But you don't believe it *was* a coincidence, do you? No more than I do. I think we've been conned, Ashley."

"By the Scotts?" she squeaked, looking so dismayed Michael wanted to take back his words.

But he couldn't. "By Bart. I'm not so certain Birdie even knows about it."

"How could she *not* know? And what if we're wrong?"

"So you do think they conned us. Or at least Bart."

She sank onto the bed and put a hand to her frowning brow. "I just can't bring myself to believe that sweet couple—that sweet man—would put us through such worry for a measly ten thousand dollars."

"Don't forget our jewelry," Michael reminded her grimly. He didn't want to think it either, but he had no choice. "That's another fifteen thousand dollars."

"Still . . ." She shot him a pleading look, as if she hoped he'd give her a reason not to believe it. "Maybe Bart's in trouble—"

"Stop making excuses for him," Michael inserted softly. He hated to see her so upset, and his anger at Bart escalated. He could very easily find himself feeling sorry for the elderly man . . . if it weren't for the fact that Ashley looked so damned betrayed. "The whole setup—the camera, the kidnapping—those weren't the actions of an amateur, Ash. I think Bart's a professional con artist."

She frowned. "And his wife doesn't know it?"

He shrugged. "Maybe. Maybe not. If he's clever enough, he could successfully hide it from her."

"When . . . when did you first suspect?"

"I thought it was odd that a thief would go to the trouble of videotaping one target, yet apparently didn't know that another was broke. I dismissed the suspicion by thinking the thief must have been clever enough to know we would help the Scotts. Then Tanya and Deckland told us that his bed hadn't been slept in. I believe now that he was with Birdie all night at the other hotel. He probably never dreamed that Tanya and Deckland would convince the desk clerk to check his room."

A spark of anger flared in her eyes. "That's pretty dirty of him, making us think that she— that she'd been kidnapped." She jumped up, paced to the door, then back again. "If this is all true, you were probably right about the thief knowing about me from the start of the cruise. Maybe . . . maybe even before."

Michael couldn't stand it any longer. He went to her, ignoring her resistance as he pulled her against his body and locked his arms around her.

Her voice was muffled against his shoulder. "What are you going to do?"

He didn't miss the fact that she'd said *you* and not *we*. He smiled inwardly, suspecting that if left to her own devices, Ashley would be tempted to forgive the couple and forget the incident had ever happened.

Rubbing her back, he said gently, "We can't let them—or him—get away with it, sweetheart.

It isn't right. You know it isn't right."

She heaved a great sigh. "I know, but they're so *old*. They don't have many years left, and they seem so sweet and happy together."

Michael deliberately hardened his voice. "If my instincts are right, they live off other people's money, money they steal by manipulating and spying on innocent people. I'm surprised they haven't been caught before." He felt her smile against his neck and was heartened by it.

"You were too smart for them."

Warmed by the compliment, he said, "If Bart hadn't slipped up by leaving the handcuffs, I might not have figured it out. Besides"—he kissed the top of her head—"you had it figured out, too. You just didn't want to believe it."

Her lips grazed his neck, sending waves of sensation pounding through him. Such a little kiss . . . such a big reaction. He'd never cease to be awed by the power she possessed to send his senses reeling.

For the first time, Michael allowed himself to wonder if he might have a tiny chance for a future with Ashley.

He was still recovering from the shock of his thought when he heard a distinctly feminine scream of rage.

"Oh, God," Ashley said, half-laughing, half-moaning. "I think that was Tanya."

Almost immediately following her words,

someone pounded on their cabin door. Michael reluctantly let go of Ashley to answer it.

Tanya shoved a sheet of paper beneath his nose, causing him to jump back. "I gave you the key to my cabin," she said through clenched teeth. "Now I find a bill on my dresser for six hundred dollars' worth of damage. What in the *hell* did you do, Michael? My carpet's wet and I've got a cabin full of dry-cleaned clothes with another huge bill!"

"Sorry," Michael said, taking the bill from her. "I'll take care of it." He started to close the door, but he should have known Tanya wouldn't let the matter rest.

She stuck her foot in the door and slapped her hands on her hips, looking past him to Ashley, then back to his deadpan face. "What did you two do to my cabin? Can you at least tell me that?"

"You don't want to know," they said simultaneously.

"Of course I want to know!"

"We broke your bathroom sink," Ashley said, surprising Michael. She joined him at the door as she added, "It was an accident."

"You broke my bathroom—" Tanya's jaw dropped. She closed it, shook her head, and said, "What could you possibly have been doing—" Once again she snapped her mouth closed. Color rushed into her face. "Why is it that I seem to be the only one on this ship who isn't having sex?"

"Oh, I don't know," Ashley said, tongue in cheek. "I don't think Deckland's having much luck, either."

Michael swallowed a chuckle at Tanya's flaming face. "Maybe you two could—"

"Don't even go there, buster," she warned before spinning on her heel and disappearing down the corridor. "If you play, you pay," she snapped over her shoulder. "I'll bring you my dry-cleaning bill, too! We'll see how long you laugh over *that* one, my friends!"

As the door closed, Ashley fell against it, laughing helplessly. Michael felt a rush of pure lust slam into him. He grabbed her wrists and held them over her head, then slowly leaned into her, pinning her against the door.

"I'll split the bill with you," she offered, making a halfhearted attempt to wriggle free. "Since I had half the fun."

"No, it was my treat. You can get the next one."

He caught her laughing mouth and kissed her, slowly, teasingly, until her breathing changed and she arched against him. When he pulled his mouth away, he was satisfied to find her regarding him through half-closed lids.

She licked her swollen lips, staring at his mouth. "I think my emotions have been on a perpetual seesaw since we sailed," she whispered. "Tanya makes me want to laugh, the Scotts make me want to laugh and cry at the same time, and you—"

"And me?" Michael prompted when she stopped, inching his mouth closer to hers. "What do I make you want to do?"

"Anything and everything," she confessed breathlessly, reaching for his mouth. "Mostly naughty things."

Michael let go of her wrists and reached behind her, locking the door.

Chapter Twenty-six

Ashley was extremely grateful to Michael when he picked her up from the floor and carried her to bed.

Crawling wouldn't have been very dignified.

She didn't think she had a solid bone left in her body after their delicious, totally satisfying bout of lovemaking.

Right there on the floor by the door.

He gently laid her on the bed and pulled the coverlet over her naked body, his lips touching her forehead. She sighed and snaked her arms around his neck—about the only part of her body she was able to move. "Are you going to talk to Bart?"

"Yes."

Her gaze met his. "Will you be gentle?"

"I'll try."

She reluctantly let him go, tucking her hand

beneath her cheek as she listened to the sounds of him getting dressed.

Finally, she heard the click of the door shutting, followed by the sound of Michael locking it from the outside. She knew that Michael was right about confronting Bart, but she couldn't shake loose the feeling that Bart must have been desperate to fool them the way he had. He was such a sweet, harmless man, a man who obviously loved his wife.

And there was no doubt that Birdie loved Bart.

If Michael turned Bart in to ship security, what would happen to Birdie? How would she make it without Bart? She'd never heard the couple discuss any family other than each other.

A rustling sound at the door jarred Ashley from her troubling thoughts.

She froze, listening. Had Michael returned? Had he forgotten something?

After a few moments of silence, she quietly rose from the bed, staring in the direction of the door. Her heart thudded, and she silently chided herself for her ridiculous reaction. The drama was over, wasn't it?

She froze, her gaze landing on the flat white object lying on the floor in front of the door.

It hadn't been there earlier, she was certain.

Dragging the coverlet with her, she silently crossed the room and bent to retrieve the paper, thinking at first that it must be the promised dry-cleaning bill from Tanya. She unfolded it, gasping as she realized it was a computer printout of the passenger list.

Not *the* passenger list, she corrected. Not the one Deckland had given her, because she had marked the passengers from her home state with a pink highlighter.

On the list she held, a single name had been circled in red ink. As if to emphasize further, someone had also drawn a red star beside it, followed by four dollar signs.

It was Michael's name they had circled.

Ashley let out a disbelieving laugh. If they expected her to believe Michael was the one she sought, they were going to be disappointed. What a joke!

But who? Who would play such a joke? Not anyone who truly knew her, she mused, because if they knew her, they would also know that she would never in a million years believe that Michael had played the lottery, much less won it. Ha!

Still chuckling at the thought, Ashley made her way to the bathroom, taking the list with her. She wasn't letting *this* list out of her sight. After a quick shower, she would pay Deckland a visit. Since he'd obtained the first list for her, maybe he could shed some light on who might have passed her the second one.

She set the list on the sink, then grabbed a

towel from the shelf above the toilet.

A piece of paper fell from the shelf to the floor.

Ashley blinked, staring first at the folded passenger list on the sink, then at the folded paper on the floor. She picked it up and quickly opened it.

It was the missing passenger list—*her* missing list, the one with all the highlights. How had it gotten into the bathroom—beneath a stack of towels? Well, obviously someone had put it there, she realized.

And since she didn't suppose the thief would have bothered, she could only think of one person who could have done it.

Michael.

But why?

She looked at the list in her hand, then at the list on the sink, then back again. Whoever had slipped her the second list had known she was no longer in possession of the first one.

Michael was the only one she'd told, she was certain. He, therefore, must have told someone else.

She blinked, sucking in a sharp breath, forcing herself to consider the impossible.

Michael had hidden the list . . . to keep her from finding out the identity of the other lottery winner. She could think of no other rational explanation.

Which meant . . .

She sat heavily on the closed commode, shock strumming along her nerve endings and sending her pulse skyrocketing. The implication was stunning and nearly impossible for her to grasp.

Yet the clues were there, glaringly obvious now.

Starting with the first clue, when she found Michael in her cabin claiming it was *his* cabin. And if *that* wasn't embarrassingly obvious enough, what about when he'd bought the expensive jewelry without blinking an eye at the cost?

Then he'd presented all that cash when Birdie was missing.

Clues she had ignored simply because the possibility of Michael playing the lottery was preposterous to her. That he might have won playing the lottery using her numbers was even more preposterous. Downright unbelievable, in fact.

Her sudden, derisive laughter echoed off the bathroom walls. She shook her head, then moaned and covered her hot face with her hands. *Oh, God.*

Deckland—very probably coached by Kim, Ashley realized with another embarrassed moan— must have been the one who'd slipped the second list beneath the door. It made sense, considering the fact that he'd given her the first one.

He was very probably—by now—exasperated

with her narrow-mindedness, her complete certainty that it couldn't be Michael who shared her winning numbers.

Michael didn't gamble. He had always teased her unmercifully about playing the lottery, reminding her on a weekly basis that the odds were impossible.

Yet here she was, holding the passenger list that someone had hidden beneath the stack of towels. It certainly hadn't gotten there on its own, and Ashley knew the maid hadn't stuck it there.

So it had to have been Michael. And the reason he'd hidden the list was outrageously obvious.

Now. After five days at sea, with clue upon clue right in front of her nose.

She took a deep breath, then forced herself to accept the truth. Michael had won the lottery, using the same numbers she had faithfully used for the past three years.

Sentimental numbers. Two of the happiest days of her life.

The day of their first real date.

Their wedding day.

Had he been playing all along? Or was it a pure fluke that he'd bought a ticket—using her numbers—on the very day her numbers had won?

Talk about long odds!

Ashley recalled watching a "Ripley's Believe it or Not" show on television in which a teenage girl had tucked a message into a bottle and thrown it into the ocean. The message had washed ashore and been found by another teenage girl with the exact same name, same age, and same birthday. Later, when they'd gotten together, they had discovered that they both owned a dog with the same name.

If something that bizarre could happen—

Another stunning realization crashed in on Ashley before the dust had settled on the first one. A rash of goose bumps spread across her arms, making her shiver. She pulled the slipping sheet around her as her heart began to fill with a delicious, dangerous, drunken joy.

To use those numbers, Michael had to have been thinking about her, their marriage. Being a couple.

Did that mean . . . oh, God, did it mean he still loved her?

"I should be buying *you* a drink," Bart said, tilting his glass in Michael's direction before he downed the contents.

They were seated at a table for two in one of the less populated lounges on the ship, back against the wall and away from nosy bartenders and curious dinner companions.

Michael didn't want to take the chance of getting interrupted until he'd said all he wanted to say, and heard all he'd wanted to hear.

He removed the lime slice from the lip of his bottled Corona and set it on his napkin.

Then he looked at Bart.

The elderly man appeared cool on the outside, but there were subtle signs Michael might not have noticed if he hadn't known the truth about Bart. Such as the slightly trembling hands, and the way Bart couldn't meet his gaze for longer than a few seconds. He was, Michael realized with a stab of satisfaction, understandably nervous about the invitation Michael had extended to join him for a drink.

Good.

It was just as he had anticipated, and it showed that Bart wasn't entirely ruthless. In Michael's experience, ruthless men were rarely nervous about their ruthless deeds.

Patiently, Michael waited until the waiter brought Bart a fresh scotch on the rocks. And out of respect, Michael also waited until Bart had swallowed his liquor before he dropped his bombshell.

As furious and disgusted as he was with Bart, he didn't want the old man choking to death.

"How long have you been ripping people off?" he asked, so casually it was a few seconds before Bart's expression changed from slightly wary to slack-jawed disbelief.

"Pardon me?"

"I asked you"—Michael deliberately pronounced each word slowly and distinctly—"how long you've been ripping people off."

Bart hastily closed his mouth. His thick brows furrowed. "If this is a joke, Michael, I have to tell you I don't think it's a funny one."

Michael sighed and shook his head. He had expected Bart to deny it, so he wasn't surprised. But it *was* an insult. "I know about the videocamera and I know about the jewelry. I also know that Birdie was never actually kidnapped. Ashley knows it, too." Michael ignored Bart's outraged sputtering and leaned across the table to whisper, as if he were confiding a secret, "Here's the six-thousand-dollar question, Bart; does *Birdie* know her husband's a thief?"

Red-faced and refusing to drop his outraged act, Bart pushed back his chair and got to his feet. "If you really believe I'm a thief, why haven't you gone to security?"

With a shrug, Michael reached for his Corona. He took a deep drink and wiped his mouth before answering. "Because Ashley has a big heart, and she believes you've got your reasons for manipulating people, then ripping them off." He inclined his head, his eyes hard. "Have a seat, Bart. For Ashley's sake, I'm willing to listen."

Bart sank into his chair again. His face had gone two shades whiter, and his trembling had increased to the point that he gave up trying to lift his glass.

There was true regret in his eyes when he finally met Michael's expectant gaze. "To answer your first question, I've been ripping people off for about a year and a half. Three years, four months, and two weeks ago, we found out that Birdie was in the early stages of Alzheimer's. She—she takes medicine, but she's not responding well. Some unfortunate people don't." Slowly, Bart reached out and picked up his glass. He managed to take a drink without spilling it, but his voice broke as he added, "I live in constant fear that I'll wake up one morning and she won't know who I am."

Michael studied the older man closely, trying to decide if he was telling the truth. If he wasn't, he was the best damned actor Michael had ever met. "She seems clear-minded to me."

"That's because you don't know her," Bart said. Pain, whether real or imagined, clouded his eyes. "Has she told you about our kids?"

When Michael shook his head, Bart continued.

"That's because she doesn't always remember that we *have* kids, and let me tell you, our kids were her life. We've got two daughters and five grandchildren. Women *always* brag about their kids, especially grandkids. She—she does okay as long as I leave little reminder notes for her to find."

Despite his determination to remain tough, Michael couldn't stop the sympathy that flooded him. He hated it when Ashley was right. The guy *did* have a good story. "Does she know?"

Bart shook his head, his eyes full of tears. "She knew when she was first diagnosed, but when she seemed to forget about it, I didn't have the heart to remind her. When she asks the nature of her medicine, I tell her it's for her blood pressure. I . . . I even transfer her medicine over to different bottles. As for the reminder notes, I tell her they're for me."

"Can you prove any of this?"

"Yes. The ship's doctor has a copy of her medical records. I could get them if you'd like."

Michael tried to resurrect his earlier fury but didn't succeed. The most he could do was make an effort to *sound* furious. "I'm sorry about Birdie, but that doesn't excuse what you did to us, or what you've been doing to other people."

"I know, I know," Bart said, following his words with a heavy sigh. "She just has such a good time on these cruises . . . meeting new people." He hesitated, picking at the coaster beneath his glass. "As long as she's always meeting new people, people she doesn't have to remember, she doesn't suspect anything."

Okay, so he was a gullible fool, but he had to ask. "So you steal money—"

"Only from people who won't miss it," Bart inserted firmly. "Rich people." He flicked a glance at Michael, then focused on the table again. "People who have money to spare, and never too much from one person."

"And you steal this money so that you can take Birdie on more cruises?"

Bart nodded. "All we have are our Social Security benefits. I, um, sold our house, but after I paid off the mortgage, there wasn't much left. We've been living in hotels in between cruises."

Michael finished his beer. He signaled for the waiter to bring another round of drinks. "You knew that Ashley had won the lottery?"

"Yes. I—I wasn't planning on taking much, I swear, I did a background check on her—"

He broke off as Michael let out a short, nasty curse.

Casting him an apologetic look, he said, "I'm sorry, but I did a background check on you, too. I have a friend who works for the FBI."

"How convenient," Michael clipped out, grateful to latch on to a thread of his earlier anger. "So you know that I won the lottery, too."

"Yes." Bart braved another look in his direction, but quickly looked away from the obvious fury in his face. "I know that your business is

348

doing well, and that Ashley is very good at selling houses."

"And knowing this soothes your conscience?"

Surprisingly, Bart nodded. "Yes, it does. I would never take money from someone who needed it more than I do."

"How noble." Michael didn't bother hiding his sarcasm. He might be sympathetic, but he hated the thought of anyone abusing Ashley in any way. "You're like a twisted Robin Hood. Take from the rich, give to yourself."

For the first time, Bart's voice held a hint of anger. "I don't take pleasure in stealing, young man. I do it for Birdie, and it's a short-term career. In another year or two—three, if I'm lucky—Birdie will be tied to a hospital bed in a nursing home somewhere. She won't know me, or herself. She'll die without the love of her family because she won't know she *has* the love of her family." He ran his hands through his remarkably thick hair. "Sometimes I can't decide if that's a blessing or a curse, and you might not believe me, but I plan to pay as many people back as I can. Birdie has life insurance. I'm keeping track of the people I owe—I have the notebook in my suitcase, if you'd like to see it."

"I just might." Michael felt himself softening again, and wondered if he was being taken for the biggest fool on earth. "And I'd like to see those medical records, too. In the meantime, you will pay Deckland and Tanya back their money. If you do that, I don't see any reason to tell them the truth."

Bart's mouth fell open. "What about—"

"I don't know, yet. A lot will depend on whether I find out you're telling the truth or not. I will also want your solemn and sincere promise that you will stop stealing." Michael made his voice hard, hoping to balance the sympathy he couldn't help feeling for this man and his wife.

With great dignity, Bart held out his hand. "That's more than fair, Michael. You're a decent, honest man, and I wish I could be more like you."

Michael didn't say that he wasn't sure he wouldn't do the same thing if it happened to him and it was Ashley who was suffering from the ugly, debilitating disease. He didn't say it because he didn't want to encourage Bart.

But he thought it. He definitely thought it.

Chapter Twenty-seven

One look at Deckland's face and Ashley knew that every improbable conclusion she'd came to while sitting in the tiny bathroom had been shockingly, impossibly, right on the nose.

And even then, she wasn't satisfied. Not until she heard a verbal confirmation.

She waved both copies of the list beneath Deckland's nose. "Is it true? Is Michael the other lottery winner—the one I've been searching for?"

With a sigh, Deckland nodded. He motioned her inside, then looked right and left along the hall before shutting the door. "If Michael finds out I've been talking to you about this, a good friend of mine could lose his job."

Ashley frowned. "You're not making sense."

"He told me if I didn't keep my mouth shut—

and stop slipping you clues, like the list, he would see that Ian lost his job."

"Who's Ian?"

"He's the guy who gave me the passenger list."

"Michael *blackmailed* you?" Ashley squeaked out, trying to wrap her mind around the thought. "But why didn't he want me to know?" And why would he go to such lengths?

Deckland gave her a shame-shame look. "Come on, Ashley. Think about it. He bought a lottery ticket using the same numbers as you, and I happen to know they're the dates of your first date and your wedding anniversary."

"Kim?"

"Yeah, but that's not the issue."

Ashley didn't agree, but she let him continue.

"He just happened to luck out by buying that ticket on the same day those numbers were picked. He's afraid of what you'll think if you find out."

She went very still, absorbing his words, trying to absorb the pain as well. "He was afraid I'd think he cared about me. That—" She swallowed hard. "That he might still love me."

"Precisely. Which, I might add, he does."

"Right." Her voice came out hoarse and wobbly. "If he loved me, why wouldn't he want me to know?"

"Come on, Ashley! You broke the man's heart, then stomped on the pieces."

Ashley gasped. "I did not! *He* broke *my* heart by sleeping with that—with that blond bimbo!"

"He didn't have sex with her."

"The hell he didn't! I saw them, Deckland, and I assure you that they were having sex." Her stomach rolled with the old familiar sick feeling she felt anytime she thought about that horrible moment. "So please, spare me your testimony. You weren't there. You didn't see what I saw. Nobody else did."

Deckland lifted his hands in an exasperated gesture. "You are so pigheaded, but then, I knew that from Kim. What I find hard to believe is that you're narrow-minded on top of being pigheaded. You didn't strike me as the type." He held up a hand when she opened her mouth to speak. "Okay, okay. So you won't believe me, either. Have you thought about just forgiving him? He obviously made a mistake. He's paid for it, don't you think?"

She didn't know how to respond. Hadn't she been thinking the same thing? That maybe it was time to forgive and forget? She still loved Michael . . . and if there was a chance that he still loved her, wouldn't she be crazy to throw the opportunity away?

"What if . . . what if I forgive and forget and he does it to me again?" She hadn't realized she'd whispered the fearful words aloud until Deckland spoke.

"I honestly don't think he will. And really, you can't go around being scared to love. You'll wind up a lonely old woman."

Ashley made a face at him. "Thanks for the insight, Doctor. Now give me another good reason to trust him again."

"Because you love him."

She swallowed hard. Okay, so he had her there. "I do, but—"

"Just leave off the but, will you? Just tell him that you love him. See if he doesn't tell you the same thing right back. You two could get married again and live happily ever after."

Narrowing her eyes, she asked suspiciously, "Are you really writing a book, or was that all a cover?"

Deckland chuckled. "Not even *Kim* has that kind of pull. Of course I'm writing a book." He wiggled his eyebrows, making her smile despite her inner turmoil. "She promised me some good research, and she was right. I think you and Michael *invented* the term 'body chemistry.' "

"Glad to be of help," she murmured sarcastically, still thinking about his suggestion. Did she have the guts to tell Michael that she still loved him and wanted to try again? What if Deckland was wrong, and all Michael wanted from her was sex?

"Don't you believe in fate?" Deckland asked, as if he sensed her hesitation. "He bought a lottery ticket using your numbers on the day those numbers were picked. If that's not fate, I don't know what is."

True, true, Ashley mused silently. Out loud, she whispered, "I'm scared, Deckland. I'm scared of getting my heart ripped apart again. I— I don't think I could live through that a second time." She took a deep breath. "You have no idea how much I love Michael. And my love gives him all sorts of power."

"It goes both ways, my dear. It goes both ways."

So it did. The question was, did Michael love her the same way she loved him? If only she could be sure.

She stared down at the passenger lists she clutched in her hand. It was proof that he hadn't forgotten her, but was it actually proof that he still loved her?

Deckland crossed the cabin and put an urgent hand on her shoulder. "Tonight's the last night of this cruise. Don't let him walk away tomorrow without telling him, Ashley. If you do, I think you'll regret it for the rest of your life."

She had a funny feeling Deckland was right.

She was dressed and ready for their last dinner aboard the ship by the time Michael returned. His tuxedo lay ready on the bed, and she'd shined his shoes.

Wifely things, she'd thought, and judging by

the glow in Michael's eyes when he saw what she'd done, he thought so, too.

She found herself blushing. "I, um, saw that you were running late, so I got everything ready for you. Did you talk to Bart? How did it go? I've been going out of my mind waiting for you to get back." Actually, she'd been going out of her mind wondering if she would get up the courage to tell him that she loved him. "Did he—admit to everything?"

Michael took his time answering, his hot, lazy gaze moving over her figure, then wandering back to her face. "You look beautiful," he said, his voice disturbingly husky.

She wore a short black dress, black high heels, and a silk shawl draped casually over her bare shoulders. She'd fashioned her hair into a loose French twist. Glittering black onyx earrings dangled from her ears, and a matching collar necklace circled her throat.

Michael made her feel as if she wore a diamond-studded evening gown and Cinderella's slippers.

Blushing again, she said softly, "Thank you. Now, please tell me about your meeting with Bart."

His heated gaze cooled a few degrees. He handed her a manila folder as he said, "You were right. He wins a medal for having the most convincing sob story."

356

"Don't be cruel," she chided, taking the folder. She opened it, scanning the contents. By the time she finished, she had to blink the tears from her eyes. She sniffed, daring Michael to laugh at her. "Poor Birdie, and poor Bart. We have to do something, Michael."

"We *have* done something," he said. "We've given them a small fortune in jewelry, and I told him that he could keep the six thousand."

"You mean eight thousand. I don't want my money back."

He turned her and finished zipping her dress, his hands lingering on her shoulders, his breath warm on her neck. "I figured you'd say that, so I told him to keep it. In return he's promised to stop stealing."

Suppressing a shiver at his touch, Ashley glanced over her shoulder at him. "Do you think he will?"

"He'd better."

"So, he's been stealing money to finance their cruises to keep Birdie happy during her last years?"

"That about sums it up, yeah. He claims that Birdie isn't aware of the disease. Meeting new people all the time keeps her in the dark. She doesn't have to remember them, like she does her family."

"They have children?"

"Yes. Two grown daughters, and five grand-children."

"She's never mentioned them," Ashley said, blinking at the tears that welled in her eyes. Poor Birdie.

"That's because—according to Bart—she doesn't remember them often."

A tear trickled down her cheek. Ashley wiped it away, but another one soon followed. So much for her careful makeup job! "That's—that's awful." She sat on the edge of the bed, watching him get dressed. "I'd like to help them, Michael. I won five hundred thousand dollars. I can afford to be generous."

Shooting her an enigmatic glance, Michael slipped into his tuxedo jacket. He began to fiddle with the bow tie.

Ashley rose and went to help him. She brushed his hands away. "Let me do it."

He gave up without a fight, watching her face intently as she worked. "He says he has a note-book in his cabin. He claims he keeps up with everyone he robs, and how much he owes them. Birdie has life insurance. . . ."

"Oh." Ashley blinked rapidly again to clear her eyes. "Maybe he's telling the truth. Maybe he *does* intend to pay everyone back. Bart doesn't strike me as the ruthless criminal type."

"Apparently," Michael said dryly, "he doesn't strike *anyone* as the ruthless criminal type. That's why he's been so successful at robbing people. I forgot to ask him, but I think that Birdie's missing brooch was the first step in pulling the wool neatly over our eyes."

Unfortunately, Michael's theory made sense. "In reporting the brooch stolen, he made sure that when another theft was discovered, he was already one of the victims, not a suspect."

"Exactly."

Ashley frowned as a new thought occurred to her. "But Birdie was so upset over her brooch."

"Birdie has Alzheimer's," he gently reminded her. "Chances are the brooch has been missing for a long time, and she doesn't remember."

"Oh." She gave the tie one last tug before putting her hands on his broad shoulders. She looked up at him, her heart climbing into her throat at the thought of telling him that she loved him. Her lips went dry; she licked them, immediately capturing his interest. "Michael?"

His hot gaze settled on her mouth, his lids lowering, giving him that sexy look that made her knees weak. The man was sinfully gorgeous.

"Ashley?" he countered.

"I, um, I just wanted you to know that I've had a great time on this cruise . . . with you."

He chuckled. "It's certainly been interesting, hasn't it?"

"I wasn't talking about the adventure part."

A mocking brow rose in teasing question. "You weren't?"

"No. I wasn't." *Here goes nothing.* "I was referring to us, as a couple. Being together, and having fun." She caught her breath when he snaked his arms around her waist and pulled her against him.

He was rock hard.

"Too bad it has to end," he whispered.

She responded to the longing in his voice by melting against him. "Does it? Have to end, I mean?" Against her, she felt other parts of his body stiffen until he was one hard wall of muscle and bone. She held her breath, anticipation driving up her heart rate.

"Are you saying what I think you're saying? That you might want to continue seeing each other after the cruise?"

It would be helpful, she thought, if he would open his eyes. What was he really thinking? Did he like the idea? Or was he just being polite? He revealed nothing, either by tone or expression.

"What—what do you think about the idea?" she asked.

"Does this mean you finally believe I'm innocent?" he countered.

"I'm saying it doesn't matter, Michael. The past doesn't matter to me anymore." It was so liberating to say the words out loud that she wanted to shout and throw her arms around his neck. What she'd said was true—she didn't care about what he'd done in the past. She was ready to walk with him into the future.

But she didn't shout. She didn't move at all. Instead, she waited, hardly daring to breathe, anxiety coursing through her. This was the moment of truth.

"So what you're saying is you're ready to forgive and forget, and give me another chance."

Uh-oh. He didn't sound thrilled at all. In fact, unless she was imagining it, he sounded angry . . . and disappointed.

His hands fell abruptly from her waist. He stepped away from her, moving to the full-length mirror hanging on the outside of the bathroom door. For a long moment, she watched him fiddle with his bow tie. She was certain she'd gotten it right, but he was yanking it around and mumbling as if she'd made a mess of it.

Yes, he was angry. And she didn't know why.

"Michael?"

He turned to her, shoving his hands in his pockets. His eyes were mocking as they raked her up and down. He smiled, but this smile didn't weaken her knees or make her mouth go dry.

This smile held no humor.

"I'm probably a fool for saying this, but I've got to say it. Without trust, there *is* no us. You've made it clear that you still don't trust me. I don't think—no; that's not right. I *know* that I can't live that way. Not again." He sighed, and just for a moment, Ashley saw the raw longing in his eyes.

She realized something then. She realized that Michael *did* truly love her. So much that he couldn't bear the thought of going through the pain of breaking up again.

She knew exactly how he felt. In fact, she thought, taking a deep angry breath into her lungs, *he* couldn't possibly know how *she* felt.

Maybe it was time she told him.

Her voice shook as she said, "You don't know what I went through in those few seconds after I opened the door to room Four-twenty-six. The man I loved with every fiber of my being, the man I would have died for, was making love to another woman."

"I wasn't—"

She held up her hand, stopping him. She was exposing her heart to him for the first time since she'd walked in on him that night, and she was going to finish. Afterward, she would let him talk.

With tears spilling unheeded down her face, she went on. "I never understood the meaning of a broken heart until that night. Until that— that moment. It hurt so bad that I knew I had to do something before I shattered into a million pieces. So I closed that area of my heart off. I shut it down, and refused to open it back up to more pain."

"Ash, you—"

"Please, Michael. Let me finish. Then I'll listen. I promise." When he clamped his mouth closed, she went on. "I know that you were drunk, and maybe you didn't realize what you were doing. I didn't want to understand then, but I do now. I believe now that if you hadn't been drunk, you wouldn't have done what you did." She offered him a tremulous smile, looking at him through tear-blurred eyes, standing there so very handsome in his black tux. "So, can we please just forget the past and try again?"

He hesitated, and then he surprised her by saying, "No."

Chapter Twenty-eight

Maybe she'd heard him wrong.

Ashley's eyes went wide. She swiped at her face, but the tears just came faster. "Wh—what did you say?" Hadn't she known it was a possibility?

"No." This time there was no mistaking his answer. He crossed the room, grabbed her shoulders, and kissed her hard on her open mouth. He was smiling when he drew back.

She was totally bewildered by his reaction.

"No," he said again. "We can't forget the past, Ashley." Suddenly, he jerked her to his chest, squeezing the breath out of her. His voice was ragged in her ear. "You little fool! If you had any idea how many times I've gone over that night, how many nights I've lain awake, trying to put myself in your shoes and visualize what you saw. I couldn't for the life of me figure out how you came to think we were having sex. I mean, I knew that it looked bad—of course it looked bad, but to be so stubbornly certain that she and I—that we—" He squeezed her again, growling in her ear. "At this point, I don't know if I should tell you or just keep my mouth shut and accept your forgiveness. It may be better for you that way," he added mysteriously.

Ashley tried to break away from his tight hold, tried to breathe, but couldn't. It seemed Michael was determined not only to squeeze her to death, but also to totally confuse her.

She didn't have the breath to speak above a squeaky whisper as she said, "Michael? Would you please tell me what the hell you're talking about?" She heard the rumbling in his chest as he chuckled, then groaned, as if he couldn't believe his own thoughts.

She stared into his sheepish face, saw and recognized the light of joy in his eyes. Her bewilderment was complete. "How can you be—be so damned happy about what I told you?"

"Because, Ash." He paused to plant a tender kiss on her tear-drenched nose. "I've just realized something momentous. Something bigger and better than winning the lottery."

"Which, by the way, I know about," she inserted, trying to glower at him. To her continued surprise, he merely smiled and shook his head, as if he wasn't the least bit concerned about her finding out about something he'd gone to great lengths to hide.

"Doesn't matter," he confirmed cheerfully. "Oh, God, Ashley, none of that matters! You see, when you told Kim, who then told me, that you saw that woman sitting on top of me, I was confounded at first. Then I got angry, believing you had embellished the scene to make your reason for divorcing me more plausible."

Ashley opened her mouth to protest. Michael picked her up and swung her around, startling her into silence.

"I thought you wanted out."

"Michael," she warned, burning with curiosity and confusion. "If you don't tell—" She landed harmless blows on his chest until he put her down again.

But he didn't let go. In fact, he held her as if he would *never* let her go. More mystery. More confusion.

Finally, he inched his head back until he could look at her. "Ashley, you're not going to handle this very well, sweetheart."

She stubbornly remained silent.

"I wasn't in room Four-twenty-six."

Her mouth went bone dry. Her heart stuttered, then lurched into a drunken rhythm. "You weren't in room—"

"No, I wasn't." He shook his head for emphasis, grinning into her stunned face. "Phil was."

"Phil was." Phil had been Michael's best friend since high school. They'd gone to the same college as well.

"Yes, Phil was. I was in room Four-twenty-seven, and I *was* in bed with a woman, but I only discovered that fact moments before someone opened the door, gasped, and then fled. Apparently it was the maid, not you. When I found out that you had left me and why, I figured you had walked in at the exact same moment I awakened to find a strange woman examining my, um, genitals. Phil, on the other hand, bragged later about having a wild time with a woman he'd met in the bar. She was from Texas, and he nicknamed her Calamity Jane because she rode him like a—Ashley? Are you okay, darlin'?"

She wasn't okay. In fact, she was fairly certain she was about to faint.

And then she did.

"Foolish, foolish woman," Michael whispered tenderly as he carried Ashley to the bed. He laid her down, then sat beside her, waiting for her to come around.

Within seconds, her lashes fluttered. She opened her eyes and immediately covered them with her hands. "Oh, God, Michael! How can you ever forgive me?"

She was crying, silent sobs that made Michael want to cry with her. "Don't, baby. Don't waste even one minute beating yourself up for something you had no control over. How could you possibly have known that at the last minute Phil traded rooms with me? *I* didn't even realize it until I got my credit card statement in the mail. I should have realized then, and I might have if it hadn't been for the maid—"

"The maid?" She peeped at him through her fingers, her face still flushed a rosy red.

"I know it was the maid now, and at the time I assumed it was the maid, but when I came home and realized you'd left me, I figured it was you who had come in just as that woman was looking at—well, never mind. All that matters now is that we've realized our mistakes."

"It wasn't your mistake, Michael!" Her voice was so thick with self-loathing that Michael winced. "It was *my* stupid mistake! I didn't even wait long enough to make sure it was *you* beneath that—that Texas trash!"

He couldn't resist a chuckle at her description of Phil's Calamity Jane. "Well, we've both been stupid and blind and pigheaded."

Slowly, she pulled her fingers away, revealing damp eyelashes and violet eyes that made his heart skip a beat. "Why—why did Phil change rooms with you?"

"I had booked the honeymoon suite—still hoping you'd change your mind and join me. When it got late and Phil realized you weren't coming, he traded keys with me. He had a date to impress. I was so drunk when I got to my room that I didn't even notice. I just glanced at the number on my room key and stumbled to that door. After I got home and found you'd left me, it was the last thing on my mind."

"Oh, God, Michael!" She rose up, grabbed his cheeks between her shaking hands, and began raining kisses all over his face. "I'm so sorry, so very, very sorry! How can you ever forgive me?"

Choking up, Michael gathered her against him, holding her tight. They sat that way for long, blissful moments before he gently pulled her back.

He stared into her beautiful, tear-drenched eyes as he said solemnly, "Maybe if you do that thing with the soap again, it would help me forget." He burst out laughing at her stunned expression. "Hey, I'm kidding, sweetheart. Just kidding." He kissed her then, long and leisurely.

When they finally drew apart, he whispered, "I love you."

She whispered back, "I love you, too, although I don't know how you can—"

He kissed her silent.

Epilogue

"Are you sure about this, honey?"

Ashley smiled up at Michael, who regarded her with ever growing concern. "I'm sure. It's been weeks since I last suffered from morning sickness. Besides, these boats are so big, you're hardly aware you're on the water."

They were standing on the dock in Ft. Lauderdale, waiting for the Scotts to arrive before they boarded the ship for a seven-day cruise. With a blissful sigh, Ashley leaned into her husband.

He immediately grew hard against her back.

Grinning, she shifted against him, making him groan. "You forgot your jacket," she teased.

"I've just realized that," he growled, biting her earlobe until she shrieked.

"Look, there they are!" She could barely keep

her feet planted, she was so excited about seeing the Scotts again.

The couple approaching them were dressed in bright, tropical colors. Both wore matching sailor's hats, and both were wearing huge smiles.

"Bart! Birdie! I'm so glad you could make it." Ashley reached for Birdie, kissing her soft cheek and squeezing her hand.

When she drew back and looked into the older woman's eyes, she realized there was no recognition, just a faint puzzled look.

Her heart took a nosedive. She swallowed a lump and forced a bright smile onto her face. When they'd sent Bart a generous check to pay for this cruise and many more, Bart had warned them that Birdie might not recognize them.

"Are you looking forward to the cruise?" Ashley asked Birdie, deliberately not using her name.

But Birdie was staring beyond Ashley.

When Ashley followed her line of vision, she had to clap a hand to her mouth to keep from laughing.

Birdie was staring at Michael . . . and this time there *was* recognition in her eyes. But Birdie wasn't looking at his face.

She was looking lower. Below his waist, to be exact.

"Don't I know you?" she asked Michael, still

frowning and baldly staring at his crotch. "You seem so familiar. . . ."

Red-faced, Michael shoved one hand into his pants pocket to deemphasize his erection and stepped gamely forward, extending his free hand to Birdie. "I'm Michael. You must be Mrs. Scott. When Bart described you to me, he didn't mention that you would be the prettiest girl on the ship."

Birdie was still staring at him in a puzzled way. "Have we met? I feel as if I know you." Her gaze dropped pointedly again, then widened. She swung around to stare at Ashley. "A-Ashley?"

Tears sprang to Ashley's eyes. The lump was still there and growing bigger by the moment. Birdie had recognized her!

"Is that you?" Birdie continued, moving closer. "You've gone and gotten yourself pregnant, I see. But then, I always suspected Michael was a stud." She pointed to Michael, her blue eyes twinkling. "I see you've forgotten your jacket."

Michael laughed and drew Ashley into the circle of his arms. "Yes, I did."

"Well," Birdie said loudly, snagging the attention of several couples walking up the gangplank to the ship, "Bart can lend you one of his. You certainly can't go around flagging everyone with that thing. . . ."

Shaking with silent laughter, Ashley and Michael followed the couple onto the waiting ship.

Those
Baby Blues

SHERIDON SMYTHE

Hadleigh Charmaine feels as though she has been cast in a made-for-TV movie. The infant she took home from the hospital is not her biological child, and the man who has been raising her real daughter is Treet Miller, a film star. But when his sizzling baby blues settle on her, the single mother refuses to be hoodwinked—even if he makes her shiver with desire.

Treet knows he's found the role of a lifetime: father to two beautiful daughters and husband to one gorgeous wife. Now he just has to convince Hadleigh that in each other's arms they have the best shot at happiness. He plans to woo her with old-fashioned charm and a lot of pillow talk, until she understands that their story can have a Hollywood ending.

Dorchester Publishing Co., Inc.
P.O. Box 6640
Wayne, PA 19087-8640

52483-X
$5.99 US/$7.99 CAN

Please add $2.50 for shipping and handling for the first book and $.75 for each additional book. NY and PA residents, add appropriate sales tax. No cash, stamps, or CODs. Canadian orders require $5.00 for shipping and handling and must be paid in U.S. dollars. Prices and availability subject to change. **Payment must accompany all orders.**

Name: _____

Address: _____

City: _____ State: _____ Zip: _____

E-mail: _____

I have enclosed $_____ in payment for the checked book(s).

For more information on these books, check out our website at www.dorchesterpub.com.
_____ *Please send me a free catalog.*

Wild About You

ROBIN WELLS

All Rand Adams wants is a ranch where he can train world-class quarter horses and the chance to lead an orderly, logical existence. But free-spirited Celeste Landry has moved in next door and opened the Wild Things Fun Farm, a children's petting zoo stocked with cast-off circus animals and misfit critters. There is about to be a problem.

The two couldn't be more different. Celeste believes in fate and destiny. Rand believes in self-determination. She thinks him headstrong. He thinks her a head case. But after they share one hot kiss, she is no longer driving him crazy; she is driving him wild. And there is only one path to true happiness: He has to start listening to his heart.

Dorchester Publishing Co., Inc.

P.O. Box 6640 $6.99 US/$8.99 CAN

Wayne, PA 19087-8640   __ 52535-6

Please add $2.50 for shipping and handling for the first book and $.75 for each book thereafter. NY and PA residents, please add appropriate sales tax. No cash, stamps, or C.O.D.s. Prices and availability subject to change.

Canadian orders require $2.00 extra postage and must be paid in U.S. dollars through a U.S. banking facility.

Name_____

Address_____

City_____ State_____ Zip_____

E-mail_____

I have enclosed $_____ in payment for the checked book(s).

Payment <u>must</u> accompany all orders. __ Check here for a free catalog.

CHECK OUT OUR WEBSITE! www.dorchesterpub.com

ROBIN WELLS
OOH, LA LA!

Kate Matthews is the pre-eminent expert on New Orleans's red-light district. It makes sense that she'd be the historical consultant for the new picture being shot on location there. So why is its director being so difficult? His last flick flopped, and he is counting on this one to resurrect his career. Maybe it is because he is so handsome. He's probably used to getting women to do as he wishes. And now he wants her to loosen up. But Kate knows that accuracy is crucial to the story Zack Jackson is filming—and finding love in the Big Easy is anything but. No, there will be no lights, no cameras and certainly no action until he proves her wrong. Then it'll be a blockbuster of a show.

Dorchester Publishing Co., Inc.
P.O. Box 6640
Wayne, PA 19087-8640

52503-8
$5.99 US/$7.99 CAN

Please add $2.50 for shipping and handling for the first book and $.75 for each additional book. NY and PA residents, add appropriate sales tax. No cash, stamps, or CODs. Canadian orders require $5.00 for shipping and handling and must be paid in U.S. dollars. Prices and availability subject to change. **Payment must accompany all orders.**

Name: _____

Address: _____

City: _____ State: _____ Zip: _____

E-mail: _____

I have enclosed $_____ in payment for the checked book(s).

For more information on these books, check out our website at www.dorchesterpub.com.
_____ *Please send me a free catalog.*

ATTENTION
BOOK LOVERS!

Can't get enough of your favorite **ROMANCE**?

Call **1-800-481-9191** to:

✳ order books,

✳ receive a **FREE** catalog,

✳ join our book clubs to **SAVE 20%!**

Open Mon.-Fri. 10 AM-9 PM EST

Visit **<u>www.dorchesterpub.com</u>**
for special offers and inside
information on the authors you love.

We accept Visa, MasterCard or Discover®.
LEISURE BOOKS ♥ LOVE SPELL